THE MYSTERY LOVERS'
BOOK OF QUOTATIONS

The Mystery Lovers' Book of Quotations

A Choice Selection from Murder Mysteries, Detective
Stories, Suspense Novels, Spy Thrillers, and Crime Fiction

Compiled and arranged by
Jane E. Horning

THE MYSTERIOUS PRESS

New York • London
Tokyo • Sweden • Milan

The Mysterious Press, 129 West 56th Street, New York, N.Y. 10019

Printed in the United States of America
First Trade Printing: November, 1989

10 9 8 7 6 5 4 3 2 1

Library of Congress Cataloging-in-Publication Data

Horning, Jane E.
   The mystery lovers' book of quotations.

   1. Quotations, English.   2. Detective and mystery
stories. 3. Spy stories.   I. Title.
PN6083.H72   1988   808.88′2   87-73208
ISBN 0-89296-948-2 (pbk.)

For James Jay Horning

PREFACE

By way of beginning. . .

I read murder mysteries and detective stories for years and collected quotations and favorite lines from the genre, considering the collecting as a minor amusement. I must have valued my small collection more than I knew, for one day I found myself thinking how nice it would be to have a book of such quotations. The pleasure of compiling it I would reserve for myself, and what a wonderful book it would be.

It would cover the genre from Voltaire's *Zadig* and William Godwin's *Caleb Williams* to the present. It would include all the famous lines and all the good lines from the major authors and good lesser-known authors. It would include every good line from the second- and third-rate authors. It would have a quotation from every major character if I could find one.

The collection would be a delight to the browser, useful to the scholar. The indexes would be impressive, the attributions impeccable. It would never be as good or as complete as I should like it to be, and of course it would take time. I could happily work on it forever, and I very nearly have, but eventually my publisher said, "Time's up."

The arrangement is alphabetical by author, with titles arranged chronologically under author's name. It should be mentioned that the title used is almost always the first title the work was published under, be it the English or the American title. Alternate titles are included in the title index at the back.

The quotations themselves are drawn mainly from the works of the genre and may be on any subject. They are not concerned only with crime and its detection, for I have never considered mysteries to be so limited. Any good line from the genre is welcome in my collection, though I do have a special regard for those dealing with its major themes. There are also quotations taken from works outside the genre; these are intended to be definitely to the point about murder and related criminous subjects.

The reader may begin anywhere in the book, and be amused or appalled, depending on the quotation and the reader's own views. The reader searching more purposely may go to an author, or may look up a specific title in the title index. If concerned with a specific topic, the reader may turn to the subject index and find references to quotations about alibis, coincidence, evidence, misdirection, or whatever. Names of fictional characters are also included in this index.

There may be people who could have compiled such a work without help, but I cannot claim to be one of them. I had a great deal of help, both direct and indirect. Friends listened to me, made suggestions, let me try out quotations on them. Every reader who loves the genre has favorite lines and passages. I have listened when people told me theirs, and many were subsequently added to the collection.

Certain people deserve special mention: My husband, Jim Horning, computer scientist and keeper of the collection's computer files. He offered suggestions and reassurance at critical moments, helped in tracing quotations down so that they could be verified, and only protested when the overflow of books and papers encroached on his closet.

Marvin Lachman, for being generous both with encouragement and with practical help in verifying the quotations in the E. Howard Hunt section. He also sent ten pages of quotations that he had collected from his own reading. All were good, some I already had, some were similar to quotations already in the collection, but I used many of them.

Ruth Satterthwaite and Ruth Lauer, for sharing books and ideas with me. Barbara Hehner, for editorial advice and for introducing me to the Haycraft-Queen Cornerstone Library list years ago. If I did this book for anyone besides myself, I did it for Ruth, Ruth, and Barbara to enjoy with me.

Jonathan Hanson, who helped with the early stages of computer input and formatting. Brian Randell, who gave the manuscript a careful reading and made useful comments and suggestions, and who found it was some weeks before he could read a thriller for the story instead of for quotations. Bill Blackbeard, of the San Francisco Academy of Comic Art, for sharing his mystery collection with me. Priscilla Ridgway, executive secretary of Mystery Writers of America, for her help in tracking down elusive details. Thomas Jefferson, for founding the Library of Congress. Sara Ann Freed, my editor at Mysterious Press; working with Sara during the past two years as the collection grew and took on its final form has been a valuable and rewarding experience. That sounds rather lofty. It has also been fun.

I am not including a formal bibliography of the secondary sources and reference works that I have made use of, because I looked at *everything* I could find, from old *Book Review Digests* to the fan magazines. I did find, however, that there were books I reached for over and over again: Howard Haycraft's *Murder for Pleasure* (1941, reprinted 1974) and *The Art of the Mystery Story* (1946, reprinted 1975); Jacques Barzun and Wendell Hertig Taylor's *A Catalogue of Crime* (1971); Julian Symons's *Bloody Murder* (1972, second edition 1985); Chris Steinbrunner and Otto Penzler's *Encyclopedia of Mystery and Detection* (1976); Allen J. Hubin's *The Bibliography of Crime Fiction* (1979, second edition 1984); John M. Reilly's *Twentieth-Century Crime and Mystery Writers* (1980, second edition 1985); Jon L. Breen's *What About Murder?* (1981); H.R.F. Keating's *Whodunit?* (1982); Walter Albert's *Detective and Mystery Fiction* (1985); and Bill Pronzini and Marcia Muller's *1001 Midnights* (1986). The last is a book to treasure. It makes you want to read and read and read. I found it exceptionally rich as a secondary source for quotations, and the fact that the title was almost always given made verifying the quotations much easier.

Though it seems I checked every quotation, every title, every date, every author's name and date of birth (not all dates were available), every possible point, then rechecked and checked again, I know how persistently wrong one can be. I am sure there are mistakes. I am equally sure they will not go undetected, for mystery fans are awesomely knowledgeable. I can only say that I never deliberately misquoted to "improve" a quotation.

Now the book is nearly done. I have just found a great line in S. T. Haymon's new detective novel, *Death of a God:* "The only real choices life offers you are different ways of making a fool of yourself." And a Eugene Ionesco passage which reads: "People like killers. And if one feels sympathy for the victims it's by way of thanking them for letting themselves be killed." I don't know which play it is in, so I will have to read until I find it to verify the quotations and attribute it correctly. I will start with *The Lesson* because that is the play where the murder weapon is the word "knife."

JANE E. HORNING
January, 1988

PETER ACKROYD 1949–

English novelist who has made use of the conventions of the murder mystery genre. In *Hawksmoor*, an eighteenth-century story alternates with similar twentieth-century events—a series of murders taking place in different London churches.

1   Christ was the Serpent who deceiv'd Eve.
>—Nicholas Dyer, stating the creed of his satanic sect, *Hawksmoor*, 1985

2   Miracles are but divine experiments.
>—Parson Pridon, ibid.

3   Forgetfulnesse is the great Mystery of Time.
>—Sir Christopher Wren, Ibid.

CLEVE F. ADAMS 1895–1949

American private eye novelist of the hard-boiled school; creator of Rex McBride, sexist, racist, sentimentalist—the opposite of Raymond Chandler's knightly hero.

4   Jealousy is worse than liquor. It biteth like an adder.
>—Rex McBride, *Up Jumped the Devil*, 1943

DOUGLAS ADAMS 1952–

English science fiction writer; author of *The Hitchhiker's Guide to the Galaxy*, and *Dirk Gently's Holistic Detective Agency*, which bridges two genres.

5   The whole thing was obvious! So obvious that the only thing which prevented me from seeing the solution was the trifling fact that it was *completely impossible*.
>—Dirk Gently, *Dirk Gently's Holistic Detective Agency*, 1987

6   It is a rare mind indeed that can render the hitherto nonexistent blindingly obvious.
>—Dirk Gently, ibid.

HAROLD ADAMS 1923–

American detective novelist; creator of Carl Wilcox, ex-con and the first person blamed for any crime in his small South Dakota town.

7   Never start an argument with your hands in your pockets.
—Carl Wilcox, *The Naked Liar*, 1985

8   The one good thing about politicians is the wise ones know when to compromise. The dumb ones don't know anything else.
—Carl Wilcox, *The Barbed Wire Noose*, 1987

SAMUEL HOPKINS ADAMS 1871–1958

American journalist and influential muckraker, author of novels and detective stories; creator of Average Jones, advertising "Ad-Visor."

9   The open eye of the open mind—that has more to do with real detective work than all the deduction and induction and analysis ever devised.
—Waldemar to Jones, "The B-Flat Trombone," *Average Jones*, 1911

10   Don't forget the fortunate coincidences. . . . In fact, detective work . . . is mostly the ability to recognize and connect coincidences.
—Average Jones, "Red Dot," ibid.

11   It would be a dull world, except for peculiar persons.
—Professor Warren, "The Man Who Spoke Latin," ibid.

12   No fellow can be on the job *all* the time.
—Average Jones, ibid.

13   Money talks.
—"The One Best Bet," ibid.

This thought is age-old. Adams used the modern catchphrase four years before the first usage recorded in Eric Partridge's A *Dictionary of Slang and Unconventional English*, 8th ed., 1984.

CATHERINE AIRD 1930–

Pseudonym of Kinn Hamilton McIntosh, who lives in England. After years of reading mystery and detective novels, she started writing them; creator of Detective Inspector C.D. Sloan, called "Seedy" by his friends.

14   The only thing worth putting on a horse in his philosophy
being Lady Godiva.
> —Said of Inspector C.D. Sloan, who is
> against betting on horses, *A Late Phoenix*,
> 1970

15   If . . . you can't be a good example, then you'll just have to
be a horrible warning.
> —Inspector C.D. Sloan to
> Detective-Constable Crosby, *His Burial
> Too*, 1973

16   Just as no man was a hero to his valet, so no member of a
profession was sea-green incorruptible to a policeman.
> —*Passing Strange*, 1980

MARTHA ALBRAND 1914–1981

Pseudonym of German-born naturalized American Heidi Huberta
Freybe, who has also used other pseudonyms. As Albrand, writer of
suspense and international intrigue novels. She considers all writing
to be a process of elimination, but "it is of utmost importance in a
suspense novel."

17   There are as many jealousies in life as there are different
flowers or trees or animals.
> —*A Taste of Terror*, 1977

THOMAS BAILEY ALDRICH 1836–1907

American man of letters, and author of several mystery and
detective stories; creator of Paul Lynde, who is quite truly out of his
head, though his observations are apt.

18   She had no more heart than there was an anatomical
necessity for.
> —Paul Lynde's opinion of Celeste, "The Cut
> on the Lips," *Out of His Head*, 1862

19   Poverty is the unpardonable sin.
> —ibid.

20   It is a way of mine to put this and that together.
> —Paul Lynde's detective method, ibid.

21   No stupid man ever suspected himself of being anything but
clever.
> —*The Stillwater Tragedy*, 1880

22   A thing cannot be weighed in a scale incapable of containing it.

> —Margaret Slocum to Richard Shackford, ibid.

23   There is a possible Nero in the gentlest human creature that walks.

> —"Leaves from a Notebook," *Ponkapog Papers*, 1903

TED ALLBEURY 1917–

English intelligence officer turned espionage novelist; he also writes using other names. He believes that "only the well-tuned coward can survive in the world of espionage."

24   There's a day in every man's life when he suddenly realizes that he's older than his father. A day when the father becomes a child in need of protection and the young man must be a shield.

> —*The Alpha List*, 1979

25   Scholars are always putting two and two together and making five.

> —James Lawler, *Shadow of Shadows*, 1982

26   When all are prisoners the jailers are free men.

> —Anatoli Petrov, ibid.

GRANT ALLEN 1848–1899

Canadian-born English writer, scientist, and philosopher; creator of Colonel Clay, the first great crook of the genre, who *repeatedly* robs his victim, Sir Charles Vandrift, the African millionaire.

27   A man of the world accepts what a lady tells him, no matter how improbable.

> —Seymour Wentworth, "The Episode of the Mexican Seer," *An African Millionaire*, 1897

28   If you wish to see how friendly and charming humanity is, just try being a well-known millionaire for a week, and you'll learn a thing or two.

> —Seymour Wentworth, "The Episode of the Diamond Links," ibid.

29   The worst of the man is, he has a method. He doesn't go out of his way to cheat us; he makes us go out of ours to be cheated.
—Sir Charles Vandrift of Colonel Clay, ibid.

30   I catch you just where you are trying to catch other people.
—Colonel Clay to Sir Charles Vandrift, "The Episode of the Drawn Game," ibid.

31   The worst of married women is—that you can't marry them; the worst of unmarried women is—that they want to marry you.
—The poet to Sir Charles Vandrift, "The Episode of the Game of Poker," ibid.

32   In life, as at cards, two things go to produce success—the first is chance; the second is cheating.
—The magazine editor, ibid.

MARGERY ALLINGHAM 1904–1966

English detective novelist, whose literary family regarded writing as the only reasonable way of passing the time, not to mention earning a living; creator of Albert Campion, who looks a silly ass, but isn't.

33   Walk softly, keep your gun ready, and for heaven's sake don't shoot unless it's a case of life or sleep perfect sleep.
—Albert Campion, The Crime at Black Dudley, 1929

34   He was a lank, pale-faced young man with sleek fair hair and horn-rimmed spectacles. His lounge suit was a little masterpiece, and the general impression one received of him was that he was well bred and a trifle absent-minded.
—Description of Albert Campion, Death of a Ghost, 1934

35   If one cannot command attention by one's admirable qualities at least one can be a nuisance.
—ibid.

36   The nicest people fall in love indiscriminately . . . while under the influence of that pre-eminently selfish lunacy they may make the most outrageous demands upon their friends with no other excuse than their painful need.
—Flowers for the Judge, 1936

37   Nearly thirty-five and nearly twenty-five are two very different kettles of fish where nervous stamina and the ability to do without sleep are concerned.
          —Albert Campion's reflection, ibid.

38   Love or money can conceal every other disturbing occurrence to be met with in civil life, but sudden death is inviolate. A body is the one thing that cannot be explained away.
          —*Dancers in Mourning*, 1937

39   I don't mind what I do so long as it's not common.
          —Mr. Lugg, ibid.

40   When I get good I'll do me own quotations.
          —Mr. Lugg, *The Fashion in Shrouds*, 1938

41   You would be surprised to know how much unnecessary worry a simple policy of polite disinterest can save one.
          —Miss Jessica Palinode, *More Work for the Undertaker*, 1948

42   He was the best of policemen, which is to say that he never for one moment assumed that he was judge or jury, warder or hangman.
          —Said of Charlie Luke, *The Tiger in the Smoke*, 1952

43   Lying wastes more time than anything else in the modern world.
          —Canon Avril, ibid.

ROBERT EDMOND ALTER 1925–1966

American short story writer, author of more than a dozen children's books, and three hard-boiled suspense novels. *Swamp Sister* and *Carny Kill* are set in Florida.

44   He felt like yesterday's newspaper left out in the rain.
          —*Swamp Sister*, 1961

ERIC AMBLER 1909–

English writer of spy and international intrigue novels, awarded the Grand Master title by Mystery Writers of America in 1975 and the O.B.E. (Officer, Order of the British Empire) in 1981. It would be difficult to overstate his influence on the genre.

45   Of the genre itself, Ambler has said:
"The thriller is an extension of the fairy tale. It is melodrama
so embellished as to create the illusion that the story being
told, however unlikely, could be true."
—*The Times*, 1974

46   Sleep is not always an unmixed blessing. It brings relief to the
nerves and strength to the body; but it also brings cold sanity.
—*Uncommon Danger*, 1937

47   "He needed the money."
It was like an epitaph.
—Josef Vadassy's reflection, *Epitaph for a
Spy*, 1938

48   Chance plays an important, if not predominant, part in
human affairs.
—*The Mask of Dimitrios*, 1939

49   If there should be such a thing as a superhuman Law, it is
administered with sub-human inefficiency.
—ibid.

50   International big business may conduct its operations with
scraps of paper, but the ink it uses is human *blood!*
—Marukakis, ibid.

51   Your passport describes you as a writer, but that is a very
elastic term.
—Mr. Peters to Mr. Latimer, ibid.

52   A little fact will sustain a lot of illusion.
—Mr. Foster, *Judgment on Deltchev*, 1951

53   Of course, I don't know what this dialectical-materialism
stuff means, but then I could never understand what the
Bible was all about either. I always used to get top marks for
Scripture. Here I'm politically reliable.
—Arthur, *The Schirmer Inheritance*, 1953

54   Games of chance are at least subject to the law of averages,
race horses do sometimes run true to form, and skill can
often qualify bad luck at poker.
—*Passage of Arms*, 1959

55   Bullshit baffles brains.
—As Arthur Simpson's father used to say,
The Light of Day, 1962

56   You'd better watch yourself; your sheep's clothing is slipping.
          —Theodore Carter, *The Intercom Conspiracy*,
          1969

57   I do not drink heavily. I drink what I *need* to drink. The need
          varies from time to time.
          —Theodore Carter, ibid.

58   What use is an honest lawyer when what you need is a
          dishonest one?
          —Professor Krom, *Send No More Roses*,
          1977

59   The warning message arrived on Monday, the bomb itself on
          Wednesday. It became a busy week.
          —Opening paragraph, *The Care of Time*,
          1981

FREDERICK IRVING ANDERSON 1877–1947

American short story writer whose ambition was to "write one story
and to tell an entirely different one between the lines"; creator of
two great crooks, the Infallible Godahl and the Notorious Sophie
Lang. *The Book of Murder* was a Haycraft-Queen Cornerstone
Library selection.

60   Abolish the lure of gold and the world will be born good
          again.
          —Godahl, "The Fifth Tube," *Adventures of
          the Infallible Godahl*, 1914

61   One's physician is a tyrant!
          —Godahl, ibid.

62   We don't detect crime. Crime detects itself.
          —Deputy Police Commissioner Parr, "The
          Signed Masterpiece," *The Notorious
          Sophie Lang*, 1925

63   There is nothing so drab as police business ninety-nine times
          out of a hundred.
          —"Beyond All Conjecture," *The Book of
          Murder*, 1930

64   Every dog has his flea—if he is a normal dog.
          —Deputy Police Commissioner Parr, "The
          Recoil," ibid.

ARISTOTLE 384–322 B.C.

Leading philosopher of ancient Greece, who had something to say about crime and its causes.

65 There are crimes of which the motive is want. . . . But want is not the sole incentive to crime. . . . The greatest crimes are caused by excess and not by necessity.
—*Politics*, Book II, Chapter 7; English translation by Benjamin Jowett, 1885

CHARLOTTE ARMSTRONG 1905–1969

American playwright and mystery novelist, winner of an Edgar for *A Dram of Poison*. In *The Seven Widows of Sans Souci*, she coined the term "li-ee" for those who emotionally blackmail others into lying to them.

66 Death was better than dishonor? What? In this year of Our Lord?
—*The Witch's House*, 1963

ISAAC ASIMOV 1920–

Russian-born naturalized American citizen, author of many scientific works, science fiction, and detective stories—most notably the Union Club and Black Widower series.

67 People use vulgarisms as general intensifiers, without any conception of the meaning. Like the woman who stepped off the curb on Park Avenue and said with deep annoyance, "Oh, *shit!* I stepped in some doggie poo-poo!"
—*Murder at the ABA*, 1976

68 To want to compose a better limerick is the mark of a man with a micro-ambition.
—Thomas Trumbull, "None So Blind," *Casebook of the Black Widowers*, 1980

PIERRE AUDEMARS 1909–

English author of detective novels; creator of Monsieur Pinaud of the French Sûreté.

69 Attempting to control one's own conduct leaves singularly little time for policing the morals of others.
—M. Poidevin, *And One for the Dead*, 1975

W. H. AUDEN 1907–1973

English poet Wystan Hugh Auden, who moved to the United States in 1939 and became a citizen. He both influenced the genre and was influenced by it; author of the oft-reprinted essay, "The Guilty Vicarage."

Auden said that writers who invented the best detective puzzles also invented the most intolerable detective heroes, but confessed to a weakness for Nicholas Blake's Nigel Strangeways, "because some of his habits were taken from mine."

70   If I have any work to do, I must be careful not to get hold of a detective story for, once I begin one, I cannot work or sleep till I have finished it.

—"The Guilty Vicarage," *Harper's Magazine*, May 1948

71   The basic formula is this: a murder occurs; many are suspected; all but one suspect, who is the murderer, are eliminated; the murderer is arrested or dies.

—Defining the detective story, ibid.

PAUL AUSTER 1947–

American writer, poet, and detective novelist; author of the New York Trilogy.

72   Our lives carry us along in ways we cannot control, and almost nothing stays with us.

—The nameless narrator, *The Locked Room*, 1986

73   What man is strong enough to reject the possibility of hope?

—The nameless narrator, ibid.

74   No one wants to be part of a fiction, and even less so if that fiction is real.

—The nameless narrator, ibid.

75   I could no longer make the right distinctions. This can never be that. Apples are not oranges, peaches are not plums. . . . But everything was beginning to have the same taste to me.

—The nameless narrator, ibid.

MICHAEL AVALLONE 1924–

American private eye novelist, who writes under many names. As Avallone, creator of Ed Noon (Hi, Noon!) and his Nooniverse.

76 When you have a bee in your bonnet, you don't start swinging a fly swatter.
—Ed Noon, *The Tall Delores*, 1953

77 Death is as pointless as having a key for an open door that you are only going to walk through once.
—*Meanwhile Back at the Morgue*, 1960

78 The next day dawned bright and clear on my empty stomach.
—Ed Noon, ibid.

H. C. BAILEY 1878–1961

English detective novelist and short story writer Henry Christopher Bailey, one of the "Big Five" of the Golden Age;* creator of Reggie Fortune, a practicing physician who acts as special consultant for Scotland Yard when medical points arise in criminal cases, and Joshua Clunk, a hymn-singing scoundrel of a lawyer.

79 Great firms don't murder inventors. It isn't worth their while. They prefer to swindle 'em. That is quite easy and legal.
—Joshua Clunk, *Garstons*, 1930

80 What a nuisance politicians would be if they weren't all cowards.
—Sydney Lomas, "The Hermit Crab," *Mr. Fortune's Trials*, 1925

81 I'm for the man that's wronged. That's all.
—Reggie Fortune, "The German Song," *Mr. Fortune Speaking*, 1930

82 He [Reggie Fortune] is wont to say that he has an old-fashioned mind. Insofar as this refers to morals it means that he holds by the standard principles of conduct and responsibility, of right and wrong, of sin and punishment.
—Introduction, *Mr. Fortune Wonders*, 1933

---

*According to Howard Haycraft in *Murder for Pleasure*, the other four were generally considered to be Dorothy L. Sayers, Agatha Christie, R. Austin Freeman, and Freeman Wills Crofts. He conceded that membership in the quintet was elusive; certainly one can argue for the inclusion of other authors.

83   There are no general rules.

> —One of Reggie Fortune's favorite maxims,
> ibid.

84   The forces of nature always bring out facts discovering the
criminal if anybody takes the trouble to notice them.

> —A fundamental principle of crime detection,
> according to Reggie Fortune, "The Brown
> Paper," *Mr. Fortune Here*, 1940

85   Indecision and hesitation are the weakness of a careful nature
always intent on the saving of face and losing it thereby.

> —*The Bishop's Crime*, 1940

86   Sympathy is the worst infirmity of muddling minds.

> —*No Murder*, 1942

87   Friend of the Family: relations discovered or destroyed;
domestic quarrels settled; mysteries solved—family skeletons
a specialty.

> —The Honorable Victoria Pumphrey's
> advertisement when she sets up as a
> private inquiry agent, "A Matter of
> Speculation," *Ellery Queen's Mystery
> Magazine*, February 1961

JOHN BALL 1911–

American detective novelist, whose *In the Heat of the Night* won an
Edgar for best first mystery; creator of Virgil Tibbs, homicide
specialist for the Pasadena Police Department, and one of the first
major black police detectives in the literature.

88   "Virgil is a pretty fancy name for a black boy like you.
What do they call you around home where you come from?"
"They call me Mr. Tibbs."

> —Chief Gillespie's taunt, and Virgil Tibbs's
> reply, *In the Heat of the Night*, 1965

EDWIN BALMER 1883–1959 and WILLIAM MacHARG 1872–1951

Two American journalists and writers of popular fiction who
collaborated to write the first volume of short stories making use of
psychology in the detection of crime; creators of Luther Trant,
"Practical Psychologist." William MacHarg (q.v.) also wrote detective stories on his own

89 In the face of misunderstanding and derision, he [Luther Trant] had tried to trace the criminal, not by the world-old method of the marks he had left on things, but by the evidences which the crime had left on the mind of the criminal himself.

—"The Eleventh Hour," *The Achievements of Luther Trant*, 1910

ELSA BARKER 1869–1954

American detective novelist; creator of Dexter Drake, a private investigator with "the manner of a *grand seigneur*."

90 You remember that Wall Street philanthropist who was killed by a can of sauerkraut thrown at his head. . . . What a pickle the police were in that day!

—Paul Howard to Dexter Drake, *The C.I.D. of Dexter Drake*, 1929

91 The art of detection is finding a common denominator for the fractions of a case.

—Dexter Drake, ibid.

92 The solving of almost every crime mystery depends on something which seems, at the first glance, to bear *no relation whatever* to the original crime.

—Dexter Drake, ibid.

ROBERT BARNARD 1936–

English mystery and detective novelist, who calls his characters "grotesques"; creator of Superintendent Perry Trethowan.

93 Barnard has said:
"I'm never obsessed with evil. . . . I'm much more interested in meanness."

—Interview, *The Armchair Detective*, Summer 1984

94 A bad smell is more interesting than a deodorizing spray.

—*Blood Brotherhood*, 1977

95 It would be the height of idiocy to deny oneself wine merely to live a little longer.

—Sir Oliver Fairleigh-Stubbs, *Unruly Son*, 1978

96   You could say they're related in a way, only we don't have a
word for it. They were both married to the same chap.
—Greg Hocking, *Posthumous Papers*, 1979

97   Blood is certainly *stickier* than water.
—Superintendent Perry Trethowan, *Sheer
Torture*, 1981

98   A conspicuous lack of self-knowledge has its dangers.
—*Little Victims*, 1983

99   Don't you think moderation in *all* things might in itself be a
sort of excess?
—Father Battersby, *Disposal of the Living*,
1985

RONALD GORELL BARNES (LORD GORELL) 1884–1963

English peer, barrister, and detective novelist.

100   The same facts can often be explained in several ways.
—Inspector Humblethorne to Evelyn Temple,
In the Night, 1917

ROBERT BARR 1850–1912

English journalist and detective story writer; creator of Eugene
Valmont, a comical French detective living in London. A later
sleuth, Agatha Christie's Hercule Poirot, would possess many of the
habits and mannerisms of Valmont.

101   In our secret hearts we all admire a great thief, and if not a
great one, then an expert one, who covers his tracks so
perfectly that the hounds of justice are baffled in attempting
to follow them.
—Lionel Dacre, "The Clue of the Silver
Spoons," *The Triumphs of Eugene
Valmont*, 1906

102   Of course, the English are a very excellent people, a fact to
which I am always proud to bear testimony, but it must be
admitted that for cold common sense the French are very
much their superiors.
—Eugene Valmont, "The Absent-Minded
Coterie," ibid.

JACQUES BARZUN 1907– and WENDELL HERTIG TAYLOR 1905–1985

American scholars, lifelong friends, and coauthors of the notable *A Catalogue of Crime*, a guide to detective fiction based on notes they kept over fifty years of reading. The following indicates the basis for their strongly held opinions.

103   Detection is a game that must be played according to Doyle.
—Introductory, *A Catalogue of Crime*, 1971

ROGER BAX. *See* Andrew Garve.

SPENCER BAYNE 1899–1978

Pseudonym of American classics scholar and wartime intelligence and criminal investigations officer·Floyd Albert Spencer. As Bayne, author of two detective novels and one spy thriller, all featuring Hendrik Van Kill, scholar and crime decoder.

104   If angels are entertained unaware, it is because they have tact.
—Hendrik Van Kill, *Murder Recalls Van Kill*, 1939

105   Murder becomes monotonous.
—Hendrik Van Kill, *The Turning Sword*, 1941

FRANCIS BEEDING

Shared pseudonym of John Leslie Palmer, 1885–1944, and Hilary Aidan St. George Saunders, 1898–1951; the pair also wrote as David Pilgrim. Of their collaborated works, *Death Walks in Eastrepps* is deservedly the best known. They wrote over thirty mysteries together, including a series of espionage thrillers; creators of Colonel Alastair Granby.

106   I am the victim of a hired car. There is something seriously wrong inside. Most of the essential parts were either left behind at the garage or have since been strewn upon the way.
—Toby Granby, *The League of Discontent*, 1930

107   It is better to be the head of a live sardine than the tail of a dead trout.
—Don Belisario, *The Big Fish*, 1938

108   The English describe necessity as the mother of invention,
            whereas the Spaniards refer to it as the enemy of chastity.
                                    —Don Belisario, ibid.

109   It is better to appear in hell than in the newspapers.
                                    —Don Belisario, ibid.

110   Murder, without cause, by a madman with his wits astray,
            monstrous, terrible. . . . It let loose the Devil among
            them, and people still believed in the Devil. He struck only
            here and there, but threatened all alike, for once he got the
            upper hand of law, order and all good things, he might regain
            the world, and use it for his ancient purposes.
                                    —*Death Walks in Eastrepps*, 1931

111   Nothing like money to keep one from brooding on the past.
                                    —ibid.

112   No man is dead till he's dead.
                                    —Colonel Alastair Granby, *The Twelve
                                    Disguises*, 1942

MARC BEHM 1925–

American actor, screenwriter, and suspense novelist, who has lived
in France for many years.

113   What does God see, Father, when he looks at us?
                                    —Unnamed private eye of the novel, to his
                                    priest, *The Eye of the Beholder*, 1980

LARRY BEINHART 1947–

American private eye novelist, winner of an Edgar for his first
novel, *No One Rides for Free*; creator of New York private eye Tony
Cassella.

114   "Will you be good while you're in Washington?"
            "Whatever do you mean?"
            "There is a certain school of thought, among men, so I've
            heard, that out-of-town doesn't count."
            "The line is, 'Under five minutes and out-of-town doesn't
            count.'"
                                    —Exchange between Glenda and Tony
                                    Cassella, *No One Rides for Free*, 1986

ROBERT LESLIE BELLEM 1902–1968

American writer for the pulps; creator of hard-boiled Dan Turner, "Hollywood's hottest hawkshaw."

115 Freeze, snoop, or I'll perforate you like a cancelled check.
—Villainous chauffeur to Dan Turner, "Drunk, Disorderly, and Dead," *Private Detective Stories*, June 1940

116 He was deader than the chicken in a hard-boiled egg.
—Dan Turner, ibid.

117 A roscoe stuttered: *Ka-Pow!* behind me. The blast was bad enough, but the slug's nearness was worse.
—Dan Turner, "Homicide Highball," *Hollywood Detective*, October 1943

118 A bullet can give a man a terrific case of indigestion, frequently ending in a trip to the boneyard.
—Dan Turner, "Diamonds of Death," *Hollywood Detective*, August 1950

SAUL BELLOW 1915–

American novelist, aware of the passion with which some people read mysteries.

119 If she had one consistent interest it was murder mysteries. Three or four a day, she'd read.
—Said of Madeleine, *Herzog*, 1964

MARGOT BENNETT 1912–1980

Postwar English detective novelist, whose books are fine period pieces.

120 "Are you as luxurious, greedy, mercenary, unscrupulous, selfish, faithless, ambitious, and lax as ever?"
"I'm a civilized woman."
—Exchange between Hugh Everton and Lucy Bath, *The Widow of Bath*, 1952

121 As time passes we all get better at blazing a trail through the thicket of advice.
—*Farewell Crown and Good-bye King*, 1953

E. C. BENTLEY 1875–1956

English journalist Edmund Clerihew Bentley, inventor of clerihews* and detective novelist, who has been called the father of the contemporary detective story.

122   Bentley said in his autobiography that he wrote his first detective novel in reaction to the artificiality of detective stories of the period:
"It should be possible, I thought, to write a detective story in which the detective was recognizable as a human being and was not quite so much the 'heavy sleuth.' . . . Why not show up the fallibility of the Holmesian method? . . . In the result, it does not seem to have been generally noticed that *Trent's Last Case* is not so much a detective story as an exposure of detective stories."
—Those Days, 1940

123   I have a sort of sneaking respect for the determination to make life interesting and lively in spite of civilisation.
—Philip Trent, *Trent's Last Case*, 1913

124   Holy, suffering Moses! What an ass a man can make himself when he thinks he's being preternaturally clever!
—Philip Trent, ibid.

125   The man has yet to be born who enjoys being made to look a fool without knowing why.
—*Trent's Own Case*, written with H. Warner Allen, 1936

PHYLLIS BENTLEY 1894–1977

English novelist and detective story writer; creator of Miss Marian Phipps, a spinster sleuth who believes the truth is the best gift you can give anyone.

126   In this complex modern world . . . the lives of all of us áre very subtly and intricately interwoven.
—Miss Phipps, "Chain of Witnesses," *Ellery Queen's Mystery Magazine*, May 1954

*Four-line biographical verses, consisting of two rhyming couplets.

ANDREW BERGMAN 1945–

American movie commentator, screenplay comedy writer, and detective novelist; creator of Jack LeVine, self-described as a "basic model 1944 prole."

127 A penny-ante chiseler can get just as trigger-happy as a big timer.
>—Jack LeVine, *The Big Kiss-off of 1944*, 1974

ANTHONY BERKELEY 1893–1971

Pseudonym of English journalist Anthony Berkeley Cox, who wrote inverted murder mysteries and mystery criticism as Francis Iles. As Berkeley, author of eighteen mysteries; creator of Ambrose Chitterwick and Roger Sheringham. *The Poisoned Chocolates Case* offers the reader six plausible solutions to the murder puzzle.

128 It would be a very good thing for the cat occasionally to find itself chased by the mouse.
>—*The Poisoned Chocolates Case*, 1929

129 That was the trouble with the old-fashioned detective story. One deduction only was drawn from each fact, and it was invariably the right deduction. The Great Detectives of the past certainly had luck. In real life one can draw a hundred plausible deductions from one fact, and they're all equally wrong.
>—Roger Sheringham, *Jumping Jenny*, 1933

130 We must take things as they are, not as we would prefer them to be.
>—Mr. Chitterwick, *Trial and Error*, 1937

131 In 1930 he wrote:
"The detective story is already in the process of developing into the novel . . . holding its readers less by mathematical than by psychological ties. The puzzle element will no doubt remain, but it will become a puzzle of character rather than a puzzle of time, place, motive, and opportunity."
>—Preface, *The Second Shot*, 1930

Writing as **FRANCIS ILES,** the next year he brought a new dimension to mystery fiction, changing the emphasis from "who?" to "why?"

132   Murder is a serious business. The slightest slip may be disastrous.
                            —*Malice Aforethought*, 1931

133   To diagnose is not to cure.
                            —As Dr. Bickleigh well knew, ibid.

134   However superior to any number of cats a mouse may feel in its own hole, it requires a good deal of self-suggestion to maintain this opinion in the presence of the cat.
                            —ibid.

135   What the mind doesn't know, the eyes don't cry over.
                            —Johnny Aysgarth, *Before the Fact*, 1932

136   Circumstances alter women.
                            —ibid.

UGO BETTI 1892–1953

Italian jurist and playwright, deeply concerned with justice.

137   Murderers, in general, are people who are consistent, people who are obsessed with one idea and nothing else. And that applies to their victims, as well.
                            —The Notary, *Struggle till Dawn*, Act I, 1949; English translation by G. H. McWilliam, 1964

138   All of us are mad. If it weren't for the fact that every one of us is slightly abnormal, there wouldn't be any point in giving each person a separate name.
                            —The Doctor, *The Fugitive*, Act II, 1953; English translation by G. H. McWilliam, 1964

EARL DERR BIGGERS 1884–1933

American newspaper columnist and mystery writer; creator of Charlie Chan. Sinister and wicked Chinese are old stuff, he thought in the mid-1920s, but an amiable Chinese on the side of law and order has never been used. So, he wrote *The House Without a Key*, the first of his six Charlie Chan adventures.

139 When in Rome, I make it a point not to do as the Bostonians do. I fear it would prove a rather thorny path to popularity.
—Miss Minerva Winterslip, *The House Without a Key*, 1925

140 If you've ever read a mystery story you know that a detective never works so hard as when he's on a vacation.
—Bob Eden, *The Chinese Parrot*, 1926

141 He who rides a tiger cannot dismount.
—Charlie Chan, ibid.

142 The man who is about to cross a stream should not revile the crocodile's mother.
—Charlie Chan, *The Black Camel*, 1929

143 The deer should not play with the tiger.
—Charlie Chan, *Charlie Chan Carries On*, 1930

144 The stupidest man in the town may point out the road to the school.
—Charlie Chan, ibid.

145 What price romance—after seeing Reno?
—Leslie Beaton, *Keeper of the Keys*, 1932

146 The fool in a hurry drinks his tea with a fork.
—Charlie Chan, ibid.

147 When money talks, few are deaf.
—Charlie Chan in the movie, *Charlie Chan in Honolulu*, 1938

JOHN BINGHAM (LORD CLANMORRIS) 1908–

English crime and spy novelist, formerly an intelligence officer, and John le Carré's primary role model for George Smiley; creator of Spymaster Vandoren.

148 We live in dangerous times. All one can do is to keep the spear ready, and a feeble thing it is, touch the amulet, and hope for the best.
—James Crompton, *A Fragment of Fear*, 1965

149 If everything is going perfectly, then the only change can be for the worse.
—Spymaster Vandoren, *God's Defector*, 1976

150   The world's full of people taking chances.
            —Spymaster Vandoren, ibid.

151   Moral: Don't try and solve all your difficulties at the same
            time. Most will solve themselves or disappear.
            —Spymaster Vandoren, ibid.

ANITA BLACKMON 1893–

American mystery novelist who wrote some splendid (or dreadful)
Had-I-But-Known passages; creator of Adelaide Adams, known as
the old battle-ax.

152   Nor at that time could any power on earth have convinced
            me that I should find myself late one terrible night, sans my
            dress and my false hair, dangling from the eaves of the
            Richelieu Hotel in pursuit of a triple slayer.
            —Adelaide Adams, *Murder à la Richelieu*,
            1937

153   Not much escapes my eyes and ears and nothing escapes my
            memory, although I may mislay it for a while.
            —Adelaide Adams, ibid.

154   Nothing so sharpens the disposition as anything which
            touches on the pocketbook.
            —Adelaide Adams, ibid.

155   The quickest way to be rid of people is to lend them money.
            —Adelaide Adams, ibid.

NICHOLAS BLAKE 1904–1972

Pseudonym of English poet laureate C. Day Lewis, who considered
the detective novel "the folk-myth of the twentieth century." As
Blake, creator of Nigel Strangeways, some of whose habits and
mannerisms were modeled after those of W. H. Auden (q.v.).

156   Love is not indiscriminate charity.
            —Hero Vale, *A Question of Proof*, 1935

157   My studies in criminology have suggested to me that only
            generals, Harley Street specialists and mine-owners can get
            away with murder successfully.
            —Felix Lane, *The Beast Must Die*, 1938

158   There are occasions when the truth is more deceptive than any lie.
> —*Malice in Wonderland*, 1940

159   When a man begins to feel protective toward a woman, it's high time for someone to start protecting *him*.
> —Nigel Strangeways's reflection, ibid.

160   I am not to be evaded by quotations.
> —Miss Cavendish, *The Case of the Abominable Snowman*, 1941

161   Every collector is a potential criminal.
> —Nigel Strangeways, *Minute for Murder*, 1947

162   To look guilty is not inevitably a sign of innocence.
> —Nigel Strangeways, *The Dreadful Hollow*, 1953

163   In every highbrow there's a Common Man screaming to get out.
> —Dominic Eyre, *The Private Wound*, 1968

OLIVER BLEECK. *See* Ross Thomas.

ROBERT BLOCH 1917–

American suspense novelist and screenwriter; author of *Psycho* and winner of a special Edgar Scroll in 1961.

164   He likes to claim:
"I have the heart of a small boy. I keep it in a jar on my desk."
> —*Twentieth-Century Crime and Mystery Writers*, 2nd ed., 1985

165   I think perhaps all of us go a little crazy at times.
> —Norman Bates to Mary Crane, *Psycho*, 1959

166   We're all not quite as sane as we pretend to be.
> —Lila Crane, ibid.

167   Mother . . . what is the phrase? . . . She isn't quite herself today.
> —Norman Bates, *Psycho*; screenplay by Joseph Stephano, based on the novel, 1960

168   We're all in our private traps, clamped in them, and none of
us can ever get out. We scratch and claw but only at the air,
only at each other. And for all of it, we never budge an inch.
—Norman Bates, ibid.

LAWRENCE BLOCK 1938–

American detective novelist, who has also used the names Chip
Harrison and Paul Kavanagh. As Block, creator of Bernie Rhodenbarr, Evan Tanner, and Matthew Scudder, each featured in his own
series.

169   Experience is as effective a teacher as she is because one does
tend to remember her lessons.
—Bernie Rhodenbarr, *The Burglar in the
Closet*, 1978

170   Whoever you are, God or anybody else, you work with the
materials at hand.
—Danny Boy, *Eight Million Ways to Die*,
1982

ANDERS BODELSEN 1937–

Danish writer of crime and suspense fiction.

171   It was dishonest to pray to a god that one didn't believe in. If
God did exist after all, then he would really punish a person
for such dishonesty.
—Martin Bendix, *Consider the Verdict*, 1973;
English translation by Nadia Christensen,
1976

M. McDONNELL BODKIN 1850–1933

Irish barrister and judge, writer of mystery and detective stories;
creator of Paul Beck, one of the early "ordinary man" detectives.

172   I have no more system than the hound that gets on the fox's
scent and keeps on it. I just go by the rule of thumb, and
muddle and puzzle out my cases as best I can.
—Paul Beck, "The Vanishing Diamonds,"
Paul Beck, the Rule of Thumb Detective,
1898

173   Hearsay evidence is often first-class evidence, though the law
doesn't think so.
—Paul Beck, "Murder by Proxy," ibid.

JOHN BONETT 1906– and EMERY BONETT 1906–

Joint pseudonym of John Hubert Arthur Coulson and Felicity Winifred Carter Coulson, English detective novelists; creators of Inspector Borges and Professor Mandrake, each featured in his own series.

174   The one thing you learn, if you're capable of learning anything, is that you can't *know* anything.
> —Professor Mandrake, *Dead Lion*, 1949

175   The reason for murder often lies as much in the murderee as in the dispatcher.
> —Inspector Borges, *The Sound of Murder*, 1970

Crime and mystery novelist F. Tennyson Jesse (q.v.) coined the useful term, "murderee."

176   Chastity's a cold bedfellow and bedsocks are no substitute for affection—even if one's man snores.
> —Pamela Ducayne, ibid.

FRANCIS BONNAMY 1906–1983

Pseudonym of American Audrey Boyers Walz; creator of criminologist Peter Shane and Francis Bonnamy, who serves as his Watson.

177   Better a rogue than a fool.
> —*Dead Reckoning*, 1943

JORGE LUIS BORGES 1899–1986

Argentinian writer, awarded a special Edgar in 1975 for his significant contribution to the mystery and detective genre.

178   Everything happens to a man precisely, precisely *now*.
> —Yu Tsun, "The Garden of Forking Paths," 1941; English translation by Donald A. Yates, 1958

179   "In a riddle whose answer is chess, what is the only prohibited word?"
I thought a moment and replied, "The word *chess*."
> —Stephen Albert, answered by Yu Tsun, ibid.

180   My blood boils when I hear it said that a man can't measure up to his fantasies.
> —Commendatore San Giacomo, "Free Will and the Commendatore," *Six Problems for Don Isidro Parodi*, 1942; written in collaboration with Adolpho Bioy-Casares; English translation by Norman Thomas di Giovanni, 1981

181   A compliment is better than the truth.
> —Mario Bonfonti, ibid.

182   The punishment lies in the sin.
> —Mario Bonfonti, ibid.

183   Reality hasn't the least obligation to be interesting.
> —Lönnrot, "Death and the Compass," 1944; English translation by Donald A. Yates, 1962

STEVEN BOSAK

American writing teacher and novelist, whose first novel, *Gammon*, introduces Vernon Bradlusky, gambler and backgammon columnist, who tries to find out why his partner has been murdered.

184   All good strategies come full circle. The game that's won with one attack can be lost with the next.
> —Vernon Bradlusky, *Gammon*, 1985

ANTHONY BOUCHER 1911–1968

Pseudonym of William Anthony Parker White, who also wrote as H. H. Holmes. As Boucher, detective novelist and three-time Edgar-winning mystery critic. The annual mystery fan conference, Bouchercon, was named in his honor.

185   It is the blatantly obvious that defies this muddle-headed world, which chooses what is quite possibly so in preference to what is obviously truth. This "quite possibly so" is rarely entirely wrong; it is simply confused. And truth can issue far more readily from error than from confusion.
> —Dr. Ashwin, *The Case of the Seven of Calvary*, 1937

186   Eliminate the impossible. Then if nothing remains, some part of the "impossible" must be possible.
> —Dr. Derringer's dictum, *Rocket to the Morgue*, 1942

187   Sex and money are the two all-dominant motives for murder, and of the two I'll lay odds on money every time.
—Detective Terry Marshall, ibid.

188   As the ostrich observed, "Where is everybody?"
—*The Case of the Seven Sneezes*, 1942

JOHN BOWEN 1924–

English playwright and suspense novelist; creator of Paul Hatcher, an ardent movie buff, who looked through his rear window and decided the woman was not a woman at all.

189   A valuable object has no value unless that value can be realized.
—Paul Hatcher, *The McGuffin*, 1984

This work pays homage to the movie *Rear Window* and to Alfred Hitchcock, a "MacGuffin" being his term for the device that serves to get the story going.

RICK BOYER 1943–

American detective novelist, winner of an Edgar for *Billingsgate Shoal*; creator of Doc Adams, oral surgeon and amateur detective.

190   Grief is its own anesthetic.
—Doc Adams, *Billingsgate Shoal*, 1982

RAY BRADBURY 1920–

Noted American science fiction author, who at sixty-five published his first detective novel. He himself is the Crazy Kid of the story.

191   Death is a lonely business.
—The dreadful whisper, heard by the Crazy Kid, *Death Is a Lonely Business*, 1985

MARY ELIZABETH BRADDON 1837–1915

Victorian editor and novelist; *Lady Audley's Secret* is the best remembered of her many works.

192   Grief is so selfish.
—*Lady Audley's Secret*, 1887

193   If you ever smoke, my dear aunt (and I'm told that many
women take a quiet weed under the rose), be very careful
how you choose your cigars.
—Robert Audley to Lady Audley, ibid.

194   Circumstantial evidence, that wonderful fabric which is built
out of straws collected at every point of the compass, and
which is yet strong enough to hang a man. Upon what
infinitesimal trifles may sometimes hang the whole secret of
some wicked mystery.
—Robert Audley, ibid.

195   Life is such a very troublesome matter, when all is said and
done, that it's as well even to take its blessings quietly.
—Robert Audley, ibid.

CARYL BRAHMS 1901–1982 and S. J. SIMON d. 1948

English writers who collaborated to write comic detective tales.
Caryl Brahms was the pseudonym of ballet critic and playwright
Caroline Abrahams. S. J. Simon was the pseudonym of Simon
Jasha Skidelsky, noted bridge expert.

196   A ballet without an audience is like a cherry orchard after
Tchekov has finished with it.
—*A Bullet in the Ballet*, 1937

197   Poof, the money it interests me not. I am an artist. How
much?
—Vladimir Stroganoff, ibid.

ERNEST BRAMAH 1868–1942

Pseudonym of Ernest Bramah Smith; creator of Max Carrados, the
first and most famous blind detective, whose "blindness has merely
impelled him to develop those senses which in most of us lie half
dormant and practically unused."

198   The best use you can make of the gallows is to cheat it.
—Max Carrados, "The Knight's Cross Signal
Problem," *Max Carrados*, 1914

199   The inevitable is the one thing I invariably accept.
—Max Carrados, "The Game Played in the
Dark," ibid.

200 There is no form of villainy that I haven't gone through in all its phases. Theoretically, of course, but so far as working out the details is concerned and preparing for emergencies, efficiently and with craftsmanlike pride. . . . The point is, that the criminal mind is rarely original, and I find that in nine cases out of ten that sort of crime is committed exactly as I have already done it.
—Max Carrados, "The Mystery of the
Vanished Petition Crown," *Max Carrados
Mysteries*, 1927

201 The most difficult person to find is one who does not exist.
—Max Carrados, "The Holloway Flat
Tragedy," ibid.

SIMON BRETT 1945–

English detective novelist; creator of Charles Paris, a middle-aged, not-very-successful actor, who stumbles across murder cases he has to solve.

202 *Feed:* I heard on the radio this morning that the police are looking for a man with one eye.
Comic: Typical inefficiency.
—Vaudeville gag used as a chapter heading,
A Comedian Dies, 1979

LYNN BROCK 1877–1943

Pseudonym of Irish-born Alister McAlister, who also wrote as Anthony Wharton. As Brock, detective novelist; creator of Colonel Gore.

203 The most deplorable variety of humbug is the kind that humbugs no one but himself.
—Sylvia Luttrell, *Colonel Gore's Second
Case*, 1926

HEYWOOD BROUN 1888–1939

American journalist and social commentator, a member of the Algonquin's famous Round Table group.

204 In the march up to the heights of fame there comes a spot close to the summit in which man reads "nothing but detective stories."
—"G. K. C.," *Pieces of Hate, and Other
Enthusiasms*, 1922

CARTER BROWN 1923–1985

Pseudonym of English-born Australian novelist Alan Geoffrey Yates, who also wrote as Peter Carter Brown and as Caroline Farr. As Carter Brown, writer of popular "pulp" novels.

205   There is nothing like a blonde to decorate a kitchen.
                      —Al Wheeler, *The Body*, 1958

206   The slug from his gun had ploughed a furrow across the top of my scalp. Close enough to hurt, but no more than that. One inch lower, and I would have been a bad verse on a chunk of granite.
                      —Al Wheeler, *The Victim*, 1959

207   "I'm Lieutenant Wheeler, from the sheriff's office," I told him.

"Only a lieutenant!" He sounded bitterly disappointed. "Is that the best they could do?"

"This is Pine City County," I snarled, "and here, with a homicide, you get me. If you don't like the idea, you can always take your corpse someplace else and start over."
                      —Al Wheeler, *Burden of Guilt*, 1970

FREDERIC BROWN 1906–1972

American mystery and suspense novelist, who also wrote fantasy and science fiction—to overcome, he said, the "too real" aspects of detective fiction; creator of Ed Hunter and Ambrose Hunter. His first detective novel, *The Fabulous Clipjoint*, won an Edgar.

208   *We are the Hunters.* The name fits. We're going hunting in the dark alleys for a killer. The man who killed pop.
                      —Young Ed Hunter, joining his Uncle
                        Ambrose in a search for a killer, *The
                        Fabulous Clipjoint*, 1947

209   Death is an incurable disease that men and women are born with; it gets them sooner or later. A murderer never really kills; he but anticipates.
                      —William Sweeney, *The Screaming Mimi*,
                        1949

210   How can anyone decide whether a given fact is important or not unless one knows *everything* about it—and no one knows everything about anything.
                      —Doc Stoeger, *Night of the Jabberwock*,
                        1950

211   He had a name, but it doesn't matter; call him the *psycho*.
　　　　　　　　　　—Opening line, *Knock Three-One-Two*, 1959

GERALD A. BROWNE

American novelist whose suspense thrillers, peopled with the rich
and powerful and the would-be rich and powerful, regularly show
up on best-seller lists.

212   Consequences determined everything.
　　　　　　　　　—Leslie Pickering, *19 Purchase Street*, 1982

213   People who steal try to make up for their lack of identity with
　　　　things that belong to others.
　　　　　　　　　　—Libby Hopkins-Hull, *Stone 588*, 1986

HOWARD BROWNE 1908–

American private eye and suspense novelist, who has also used the
name John Evans; creator of Paul Pine, who wonders "what kind of
reception private detectives get from St. Peter." The first three Paul
Pine "Halo" novels were written under the John Evans pseudonym,
the fourth under his own name, as was *Thin Air*, his classic
suspense novel.

214   I used to be a trusting soul. . . . But after a few years of
　　　　being lied to and cheated and double-crossed—well, I quit
　　　　handing out halos. Too many of them were turning out to be
　　　　tarnished instead of glowing; red instead of gold . . . halos
　　　　in blood.
　　　　　　　　　　—Paul Pine, *Halo in Blood*, 1946

215   It was the kind of street where people lived who had hardly
　　　　anything except their lives.
　　　　　　　　　　—Paul Pine, *Halo for Satan*, 1948

216   I sat there woolgathering—and an inferior grade of wool at
　　　　that.
　　　　　　　　　　—Paul Pine, ibid.

217   You sat and you listened or you stood and you listened. And
　　　　when the calluses got thick enough so you didn't fidget, then
　　　　you could be a private detective.
　　　　　　　　　　—Paul Pine, *Halo in Brass*, 1949

JOHN BUCHAN (LORD TWEEDSMUIR) 1875–1940

Scottish diplomat, lawyer, author of historical works and adventure-espionage fiction, which he called "shockers"; creator of Richard Hannay and Edward Leithen.

218 As Graham Greene said:
"John Buchan was the first to realize the enormous dramatic value of adventure in familiar surroundings happening to unadventurous men."
—"The Last Buchan," *The Spectator*,
May 18, 1941

219 If you are playing a part, you will never keep it up unless you convince yourself that you are *it*.
—Maxim adopted by Richard Hannay, *The Thirty-nine Steps*, 1915

220 Every man at the bottom of his heart believes that he is a born detective.
—Edward Leithen, *The Power-House*, 1916

221 Civilization is a conspiracy. . . . Modern life is the silent compact of comfortable folk to keep up pretenses.
—Ibid.

222 The world is full of clues to everything, and if a man's mind is sharpened on any quest, he happens to notice and take advantage of what otherwise he would miss.
—Edward Leithen, ibid.

223 How thin is the protection of civilisation. An accident and a bogus ambulance—a false charge and a bogus arrest—there were a dozen ways of spiriting one out of this gay, bustling world.
—Edward Leithen, ibid.

224 These shockers are too easy. . . . The author writes the story inductively, and the reader follows it deductively.
—Dr. Greenslade to Richard Hannay, *The Three Hostages*, 1924

225 Let there come a time of great suffering or discontent, when the mind of the ordinary man is in desperation, and the rational fanatic will come by his own.
—Sandy Arbuthnot, ibid.

GERALD BULLETT 1893–1958

English crime fiction novelist, who also wrote as Sebastian Fox.

226   Love isn't words: it is something that happens.
—*The Jury*, 1935

ALAN DENNIS BURKE 1949–

American crime and suspense novelist; creator of Jack Meehan, Assistant District Attorney.

227   It [a crime] only has to be logical in the mind of the killer.
—Jack Meehan, *Driven to Murder*, 1986

THOMAS BURKE 1866–1945

English writer, best remembered for *Limehouse Nights*, a collection of short stories capturing the essence of London's Chinese district; creator of Quong Lee.

228   To be immoral, you must first subscribe to some convention-al morality.
—"The Father of Yoto," *Limehouse Nights*, 1916

229   What is commonly called a miracle is only a fact of applied knowledge.
—"Miracle in Suburbia," *Night-Pieces*, 1935

W. R. BURNETT 1899–1982

American crime novelist William Riley Burnett, awarded the Grand Master title by Mystery Writers of America in 1980.

230   Mother of God, is this the end of Rico?
—Cesare Bandello, known as Rico, *Little Caesar*, 1929

231   I steal and I admit it.
—Roy Earle, *High Sierra*, 1940

232   The biggest rat we had in prison was a preacher who'd gypped his congregation out of the dough he was supposed to build a church with.
—Roy Earle, ibid.

233   Why don't all them people who haven't got any dough get together and take the dough? It's a cinch.
—Roy Earle, ibid.

234   Barmy used to talk to me about earthquakes. He said the old earth just twitches its skin like a dog. We're the fleas, I guess.
—Roy Earle, ibid.

235   The truth is always the perfect alibi.
—Alonzo Emmerich, *The Asphalt Jungle*, 1949

ROBERT BURTON 1577–1640

English clergyman and writer, whose *Anatomy of Melancholy* is a guide to the philosophical and psychological ideas of his time.

236   Carcasses bleed at the sight of the murderer.
—*Anatomy of Melancholy*, 1621–1651

It was also believed that the murderer's image was reflected in the eyes of the victim.

GWENDOLINE BUTLER 1922–

English detective novelist, who also writes as Jennie Melville. As Butler, winner of a Silver Dagger for A *Coffin for Pandora*; creator of Inspector John Coffin.

237   Nature may emulate art but is never so satisfying.
—*A Coffin from the Past*, 1970

MICHAEL BUTTERWORTH 1924–

English suspense novelist, who also writes as Sarah Kemp. His novels are witty and bizarre, as might be expected from a man who says he believes in ghosts and lives in a haunted house.

238   They sinned without fear and—because guiltless sin follows the law of diminishing returns—without pleasure.
—*The Black Look*, 1972

239   Extravagance is a two-dollar cigar. Waste is to light it with a dollar bill.
—*The Man Who Broke the Bank at Monte Carlo*, 1983

240   Thou shalt not get found out committing any of the previous
ten.
—The Eleventh Commandment, *The Five
Million Dollar Prince*, 1986

MAX BYRD 1942–

Professor of English literature and detective novelist, whose first
book, *California Thriller*, won an Edgar for best paperback original;
creator of private eye Mike Haller, originally from Boston, now
working in San Francisco.

241   You're a cop of sorts, yes. . . . You have your own private
code as well. Some inscrutable combination of New England
Puritan and bleeding heart.
—Dinah Farrell to Mike Haller, *California
Thriller*, 1981

242   "A p. i. in Boston named Parker is so good he's writing a
cookbook."
"What's it called?"
"The Thin Man."
—Exchange between Mike Haller and Dinah
Farrell, *Finders Weepers*, 1983

JAMES M. CAIN 1892–1977

American suspense novelist, one of the masters of the hard-boiled
school, though he claimed he belonged to no school. Mystery
Writers of America awarded him the Grand Master title in 1969.
Cain thought his works had some quality of the opening of a
forbidden box, and that this, rather than violence or sex, gave them
the drive so often noted.

243   They threw me off the hay truck about noon.
—Frank Chambers's famous opening
sentence, *The Postman Always Rings
Twice*, 1934

244   I kissed her. . . . It was like being in church.
—Frank Chambers, of his passion for Cora,
ibid.

245   Hell could have opened for me then, and it wouldn't have
made any difference. I had to have her, if I hung for it.
—Frank Chambers, ibid.

246   I knew I couldn't have her and could never have had her. I couldn't kiss the girl whose father I killed.
> —Walter Huff, *Double Indemnity*, 1943

PEDRO CALDERÓN DE LA BARCA 1600–1681

Seventeenth-century Spanish dramatist, author of swashbuckling plays full of adventure and fight which came to be known as cloak-and-dagger plays—*Comedias de capa y espada*. The intrigue, undercover, and melodramatic action has become associated with espionage, especially since World War II, when the phrase was widely used for secret service work.

247   The treason past, the traitor is no longer needed.
> —*Life Is a Dream*, Act III, 1636; English translation by Edward and Elizabeth Huberman

ROBERT WRIGHT CAMPBELL 1927–

American screenwriter and detective novelist, whose paperback original, *The Junkyard Dog*, won an Edgar; creator of Jimmy Flannery, a small-time Chicago politician and amateur detective, and Bosco Silverlake, a Hollywood street philosopher.

248   Never try to eat the holes in Swiss Cheese.
> —Bosco Silverlake, *In La-La Land We Trust*, 1986

249   When you got nothing, a feather looks like a club.
> —Jimmy Flannery, *The Junkyard Dog*, 1986

DOROTHY CANNELL 1943–

English-born mystery novelist with a light touch; now living in the United States. Her first novel, *The Thin Woman*, turned out to be a mystery, although she thought she had been writing a gothic.

250   The trouble with acquiring your sex education through romantic novels is you don't realize that love is miserably hard work.
> —Ellie Simons, *The Thin Woman*, 1984

251   Dig up an old grave, and you'll find maggots.
> —Fergy's warning, *Down the Garden Path*, 1985

252   Don't poke your nose through other people's keyholes. You
may get it stuck.
—Another of Fergie's warnings, ibid.

253   God pays debts without money.
—Fergy, ibid.

MARJORIE CARLETON 1897–1964

American composer and writer of mysteries and suspense thrillers,
often set in Boston or the New England countryside.

254   There's always a psychological moment to dig into capital.
—Taynor Harrison, *The Swan Sang Once*,
1947

255   One thing is as sure as death and taxes, and that's the law of
cause and effect.
—Ethan Arnold, *Vanished*, 1955

HARRY CARMICHAEL 1908–1979

Pseudonym of Canadian-born Englishman Leopold Horace Og-
nall, who also wrote as Hartley Howard. As Carmichael, creator of
insurance assessor John Piper and crime reporter Quinn, "a slave to
accuracy of detail."

256   It doesn't pay to practice perfectionism in murder.
—John Piper, *Alibi*, 1961

257   There's an old adage that tomorrow's another day. At this
time of night it's quite a comfort.
—Detective-Inspector Rillett, *Naked to the
Grave*, 1972

258   It's beyond my conception . . . as her ladyship said when
she was asked if she had bred her own poodles.
—Ibid.

Writing as **HARTLEY HOWARD**, creator of private eye Glenn
Bowman.

259   Half the truth can be worse than a straight lie.
—*The Sealed Envelope*, 1979

JOHN DICKSON CARR 1906–1977

American mystery and detective novelist, master of the impossible
puzzle, expert on locked room murders, awarded the Grand Master

title by Mystery Writers of America in 1962. He also wrote as Carr Dickson, Carter Dickson, and Roger Fairbairn; creator of Dr. Gideon Fell, Henri Bencolin, and Sir Henry Merrivale.

260   Carr said:

"The perfect impossible solution . . . would be one whose secret could be explained in four or five lines."

—Quoted by Ellery Queen, *In the Queen's Parlor*, 1957

261   There is often a great deal to be said in favor of looking for a clue in the place where you know it isn't. You see things you would never have noticed otherwise.

—Dr. Fell, *The Arabian Nights Murder*, 1936

262   There can be no good detective fiction which is not bound by the rule of fair play with regard to presenting the evidence . . . real life is bound by no rule of fair play with regard to anything.

—"A Preface for Connoisseurs in Murder," *The Murder of Sir Edmund Godfrey*, 1936

263   Financiers make money and then go to prison. Authors go to prison and then make money.

—Guadan Cross, *The Burning Court*, 1937

264   I can tamper with the law when, where, and how I like. I have tampered with the law when, where, and how I liked; and I will do it again.

—Henri Bencolin, *The Four False Weapons*, 1937

265   Facts are piffle.

—Dr. Fell, *The Crooked Hinge*, 1938

266   Heaven pity the person who tries to tell all the truth.

—Dr. Fell, ibid.

JOHN CARTER 1905–1975

Noted English bibliographer, the first to pay serious attention to detective stories.

267   If we err, therefore, in our liking for detective stories, we err with Plato.

—"Collecting Detective Fiction," *New Paths in Book Collecting*, 1934

HERON CARVIC d. 1980

English actor and writer; creator of Miss Seeton, an elderly art teacher with an unexpected talent for police work, sometimes called the "battling brolly."

268   If there were no such thing as coincidence, there would be no such word.

> —Miss Seeton to Superintendent Delphick,
> *Picture Miss Seeton*, 1968

269   Crime may pay, but the large rewards are reaped by the barons of the industry. . . . It is a sad comment on the progress in industrial relations that little thought and no effective action has been taken to improve the lot of the evildoer. . . . Society has yet to evolve a law to safeguard the career of the lawbreaker.

> —*Miss Seeton Sings*, 1973

270   To vice innocence must always seem only a superior kind of chicanery.

> —*Odds on Miss Seeton*, 1975

VERA CASPARY 1899–1987

American screenwriter and mystery novelist; *Laura*, her first mystery, is a masterpiece.

271   If the dreams of any so-called normal man were exposed . . . there would be no more gravity and dignity left for mankind.

> —Waldo Lydecker, *Laura*, 1943

272   There are a lot of people who haven't got the brains for their college educations.

> —Mark McPherson, ibid.

SARAH CAUDWELL

Pseudonym of English barrister Sarah Cockburn; creator of Hilary Tamar, a legal historian who enjoys "speaking ill of the dead." Tamar's gender, never explicitly stated, is a matter of debate. The author says she doesn't know.

273   Little as I liked the prospect of the evening newspaper containing the headline "Barristers Shot in Fulham Fracas,"

I did not think it would be improved by the insertion of the words "and Oxford Don".

> —Hilary Tamar, *Thus Was Adonis Murdered*, 1981

274 "Parents can be very difficult."

"They have suffered a traumatic experience—you must make allowances."

> —A young man, making ill-advised remarks about his parents to Hilary Tamar, who has a tart response, *The Shortest Way to Hades*, 1985

RAYMOND CHANDLER 1888–1959

One of the finest and most influential American detective novelists, who saw the detective as a modern knight searching for a hidden truth; creator of Philip Marlowe, the shop-soiled Galahad. *The Long Goodbye* won an Edgar in 1954.

275 Of his craft, Chandler said:

"When a book, any sort of book, reaches a certain intensity of artistic performance it becomes literature."

> —In a letter to Erle Stanley Gardner, January 29, 1946

276 And about readers:

"Show me a man or woman who cannot stand mysteries and I will show you a fool, a clever fool—perhaps—but a fool just the same."

> —"Casual Notes on the Mystery Novel," 1949, in *Raymond Chandler Speaking*, 1977

277 Six years after creating Philip Marlowe, Chandler wrote a now-famous essay, stating the code of the private eye:

"Down these mean streets a man must go who is not himself mean, who is neither tarnished nor afraid. . . . He is the hero, he is everything. He must be a complete man and a common man and yet an unusual man."

> —"The Simple Art of Murder," *Atlantic Monthly*, December 1944

278 Trouble is my business.

> —Philip Marlowe, for $25 a day, and a guarantee of $250 if he pulls the job off, "Trouble Is My Business," *Dime Detective Magazine*, August 1939

279   What did it matter where you lay once you were dead? . . . You were dead, you were sleeping the big sleep, you were not bothered by things like that.
—Philip Marlowe, *The Big Sleep*, 1939

280   Somebody ought to sew buttons on his face.
—To keep his mouth shut, *Farewell, My Lovely*, 1940

281   Law is where you buy it in this town.
—Philip Marlowe, ibid.

Chandler considered using *Law Is Where You Buy It* as the title for this novel.

282   They say money doesn't stink. I sometimes wonder.
—The hot dog man, ibid.

283   I've never liked this scene. Detective confronts murderer. Murderer produces gun, points same at detective. Murderer tells detective the whole sad story, with the idea of shooting him at the end of it. Thus wasting a lot of valuable time, even if in the end murderer did shoot detective. Only murderer never does. Something always happens to prevent it.
—Philip Marlowe to Muriel Chess, *The Lady in the Lake*, 1943

284   When a guy gets too complicated he's unhappy. And when he's unhappy—his luck runs out.
—Leo, "The Blue Dahlia" (screenplay), 1945; edited by Matthew J. Bruccoli, 1976

285   Something isn't what it seems and the old tired but always reliable hunch tells me that if the hand is played the way it is dealt the wrong person is going to lose the pot.
—Philip Marlowe, *The Little Sister*, 1949

286   There is no trap so deadly as the trap you set for yourself.
—Philip Marlowe, *The Long Goodbye*, 1953

287   I'm a licensed private investigator and have been for quite a while. I'm a lone wolf, unmarried, getting middle-aged, and not rich. I've been in jail more than once and I don't do divorce business. I like liquor and women and chess and a few other things. The cops don't like me too well, but I know a couple I get along with. I'm a native son, born in Santa

Rosa, both parents dead, no brothers or sisters, and when I get knocked off in a dark alley sometime, if it happens, as it could to anyone in my business, and to plenty of people in any business or in no business at all these days, nobody will feel that the bottom has dropped out of his or her life.
—Philip Marlowe, ibid.

288 You can't win them all.
—Roger Wade to Edward Loring, ibid.

This is the first recorded use of this catch phrase, according to *The Concise Oxford Dictionary of Proverbs* (1982). It was not in general usage until the mid-1960s.

GEORGE CHAPMAN 1559?–1634

Seventeenth-century English playwright, who penned one of the classic lines about murder.

289 Blood, though it sleep a time, yet never dies.
The gods on murtherers fix revengeful eyes.
—*The Widdowes Tears*, Act V, scene iv, 1612

LESLIE CHARTERIS 1907–

Naturalized American writer, born Leslie Charles Bowyer Yin in Singapore of a Chinese father and an English mother; creator of Simon Templar, better known as The Saint, a great rogue on the side of the angels.

290 We Saints are normally souls of peace and goodwill towards men. But we don't like crooks, blood-suckers, traders in dope and damnation and other verminous escrescences of that type—such as yourself. We're going to beat you up and do you down, skin you and smash you, and scare you off the face of Europe. We are not bothered about the letter of the Law, we act exactly as we please, we inflict what punishment we think suitable, and no one is going to escape us.
—The Saint, "The Man Who Was Clever," *Enter the Saint*, 1930

291 I'm just a born-an'-bred fighting machine, and a quiet life of the moss-gathering would just be hell for me. I'm not a dick, because I can't be bothered with red tape, but I'm on the same side.
—The Saint, ibid.

292 As a general rule, problems in detection bore me stiff—it's so much more entertaining to commit the crime yourself.
—The Saint, "The Appalling Politician," *The Brighter Buccaneer*, 1933

293 That childish haloed figure had stood for an ideal, for a justice that struck swiftly where the law could not strike, a terror which could not be turned aside by technicalities: it had never been used wantonly.
—"The Art of the Alibi," *The Misfortunes of Mr. Teal*, 1934

294 "Do you think you can make a monkey out of me?"
"Certainly not. I wouldn't try to improve on God's creation."
—Mr. Teal, answered in Saintly fashion, ibid.

295 You need brains in this life of crime, but I often think you need luck even more.
—The Saint, "The Damsel in Distress," *Boodle*, 1934

296 Successful crime is simply The Art of The Unexpected.
—The Saint, "The Mixture as Before," ibid.

297 Charteris, speaking for himself and the Saint, said in a 1935 radio broadcast: "I'm mad enough to believe in romance. And I'm sick and tired of this age—tired of the miserable little mildewed things that people racked their brains about, and wrote books about, and called life. I wanted something more elementary and honest—battle, murder, sudden death, with plenty of good beer and damsels in distress, and a complete callousness about blipping the ungodly over the beezer. It mayn't be life as we know it, but it ought to be."

GEOFFREY CHAUCER 1343?–1400

Great English poet, whose narrative poem, *The Canterbury Tales*, enriches our knowledge of human nature as much today as it did in centuries past.

298 Mordre wol out, certeyn, it wol nat faille.
—"The Prioress's Tale," *The Canterbury Tales*,* c. 1390

*Text used: F. N. Robinson, *The Works of Geoffrey Chaucer*, 2nd ed., Boston: Houghton Mifflin Company, 1957.

Chaucer repeats the proverbial expression four tales later:

299   Mordre wol out, that se we day by day.
—"The Nun's Priest's Tale," ibid.

G. K. CHESTERTON 1874–1936

English journalist, poet, novelist, and detective story writer Gilbert Keith Chesterton; creator of Father Brown, whose head was never better than when he lost it.

300   There are no words to express the abyss between isolation and having one ally.
—*The Man Who Was Thursday*, 1908

301   The most incredible thing about miracles is that they happen.
—"The Blue Cross," *The Innocence of Father Brown*, 1911

302   The criminal is the creative artist; the detective only the critic.
—Valentin, ibid.

303   Cheerfulness without humour is a very trying thing.
—Father Brown, "The Three Tools of Death," ibid.

304   To be clever enough to get all that money, one must be stupid enough to want it.
—Muscari, "The Paradise of Thieves," *The Wisdom of Father Brown*, 1914

305   An artist will betray himself by some sort of sincerity.
—Father Brown, "The Dagger with Wings," *The Incredulity of Father Brown*, 1926

306   You see, it was I who killed all those people.
—Father Brown, in the title story of the collection, *The Secret of Father Brown*, 1927

And then he explains:

307   I had planned out each of the crimes very carefully. I had thought out exactly how a thing like that could be done, and in what style or state of mind a man could really do it. And when I was quite sure that I felt exactly like the murderer myself, of course I knew who he was.
—Father Brown, ibid.

308   If you convey to a woman that something ought to be done,
there is always a dreadful danger that she will suddenly do it.
—Father Brown, "The Song of the Flying
Fish," ibid.

PETER CHEYNEY 1896–1951

English novelist who tried to write in the tradition of the American
hard-boiled school; creator of Lemmy Caution and others.

309   Life is like a pack of cards. Every time you think you've got
the ace you find you haven't.
—*Another Little Drink*, 1940

310   You never knew any trouble in this world that some dame
wasn't at the bottom of.
—*You Can't Keep the Change*, 1940

311   When in doubt don't do anything.
—Ibid.

312   All the good guys go nutty in their old age thinkin' about the
good times they mighta had if they hadn't been so good.
—*Sorry You've Been Troubled*, 1942

ERSKINE CHILDERS 1870–1922

Anglo-Irish author whose only work of fiction, *The Riddle of the
Sands*, is one of the early espionage classics. "The game," as
intelligence work was beginning to be called, turns deadly serious as
two young Englishmen sail over the tidal sands of the North
German coast, and gradually uncover the beginnings of a German
plan to invade England.

313   It was the passionate wish of his heart, somehow and
somewhere, to get a chance of turning his knowledge of this
coast to practical account in the war that he felt was bound to
come, to play that "splendid game" in this, the most
fascinating field for it.
—Davies' hope, *The Riddle of the Sands*,
1903

314   When at a loss, tell the truth.
—An axiom Carruthers found sound, ibid.

315   To reduce a romantic ideal to a working plan is a very
difficult thing.
—Carruthers, ibid.

Childers himself volunteered for British service when World War I began, serving in the British Royal Air Service. After the war, deeply troubled by the Irish question, he returned to Ireland to fight for home rule. As a member of the Irish Republican Army he was captured, court-martialed, and executed by firing squad. His last words were:

316   Come closer, lads; it will be easier for you.
                        —Quoted by Norman Donaldson in his
                        excellent 1976 introduction to *The Riddle
                        of the Sands*, 1903

DAME AGATHA CHRISTIE 1890–1976

English mystery novelist and playwright; creator of many sleuths, including two of the most famous in detective fiction, Hercule Poirot and Miss Jane Marple. Her first novel, *The Mysterious Affair at Styles*, marks the beginning of the Golden Age of British mystery fiction. She received the first Grand Master title ever awarded by Mystery Writers of America.

317   Poirot was an extraordinary-looking little man. He was
           hardly more than five feet four inches, but carried himself
           with great dignity. His head was exactly the shape of an egg,
           and he always perched it a little on one side. His moustache
           was very stiff and military. The neatness of his attire was
           almost incredible; I believe a speck of dust would have caused
           him more pain than a bullet wound.
                        —Captain Hastings, giving the first
                        description of the little Belgian who came
                        to England as a refugee in 1914, *The
                        Mysterious Affair at Styles*, 1920

318   Two young adventurers for hire. Willing to do anything, go
           anywhere. Pay must be good. No unreasonable offer refused.
                        —Tuppence Cowley and Tommy Beresford,
                        henceforth to be known as The Young
                        Adventurers, Ltd., *The Secret Adversary*,
                        1922

319   With method and logic one can accomplish anything.
                        —Hercule Poirot, "The Kidnapped Prime
                        Minister," *Poirot Investigates*, 1924

320   It is really a very hard life. Men will not be nice to you if you are not good-looking and women will not be nice to you if you are.
—Anne Beddingfeld, *The Man in the Brown Suit*, 1924

321   It is completely unimportant. That is why it is so interesting.
—Hercule Poirot to Dr. Sheppard, *The Murder of Roger Ackroyd*, 1926

322   Never worry about what you say to a man. They're so conceited that they never believe you mean it if it's unflattering.
—Caroline Sheppard to Ursula Bourne, ibid.

323   Very few of us are what we seem.
—Tommy Beresford, *Partners in Crime*, 1929

324   She's the worst cat in the village.
—Griselda Clement of Jane Marple, *The Murder at the Vicarage*, 1930

Jane Marple was an elderly spinster whose hobby was human nature—and she wasn't above using binoculars to find out about it.

325   There is no detective in England equal to a spinster lady of uncertain age with plenty of time on her hands.
—Leonard Clement, ibid.

326   When the *mal de mer* seizes me, I, Hercule Poirot, am a creature with no gray cells, no order, no method—a mere member of the human race of somewhat below average intelligence.
—*Death in the Clouds*, 1935

327   No crime can be successful without luck!
—Hercule Poirot, *The A.B.C. Murders*, 1936

328   Speech . . . is an invention of man's to prevent him from thinking.
—Hercule Poirot, ibid.

329   It's very easy to kill, so long as no one suspects you.
—Miss Fullerton, *Murder Is Easy*, 1939

330   Anyone's safety depends principally on the fact that nobody wishes to kill them. . . . We have come to depend upon what has been called the good will of civilization.
—Ibid.

Murder Is Easy was the last of Agatha Christie's Golden Age mysteries.

331 Few men are heroes to themselves at the moment of visiting their dentist.
—*One, Two, Buckle My Shoe*, 1940

332 You can only really get under anybody's skin if you are married to them.
—Jane Marple, *The Body in the Library*, 1942

333 Never do anything yourself that others can do for you.
—Hercule Poirot, "The Apples of Hesperides," *The Labors of Hercules*, 1947

334 The worst is so often true.
—Jane Marple, *They Do It with Mirrors*, 1952

335 Of course I despise money when I haven't got any. It's the only dignified thing to do.
—Cedric Crackenthorpe to Lucy Eyelesbarrow, *4:50 from Paddington*, 1957

336 Never say anything your mother shouldn't hear about!
—Mr. Bradley to Mark Easterbrook, *The Pale Horse*, 1961

337 Don't worry. Surely the most fatuous words in the English or any other language.
—Colin Lamb, *The Clocks*, 1963

338 In her autobiography, Christie said:
"I think it is possible that Miss Marple arose from the pleasure I have taken in portraying Dr. Sheppard's sister in *The Murder of Roger Ackroyd*. She had been my favorite character in the book—an acidulated spinster, full of curiosity, knowing everything, hearing everything: the complete detective service in the home."
—*Agatha Christie: An Autobiography*, 1977

339 "One of the pleasures of writing detective stories is that there are so many types to choose from: the light-hearted thriller, which is particularly pleasant to do; the intricate detective story with an involved plot which is technically interesting and requires a great deal of work, but is always rewarding; and then what I can only describe as the detective story that has a kind of passion behind it—that passion being to help save innocence. Because it is *innocence* that matters, not *guilt.*"

—Ibid.

DOUGLAS CLARK 1919–

English pharmaceutical executive and detective novelist; creator of Chief Superintendent George Masters, called the "Great-I-Am" of Scotland Yard, and Chief Inspector Green.

340   Hard facts are just the kernel of the nut. What surrounds them has to be cracked.
—Detective Chief Inspector George Masters, *Nobody's Perfect*, 1969

341   Impudence and fortitude will get you anywhere.
—*The Gimmel Flask*, 1977

342   You call subjecting an innocent man to the business of a murder trial justice? That is law, not justice.
—Bella Bartholomew, *Poacher's Bag*, 1980

BRIAN CLEEVE 1921–

Anglo-Irish mystery and espionage novelist; creator of Sean Ryan.

343   Cleeve has said:
"Crime and thriller stories have always appealed to me for the same reason that fairy stories do, and folk tales and myths. They deal directly with the conflict between good and evil, and for that reason touch the most fundamental levels of human experience."
—*Twentieth-Century Crime and Mystery Writers*, 2nd ed., 1985

344   One should never think too much, or one would inevitably kill one's self.
—Lt. Niccolò Tucci, *Violent Death of a Bitter Englishman*, 1967

EDWARD CLINE 1946–

American private eye novelist; creator of Chess Hanrahan, who makes his first appearance in *First Prize*.

345   You can buy the most unpleasant surprises.
                —Chess Hanrahan, *First Prize*, 1987

346   Nothing that is observable in reality is exempt from rational
           scrutiny.
                —Chess Hanrahan's motto, ibid.

V. C. CLINTON-BADDELEY 1900–1970

English historian and editor, playwright, poet, and detective
novelist Victor Clinton Clinton-Baddeley; creator of Professor R. V.
Davie, elderly, donnish sleuth.

347   A rudery is only a rudery when it has power to shock.
                —Professor Davie, *Death's Bright Dart*, 1967

348   Fashion and tradition are continually at war, and fashion
           always wins.
                —Professor Davie, *My Foe Outstretch'd
                beneath the Tree*, 1968

349   Money 's the root of all comfort.
                —Professor Davie, *No Case for the Police*,
                1970

TUCKER COE. *See* Donald Westlake.

G.D.H. COLE 1889–1959 and MARGARET COLE 1893–1980

English social and political historians, who coauthored detective
stories as a sideline.

350   Uncertainty is a killing business.
                —Carter Woodman, *The Brooklyn Murders*,
                1923; written by G.D.H. Cole alone

351   A man who pretends to be a fool when he isn't is a public
           nuisance.
                —Lord Blatchington, *The Blatchington
                Tangle*, 1926

352   Murders *do* break up a house party.
                —A plaintive houseguest, ibid.

MANNING COLES

Joint pseudonym of Cyril Henry Coles, 1899–1965, and Adelaide
Frances Oke Manning, 1891–1959; creators of Tommy Hamble-
don of British intelligence.

353 If a country is worth living in, it is worth fighting for.
> —Tommy Hambledon, *Drink to Yesterday*,
> 1940

354 One should, however, distinguish between what really shocks one's conscience and what only shocks one's prejudices.
> —Hendrik Brandt, ibid.

355 Beauty draws me with a single hair if it is blonde enough.
> —Tommy Hambledon, *They Tell No Tales*,
> 1941

JOHN COLLIER 1901–1980

English writer of novels and short stories; *Fancies and Goodnights* contains many of his best stories, and was a Queen's Quorum selection.

356 If ever you are charged with murder, hang yourself in your cell the first night.
> —"The Touch of Nutmeg Makes It," *Fancies
> and Goodnights*, 1951

MARY COLLINS 1908–

American author of half a dozen mysteries, all set in California in the 1940s.

357 The tension in Iris' chest built up unbearably. By rights, the hooks on her bra ought to snap.
> —*Dog Eat Dog*, 1949

MAX ALLAN COLLINS 1948–

American crime and suspense novelist, who also writes the Dick Tracy comic strip; creator of Quarry, Vietnam veteran turned hit man, and, in another series, Nate Heller, Chicago ex-policeman turned private eye.

358 Certain people are going to want certain other people dead. . . . Anybody I ever hit was set to go anyway. I saw to it that it happened fast and clean.
> —Quarry's chilling rationalization, *The Broker*,
> 1976

359   If I thought life was cheap, I wouldn't charge so much to take
          one.
                                        —Quarry, *The Broker's Wife*, 1976

360   I haven't killed anybody all day. Help me keep it that way.
                                        —Nate Heller, *True Detective*, 1983

WILKIE COLLINS 1824–1889

English novelist who wrote the Victorian mystery masterpiece, *The
Woman in White*, and the Victorian detective novel masterpiece,
The Moonstone. Though he wrote many other novels and short
stories, he is best remembered for these two. His chosen epitaph
was, "Author of *The Woman in White* and other works of fiction."

361   From the beginning, reviewers scorned the genre:
          "Mr. Collins is in the habit of prefixing prefaces to his stories
          which might almost lead one to think he looks on himself as
          an artist."
                                        —*Pall Mall Gazette*, contemptuously
                                        reviewing *The Moonstone*; quoted by
                                        Julian Symons, *Bloody Murder*, 1972

362   Collins was an artist, and his prefaces worth noting:
          "The business of fiction is to exhibit human life."
                                        —Preface, *Basil*, 1852

363   And:
          "I have always held the old-fashioned opinion that the
          primary object of a work of fiction should be to tell a story."
                                        —Preface, *The Woman in White*, 1861

364   It is truly wonderful how easily Society can console itself for
          the worst of its shortcomings with a little bit of claptrap.
                                        —Count Fosco, ibid.

365   Crimes cause their own detection, do they? And murder will
          out (another moral epigram), will it?
                                        —Count Fosco, scoffing at Laura's beliefs,
                                        ibid.

366   English Society is as often the accomplice as it is the enemy
          of crime.
                                        —Count Fosco to Marian Halcombe, ibid.

367   When an English jury has to choose between a plain fact, *on*
          the surface, and a long explanation *under* the surface, it
          always takes the fact in preference to the explanation.
                                        —Mr. Kyrle to Walter Hartright, ibid.

368   The best men are not consistent in good—why should the worst men be consistent in evil?
—Walter Hartright, ibid.

369   Suffering can, and does, develop the latent evil that there is in humanity, as well as the latent good.
—*Armadale*, 1866

370   Crime brings its own fatality with it.
—Prologue, *The Moonstone*, 1868

371   A grizzled, elderly man, so miserably lean that he looked as if he had not got a ounce of flesh on his bones. . . . His eyes, of a steely gray, had a disconcerting trick, when they encountered your eyes, of looking as if they expected something more from you than you were aware of yourself.
—Sergeant Cuff, making his first
appearance, ibid.

372   I haven't much time to be fond of anything. But when I *have* a moment's fondness to bestow, most times, Mr. Betteredge, the roses get it.
—Sergeant Cuff, ibid.

373   At one end of the inquiry there was a murder, and at the other end there was a spot of ink on a tablecloth that nobody could account for. In all my experience along the dirtiest ways of this dirty little world I have never met with such a thing as a trifle yet.
—Sergeant Cuff, ibid.

374   Human life is a sort of target—misfortune is always firing at it, and always hitting the mark.
—Sergeant Cuff to Mr. Betteredge, ibid.

375   If there is such a thing known at the doctor's shop as a *detective fever*, that disease had now got fast hold of your humble servant.
—Gabriel Betteredge, ibid.

376   I don't suspect, I know.
—Sergeant Cuff, ibid.

377   Do you feel an uncomfortable heat at the pit of your stomach, sir? and a nasty thumping at the top of your head? . . . I call it the detective fever; and *I* first caught it in the company of Sergeant Cuff.
—Gabriel Betteredge, complaining of his new
disease, ibid.

378   We often hear (almost invariably, however, from superficial observers) that guilt can look like innocence. I believe it to be infinitely the truer axiom of the two that innocence can look like guilt.
>   —Franklin Blake, ibid.

379   It is only in books that the officers of the detective force are superior to the weakness of making a mistake.
>   —Sergeant Cuff, ibid.

380   Suspect the very last person on whom suspicion could possibly fall.
>   —Old Sharon's advice, *My Lady's Money*, 1878

RICHARD CONNELL 1893–1949

Prolific American writer, author of the classic suspense story "The Most Dangerous Game."

381   The world is made up of two classes—the hunters and the hunted.
>   —Sanger Rainsford, "The Most Dangerous Game," *Variety*, 1925

J. J. CONNINGTON 1880–1947

Pseudonym of Scottish professor of chemistry Alfred Walter Stewart. As Connington, writer of meticulously crafted detective novels in the Freeman Wills Crofts tradition; creator of Chief Constable Sir Clinton Driffield and Squire Wendover, and in a second series, Mark Brand.

382   There's only one length for a story and that's the right length.
>   —*The Four Defenses*, 1940

383   Since that inquest, I've been regularly oysterized.
>   —Ibid.

JOSEPH CONRAD 1857–1924

Polish-born, naturalized British citizen, master mariner, novelist, and story writer, best known for *Lord Jim*. His thrillers, to use the word in its finest sense, are among the first and the best ever written.

384   The terrorist and the policeman come from the same basket.
            —*The Secret Agent*, 1907

385   All a man can betray is his conscience.
            —Razumov, *Under Western Eyes*, 1911

386   A man's most open actions have a secret side to them.
            —Razumov, ibid.

387   Let a fool be made serviceable according to his folly.
            —Ibid.

388   The scrupulous and the just, the noble, humane, and
            devoted natures; the unselfish and intelligent may begin a
            movement—but it passes away from them. They are not the
            leaders of a revolution. They are its victims.
            —Ibid.

389   A belief in a supernatural source of evil is not necessary; men
            alone are quite capable of every wickedness.
            —Nathalie Haldin, ibid.

390   Do you conceive the desolation of the thought—no-one-to-
            go-to?
            —Razumov to Nathalie Haldin, ibid.

K. C. CONSTANTINE

Well-kept pseudonym of American police procedural novelist;
creator of Mario Balzic, police chief of Rocksburg, Pennsylvania.

391   Nobody loves like one coward loves another.
            —Mario Balzic, *The Rocksburg Railroad
            Murders*, 1972

392   I told myself then that whenever I didn't know what to do, I'd
            never make the mistake of doing something.
            —Lieutenant Moyer's rule, ibid.

393   Opportunity knocks several times, but chance never knocks.
            Doesn't have to.
            —Iron City Steve, ibid.

394   For everything there's a price. You pay in money or time or
            sweat or blood, but you pay.
            —Mario Balzic, *A Fix Like This*, 1975

DESMOND CORY 1928–

Pseudonym of English crime novelist and university lecturer Shaun Lloyd McCarthy, who also writes under his own name and as Theo Callas. As Cory, creator of Johnny Fedora.

395   Bony thought that he himself was perfectly normal and that the psychiatrist was a bearded weirdie who couldn't have told him breakfast time from Thursday.

> —Bony Wright, a convicted murderer whom the prison psychiatrist has called an "affective schizoid sociopath," *A Bit of a Shunt Up the River*, 1974

396   If you're self-satisfied at twenty-five, you might as well be dead.

> —*Bennett*, 1977

397   No Christian society has ever known what to do with people who go round taking the Bible literally.

> —Ibid.

398   Detective stories—aren't they jokes, basically, at the expense of the reader?

> —Ibid.

FRANCIS CRANE 1896–1981

American mystery novelist; creator of Pat and Jean Abbott, the widely traveled husband-and-wife detective team.

399   A bath always makes me very logical.

> —Jean Abbott, *The Indigo Necklace*, 1945

EDMUND CRISPIN 1921–1978

Pseudonym of English musician Robert Bruce Montgomery. As Crispin, detective novelist; creator of Gervase Fen, self-proclaimed literary critic turned detective, who passes the time playing games such as "Detestable Characters in Fiction," "Awful Lines from Shakespeare," and "Unreadable Books."

400   Most of our decisions are forced on us by laziness.

> —Gervase Fen's reflection, *Holy Disorders*, 1945

401   Psychology is wrong in imagining that when it has analysed evil it has somehow disposed of it.

> —Dallow, ibid.

402   This is a book everyone can afford to be without.
—Gervase Fen, reviewing a friend's book of
poetry, *The Moving Toyshop*, 1946

403   Don't spurn coincidence in that casual way. . . . You say
the most innocent encounter in a detective novel is unfair,
and yet you're always screaming out about having met
someone abroad who lives in the next parish and what a
small world it is.
—Gervase Fen, ibid.

404   One's plots are necessarily *improbable*, but I believe in
making sure they are not *impossible*.
—Mr. Judd, to Gervase Fen, *Buried for
Pleasure*, 1948

405   Like most people, you over-estimate the refining powers of
tribulation.
—Mr. Datchery, *The Long Divorce*, 1951

FREEMAN WILLS CROFTS 1879–1957

Irish engineer and detective novelist whose specialty was to create
and destroy the "perfect alibi"; creator of Inspector French, who
never failed to bring a case to a successful conclusion in his thirty-
year career.

406   Common sense was right ninety-nine times out of a
hundred.
But there was always the hundredth chance.
—*Inspector French's Greatest Case*, 1925

407   If we were all as wise as we should be . . . we should have
no stories to tell.
—Inspector French, *The Box Office Murders*,
1929

408   In vain he longed for the skill of Dr. Thorndyke, who might
have been able with his vacuum extractor to secure micro-
scopic dust from its fibres, which would have solved the
problem.
—Inspector French's wish, ibid.

409   Come on now: use your grey cells, as that Belgian would say.
—Inspector French, *Sir John Magill's Last
Journey*, 1930

410   We prefer the evils we know.
> —Merle Weir, *James Tarrant, Adventurer*,
> 1941

411   There's more in most things than meets the eye.
> —*The Affair at Little Wokeham*, 1943

AMANDA CROSS 1926–

Pseudonym of American Carolyn Heilbrun, professor of English at Columbia University, whose mystery novel authorship was not revealed until she was granted tenure; creator of Professor Kate Fansler, a "sort of over-age Nancy Drew," to use her husband's expression.

412   In former days, everyone found the assumption of innocence so easy; today we find fatally easy the assumption of guilt.
> —Professor Kate Fansler, *Poetic Justice*,
> 1970

413   That's the point of quotations, you know: one can use another's words to be insulting.
> —Professor Kate Fansler, *The Theban
> Mysteries*, 1971

414   Shifting problems is the first rule for a long and pleasant life.
> —Professor Kate Fansler, ibid.

415   "Cynic" is the sentimentalist's name for the realist.
> —Max Reston, *The Question of Max*, 1976

416   One hires lawyers as one hires plumbers, because one wants to keep one's hands off the beastly drains.
> —Max Reston, admitting that plumbers are
> harder to find than lawyers, ibid.

417   I see nothing wrong with acting out one's dreams, if only to discover that they never had a shred of reality about them.
> —Reed, ibid.

418   Odd, the years it took to learn one simple fact: that the prize just ahead, the next job, publication, love affair, marriage always seemed to hold the key to satisfaction but never, in the longer run, sufficed.
> —Professor Kate Fansler, *Death in a
> Tenured Position*, 1981

419   Quoting, like smoking, is a dirty habit to which I am devoted.
> —Professor Kate Fansler, *Sweet Death, Kind
> Death*, 1984

420   Most full lives are filled with empty gestures.
—*No Word from Winifred*, 1986

JAMES CRUMLEY 1939–

American detective novelist; creator of Milton Chester Milodragovitch, more often called "Milo."

421   Crumley says:
"I always introduce my work by explaining that I am a
bastard child of Raymond Chandler—without his books, my
books would be completely different."
—*Twentieth-Century Crime and Mystery
Writers*, 2nd ed., 1985

422   Youth endures all things. . . . Everything but time.
—C. W. Sughrue, *The Last Good Kiss*, 1978

423   Ignorance may not be bliss, but too often knowledge took the
fun out of some parts of life.
—"Milo" Milodragovitch, *Dancing Bear*, 1983

424   I was surprised to find out how few strangers, when I watched
their lives for a few days, turned out to be perfectly boring.
Almost everyone, it seemed, led at least one secret life.
—"Milo" Milodragovitch, ibid.

425   I've always got enough money, but nobody ever has enough
love.
—The fat girl to "Milo" Milodragovitch, ibid.

426   Sometimes you eat the bear, but sometimes the bear eats
you.
—Something they say in Montana, ibid.

427   Life has consequences.
—"Milo" Milodragovitch, ibid.

MARTEN CUMBERLAND 1892–1972

English journalist and detective novelist, who also wrote as Kevin
O'Hara. As Cumberland, creator of Commissaire Saturnin Dax.

428   The most remarkable thing about a coincidence is that it
happens. Yet, to me, a coincidence must always be held
suspect until it proves itself innocent.
—Commissaire Saturnin Dax, *Not Expected
to Live*, 1945

429   As a rule authors are satisfied with murdering language.
> —Chief of Judicial Police, *A Dilemma for
> Dax*, 1946

E. V. CUNNINGHAM 1914–

Pseudonym of American novelist Howard Fast. As Cunningham,
writer of mystery and detective novels; creator of Masao Masuto, a
Japanese-American homicide officer for the Beverly Hills Police
Department.

430   An unwillingness to believe in impending danger is a very
human quality.
> —*The Case of the Poisoned Eclairs*, 1979

CLIVE CUSSLER 1931–

American suspense and espionage novelist; creator of Dirk Pitt,
super-capable government agent.

431   Cussler's advice to the would-be thriller writer:
"If your hero must save the world, make him act human
while he goes about it."
> —"Writing the Suspense-Adventure Novel,"
> *The Writer*, February 1978

432   There are times when even a dedicated feminist needs a
chauvinist to lean on.
> —Dirk Pitt, *Vixen 03*, 1978

433   The Russians haven't built a car that can take a 'fifty-seven
Chevy.
> —Dirk Pitt, putting his foot to the pedal and
> the Cold War into perspective, *Cyclops*,
> 1986

CARROLL JOHN DALY 1889–1958

American writer, most popular *Black Mask* writer of his time;
creator of Race Williams, one of the first hard-boiled detectives.

434   I ain't a crook; just a gentleman adventurer and make my
living working against the law breakers.
> —The nameless narrator, who prefigures
> Race Williams, "The False Burton Combs,"
> *Black Mask*, December 1922

435   The simplest people in the world are crooks.
> —The nameless narrator, ibid.

436   I'm what you might call the middle-man—just a halfway house between the cops and the crooks. . . . But my conscience is clear; I never bumped off a guy what didn't need it.
> —Race Williams, "Knights of the Open Palm," *Black Mask*, June 1, 1923

437   Right and wrong are not written on the statutes for me. . . . My ethics are my own. I'm not saying they're good and I'm not admitting they're bad, and what's more I'm not interested in the opinions of others on that subject.
> —Race Williams, *The Snarl of the Beast*, 1927

438   It's generally people with money who have time to find the pitfalls of life and drop into them. It's up to me to get the rope and haul them out.
> —Race Williams, ibid.

439   I'm sorry if I appear hard boiled or cold blooded, but . . . them that live by the gun should die by the gun.
> —Race Williams, ibid.

440   In the heart of every man there lurks the germ of a crook.
> —Race Williams, *The Tag Murders*, 1930

ELIZABETH DALY 1878–1967

American mystery novelist, awarded an Edgar in 1960 for the body of her work; creator of Henry Gamadge, the New York bibliophile who was Agatha Christie's favorite American amateur detective.

441   We all have at least one book in us.
> —*Deadly Nightshade*, 1940

442   Always act as if there were going to be a murder.
> —Henry Gamadge, *Night Walk*, 1947

CLEMENCE DANE 1888–1965 and HELEN SIMPSON 1897–1940

Clemence Dane is the pseudonym of English novelist Winifred Ashton, who collaborated with English novelist Helen Simpson (q.v.) on several detective novels; creators of Sir John Saumarez, famous actor-manager and amateur sleuth.

443   Women haven't yet completely exchanged their privileges for
their rights.
—Miss Lampeter, *Enter Sir John*, 1928

LIONEL DAVIDSON 1922–

English crime fiction writer, winner of three Gold Daggers for
Night of Wenceslas, *A Long Way to Shiloh*, and *The Chelsea
Murders*.

444   Indecision argues an alternative.
—*Night of Wenceslas*, 1960

445   Between a sin and a crime there's a difference
—James Raison, *Making Good Again*, 1968

DOROTHY SALISBURY DAVIS 1916–

American crime novelist and short story writer, awarded the Grand
Master title by Mystery Writers of America in 1985, who is troubled
by the problem of violence in the mystery genre, yet believes the
pursuit of truth "shines best in the dark excesses of human
behavior"; creator of Julie Hayes.

446   Don't sell your soul to buy peanuts for the monkeys.
—Mrs. Moran, *A Gentle Murderer*, 1951

447   We reveal more of ourselves in the lies we tell than we do
when we try to tell the truth.
—Julie Hayes, *A Death in the Life*, 1976

448   Flattery makes fools of the best of us.
—Sean O'Grady, *Scarlet Night*, 1981

WILLIAM L. DeANDREA 1952–

American detective novelist, married to Orania Papazoglou (q.v.).
His first two novels, *Killed in the Ratings* and *The Hog Murders*,
won back-to-back Edgars; creator of Matt Cobb, whose job with
Special Projects for a TV network is to "keep the real world from
spoiling everybody's fun."

449   If anyone ever offers you a choice between luck and brains,
take luck every time.
—Matt Cobb, *Killed in the Ratings*, 1978

450   Life's two Great Questions: "Why me?" and "What do I do
now?"
—Ibid.

LEN DEIGHTON 1929–

English writer, war historian, and espionage thriller novelist; creator of the unnamed narrator of his early thrillers (who became Harry Palmer in the movies) and Bernie Sampson.

451   What chance did I stand between the communists on the one side and the establishment on the other?
        —The narrator, *The Ipcress File*, 1962

452   The image of illusion is shattered by the hammer of reality.
        —*Funeral in Berlin*, 1964

453   There isn't a man, woman or child in this world who can say they have never conned someone out of something. Babies smile for a hug, girls for a mink, men for an empire.
        —Silas Lowther, quintessential confidence
        man, *Only When I Laugh*, 1968

454   We are part of the process of natural selection; for we deprive the stupid and inefficient of wealth and prestige. Without us the balance of nature would be upset.
        —Silas Lowther, ibid.

455   "How long have we been sitting here?"
        "Nearly a quarter of a century."
        —Bernie Sampson's question and his friend's
        answer as they wait at Checkpoint Charlie,
        Berlin Game, 1983

        This exchange is an allusion to the opening scene of *The Spy Who Came in From the Cold* by John le Carré (q.v.).

456   The tragedy of marriage is that while all women marry thinking that their man will change, all men marry believing their wives will never change. Both are invariably disappointed.
        —Bernie Sampson, *London Match*, 1985

LILLIAN DE LA TORRE 1902–

Pseudonym of American novelist and playwright Lillian McCue. As de la Torre, creator of Dr. Sam: Johnson, who had some successes as a detector of cheats. Boswell, of course, serves as his Watson.

457 de la Torre has written:

"I call myself a 'histo-detector.' The name comes from the funny papers, but the calling is a serious one, the craft of solving the mysteries of long-ago. . . . Thoughtful consideration of such mysterious moments in history, in my opinion, is uniquely fitted to illuminate the human condition, probing as it does man's behavior under stress."

—*Twentieth-Century Crime and Mystery Writers*, 2nd ed., 1985

458 He who affects singularity, must not complain if he becomes the object of publick curiosity.

—Dr. Sam: Johnson, "The Monboddo Ape Boy," *Dr. Sam: Johnson, Detector*, 1946

459 He who is capable of memory and reason . . . needs no seer's crystal ball.

—Dr. Sam: Johnson, "The Conveyance of Emeline Grange," ibid.

460 If in spite of evidence a mystery remains unsolved, then the truth has never been suspected, and neither side is right. *The solution lies somewhere down the middle.*

—de la Torre's Law, *The Heir of Douglas*, 1952

JANE DENTINGER 1951–

American actress, acting teacher, mystery bookstore manager, and novelist; creator of Jocelyn O'Roarke, actress and amateur sleuth.

461 No one can be as dignified as the near-drunk.

—*Murder on Cue*, 1983

462 Talent can cover up a multitude of sins.

—Ibid.

463 Luck is when preparation meets opportunity.

—*First Hit of the Season*, 1984

THOMAS DE QUINCEY 1785–1859

English writer, best known for *Confessions of an English Opium-Eater* and his macabre essay series, "On Murder, Considered as One of the Fine Arts."

464   Murder is an improper line of conduct.
—"On Murder, Considered as One of the
Fine Arts," *Blackwood's Magazine*,
February 1827

465   Even imperfection itself may have its ideal or perfect state.
—Ibid.

466   If once a man indulges himself in murder, very soon he
comes to think little of robbing; and from robbing he comes
next to drinking and Sabbath-breaking, and from that to
incivility and procrastination.
—"Supplementary Paper on Murder,
Considered as One of the Fine Arts,"
Blackwood's Magazine, November 1827

This was paraphrased by Martin Cruz Smith (q.v.) in
Gorky Park.

D. M. DEVINE 1920–1980

Scottish author David McDonald Devine, writer of classic detective
novels, who also writes as Dominic Devine.

467   When a person tampers with the truth there is nearly always
some unexpected little detail to trip him up.
—*My Brother's Killer*, 1961

COLIN DEXTER 1930–

English detective novelist, crossword puzzle solver and creator,
twice awarded the Silver Dagger, for *Service of All the Dead* and *The
Dead of Jericho*; creator of Inspector Morse of Oxford.

468   Judge not—at least until the evidence is unequivocal.
—*Service of All the Dead*, 1979

FRANK DIAMOND

American espionage novelist; creator of Vicky Gaines and Ransome
V. Dragoon, known as "The Dish" and "Drag."

469   I want a lawyer. Get me Danglewrit and Loophole. On
second thought, get me Dragoon. He's better than a lawyer.
—Vicky Gaines, *Murder Rides a Rocket*,
1946

470   After I slave over a hot tommy gun all day!
—Vicky Gaines, ibid.

471   "You mean I'm a desperado?" said Vicky in delight. "Shall
I start going around with a six-gun on each hip?"
"No, the hips themselves are quite dangerous enough."
—Petersen of the FBI, ibid.

472   Dangle my remains from the ramparts!
—Ransome V. Dragoon, ibid.

473   You monster! You put me to bed with my clothes on.
—Vicky Gaines, ibid.

CHARLES DICKENS 1812–1870

The greatest of England's Victorian novelists, whose works were
often concerned with sham respectability, crime, mystery, and
detection.

474   Stick to the alleybi. Nothing like an alleybi, nothing.
—The elder Mr. Weller's advice, *The
Pickwick Papers*, 1837

475   Rather a tough customer in argeyment, Joe, if anybody was
to try and tackle him.
—Parkes, *Barnaby Rudge*, 1841

476   Something will come of this. I hope it mayn't be human
gore!
—Simon Tappertit, ibid.

477   It was a maxim with Foxey—our revered father, gentlemen—"Always suspect everybody." ·
—Sampson Brass, *The Old Curiosity Shop*,
1841

Bleak House gives us one of the first official detectives in English
fiction, Inspector Bucket of the Detective, as he likes to refer to
himself. Oddly memorable as a character, he presents a suitable
model for the many hardworking, serious police detectives who
followed him, but especially for Wilkie Collins's Sergeant Cuff and
Anna Katharine Green's Inspector Gryce. Inspector Bucket is
unspectacular but shrewd, and he becomes a major character in the
various plots and subplots as he investigates Tulkinghorn's murder
and searches for the missing Lady Dedlock. He does have his
dramatic moments.

478   I am damned if I am a going to have my case spoilt, or
interfered with, or anticipated by so much as half a second of

time, by any human being in creation. *You* want more pains-taking and search-making? *You* do? Do you see this hand, and do you think that *I* don't know the right time to stretch it out, and put it on the arm that fired that shot?
—Inspector Bucket, *Bleak House*, 1853

This was no idle boast, but there were limits to Inspector Bucket's powers.

479   "Listen then, my angel. You are very spiritual. But can you re-store him back to life?"
"Not exactly."
—Tulkinghorn's killer, sarcastically taunting Inspector Bucket, ibid.

480   If a murder, anybody might have done it. Burglary or pocket-picking wanted 'prenticeship. Not so murder. We're all of us up to that.
—Mr. Inspector, *Our Mutual Friend*, 1865

481   It was always more likely that a man had done a bad thing than that he hadn't.
—Mr. Inspector, ibid.

482   Circumstances alter cases.
—*The Mystery of Edwin Drood*, 1870, unfinished

PETER DICKINSON 1927–

English detective novelist who thinks of himself as "writing science fiction with the science left out," twice awarded the Gold Dagger, for *Skin Deep* and *A Pride of Heroes*; creator of Superintendent James Pibble, "a copper's copper" who has a talent for solving bizarre cases.

483   If you'd done thirty-five years of police work, as I have—you'd know that *any* motive is credible.
—Superintendent James Pibble, *The Seals*, 1970

484   The only possible way to behave is to take people as they are now—they're part of your life and you're part of theirs, and you've got to accept that. It doesn't matter what they were or what they've done.
—Lady Lydia Timms, *The Lively Dead*, 1975

485   The Lord give, and then He rob you blind with his free
hand.
—Mrs. Trotter's motto, *Walking Dead*, 1977

DOROTHY CAMERON DISNEY 1903–

American mystery novelist, called a "woman's writer," because her
focus is often the family unit. She was Marriage Editor of *Ladies'
Home Journal*.

486   Curiosity has a spiteful way of turning back on the curious.
—Selby Blake, *Crimson Friday*, 1943

FYODOR DOSTOEVSKY 1821–1881

There is a long-running, honorable, and enjoyable argument as to
the limits to be placed on a murder mystery. Can a murder mystery
be a great novel? Can a great novel be a murder mystery? In *Crime
and Punishment* Dostoevsky studies the psychological consequences
of murder on the murderer rather than the act itself or its detection.
Still, *Crime and Punishment* belongs to the genre, in part because
its haunting echoes can still be heard in the crime novels and
thrillers of today.

487   Man grows used to everything, the scoundrel!
—Raskolnikov, *Crime and Punishment*, 1866;
English translation by Constance Garnett,
1938

488   Do you understand what it means when you have absolutely
nowhere to turn?
—Marmeladov, ibid.

SIR ARTHUR CONAN DOYLE 1859–1930

The first Sherlock Holmes adventure was *A Study in Scarlet*, with
the title coming from Holmes's reference to "the scarlet thread of
murder running through the colorless skein of life." By his own
count, Holmes would have to do with fifty murders in his career,
and some five hundred cases of capital importance. But never once,
in any of his adventures, did he say, "Elementary, my dear
Watson."

A Study in Scarlet passed almost unnoticed on its first publication.
Fortunately, two years later an American editor of *Lippincott's*

Magazine who admired the work asked Conan Doyle to write another Sherlock Holmes story. *The Sign of Four* was an immediate success, and brought the editor of *Strand Magazine* asking for a dozen short stories. The game was afoot!

489   In his autobiography, Conan Doyle tells how he plotted his stories:
"The first thing is to get your idea. Having got that key idea one's next task is to conceal it and lay emphasis upon everything which can make for a different explanation."
—*Memories and Adventures*, 1924

490   "Wonderful!" I ejaculated.
"Commonplace," said Holmes.
—*A Study in Scarlet*, 1888

491   They say that genius is an infinite capacity for taking pains. It is a very bad definition, but it does apply to detective work.
—Sherlock Holmes to Watson, ibid.

492   There is nothing like first-hand evidence.
—Sherlock Holmes to Watson, ibid.

493   To a great mind, nothing is little.
—Sherlock Holmes to Watson, ibid.

494   Eliminate all other factors, and the one which remains must be the truth.
—Sherlock Holmes to Watson, *The Sign of Four*, 1890

495   I never guess. It is a shocking habit—destructive to the logical faculty.
—Sherlock Holmes to Watson, ibid.

496   An exception disproves the rule.
—Sherlock Holmes to Watson, ibid.

497   Women are never to be entirely trusted—not the best of them.
—Sherlock Holmes to Watson, ibid.

498   You can, for example, never foretell what any one man will do, but you can say with precision what an average number will be up to.
—Sherlock Holmes, to Watson, ibid.

499   To Sherlock Holmes she is always *the* woman.
> —Said of Irene Adler, who used her wits to
> overset his plans, "A Scandal in
> Bohemia," *The Adventures of Sherlock
> Holmes*, 1892

500   You see, but you do not observe.
> —Sherlock Holmes to Watson, ibid.

501   It is a capital mistake to theorise before one has data.
Insensibly one begins to twist facts to suit theories, instead of
theories to suit facts.
> —Sherlock Holmes to Watson, ibid.

502   As a rule, the more bizarre a thing is the less mysterious it
proves to be.
> —Sherlock Holmes to Watson, "The
> Red-Headed League," ibid.

503   It is quite a three-pipe problem.
> —Sherlock Holmes to Watson, ibid.

504   Life is infinitely stranger than anything which the mind of
man could invent.
> —Sherlock Holmes to Watson, "A Case of
> Identity," ibid.

505   Depend upon it there is nothing so unnatural as the
commonplace.
> —Sherlock Holmes to Watson, ibid.

506   It has long been an axiom of mine that the little things are
infinitely the most important.
> —Sherlock Holmes to Mary Sutherland, ibid.

507   Singularity is almost invariably a clue. The more featureless
and commonplace a crime is, the more difficult it is to bring
it home.
> —Sherlock Holmes to Watson, "The
> Boscombe Valley Mystery," ibid.

508   Circumstantial evidence is a very tricky thing. It may seem to
point very straight to one thing, but if you shift your own
point of view a little, you may find it pointing in an equally
uncompromising manner to something entirely different.
> —Sherlock Holmes to Watson, ibid.

509   There is nothing more deceptive than an obvious fact.
> —Sherlock Holmes to Watson, ibid.

510   You know my method. It is founded upon the observance of trifles.
—Sherlock Holmes to Watson, ibid.

511   When a doctor goes wrong, he is the first of criminals. He has nerve and he has knowledge.
—Sherlock Holmes to Watson, "The Adventure of the Speckled Band," ibid.

512   How dangerous it always is to reason from insufficient data.
—Sherlock Holmes to Watson, ibid.

513   It is an old maxim of mine that when you have excluded the impossible, whatever remains, however improbable, must be the truth.
—Sherlock Holmes to Mr. Holder and Watson, "The Adventure of the Beryl Coronet," ibid.

514   Crime is common. Logic is rare. Therefore it is upon the logic rather than upon the crime that you should dwell. You have degraded what should have been a course of lectures into a series of tales.
—Sherlock Holmes to Watson, "The Adventure of the Copper Beeches," ibid.

515   Data! Data! Data! I can't make bricks without clay.
—Sherlock Holmes, impatiently, to Watson, ibid.

516   "Is there any other point to which you would wish to draw my attention?"
"To the curious incident of the dog in the night-time."
"The dog did nothing in the night-time."
"That was the curious incident."
—Exchange between Inspector Gregory and Sherlock Holmes, "The Adventure of Silver Blaze," The Memoirs of Sherlock Holmes, 1894

517   Any truth is better than indefinite doubt.
—Sherlock Holmes to Grant Munro, "The Adventure of the Yellow Face," ibid.

518   Watson, if it should ever strike you that I am getting a little over-confident in my powers, or giving less pains to a case than it deserves, kindly whisper "Norbury" in my ear, and I shall be infinitely obliged to you.
—Sherlock Holmes, ibid.

519 A man always finds it hard to realize that he may have finally lost a woman's love, however badly he may have treated her.

—Sherlock Holmes to Watson, "The Adventure of the Musgrave Ritual," ibid.

520 It is of the highest importance in the art of detection to be able to recognize out of a number of facts which are incidental and which vital. Otherwise your energy and attention must be dissipated instead of being concentrated.

—Sherlock Holmes to Colonel Hayter, "The Adventure of the Reigate Squires," ibid.

521 Art in the blood is liable to take the strangest forms.

—Sherlock Holmes to Watson, "The Greek Interpreter," ibid.

522 I cannot agree with those who rank modesty among the virtues.

—Sherlock Holmes to Watson, ibid.

523 "Excellent," I cried.
"Elementary," said he.

—Watson, answered by Sherlock Holmes, "The Adventure of the Crooked Man," ibid.

524 The most difficult crime to track is the one which is purposeless.

—Sherlock Holmes to Watson, "The Adventure of the Naval Treaty," ibid.

525 It is stupidity rather than courage to refuse to recognize danger when it is close upon you.

—Sherlock Holmes to Watson, "The Adventure of the Final Problem," ibid.

526 He is the Napoleon of crime, Watson. He is the organizer of half that is evil and of nearly all that is undetected in this great city. He is a genius, a philosopher, an abstract thinker. He has a brain of the first order. He sits motionless, like a spider in the centre of its web, but the web has a thousand radiations.

—Sherlock Holmes's description of Professor Moriarty, ibid.

527 If I have one quality upon earth it is common sense.

—Watson, *The Hound of the Baskervilles*, 1902

528 The more *outré* and grotesque an incident is the more carefully it deserves to be examined, and the very point which appears to complicate a case is, when duly considered and scientifically handled, the one which is most likely to elucidate it.
> —Sherlock Holmes, reviewing the case, ibid.

529 One should always look for a possible alternative and provide against it. It is the first rule of criminal investigation.
> —Sherlock Holmes to Watson, "The Adventure of Black Peter," *The Return of Sherlock Holmes*, 1905

530 You will remember, Watson, how the dreadful business of the Abernetty family was first brought to my notice by the depth to which the parsley had sunk into the butter upon a hot day.
> —Sherlock Holmes, "The Adventure of the Six Napoleons," ibid.

531 The fair sex is your department.
> —Sherlock Holmes to Watson, "The Adventure of the Second Stain," ibid.

532 Mediocrity knows nothing higher than itself; but talent instantly recognizes genius.
> —*The Valley of Fear*, 1914

533 The temptation to form premature theories upon insufficient data is the bane of our profession.
> —Sherlock Holmes to Inspector MacDonald, ibid.

534 Only a man with a criminal enterprise desires to establish an alibi.
> —Sherlock Holmes to Watson, "The Adventure of Wisteria Lodge," *His Last Bow*, 1917

535 There is an East wind coming all the same, such a wind as never blew on England yet. It will be cold and bitter, Watson, and a good many of us may wither under its blast.
> —Sherlock Holmes, "His Last Bow," ibid.

"His Last Bow," written in 1917, was set in 1914.

536 I can discover facts, Watson, but I cannot change them.
—Sherlock Holmes, "The Problem of the
Bridge," *The Case-Book of Sherlock
Holmes*, 1927

JOHN DRYDEN 1631–1700

Seventeenth-century English poet and dramatist. "The Cock and
the Fox" reworks Chaucer's "The Nun's Priest's Tale."

537 Murther may pass unpunished for a time,
But tardy justice will o'ertake the crime.
—"The Cock and the Fox," 1700

FORTUNÉ DU BOISGOBEY 1821–1891

French mystery novelist; the most famous of his sensational novels
being *The Crime of the Opera House*.

538 It has been discovered even in official circles that for a spy or
a detective to achieve success he must in no wise resemble
what he really is. It is not enough to don a costume; he must
assume the ways of the person he wishes to represent.
—*The Crime of the Opera House*, 1880; first
English translation, 1881

WINIFRED DUKE 1890?–1962

English historian, detective novelist, and true crime writer.

539 "A man who can listen at doors—"
"Is worse than a poisoner."
—Exchange between Lewis Powell and his
sister Gwyn, wife of Harold Fieldend,
acquitted of poisoning his first wife,
Bastard Verdict, 1934

540 If we were in Scotland, we could bring it in Not Proven.
That's Not Guilty, but don't do it again.
—Andrew Brodie, the only Scot on the jury,
Unjust Jury, 1941

ALEXANDRE DUMAS 1802–1870

French novelist, author of *The Three Musketeers* and other
historical novels and romances. Early in his career, Dumas showed
his interest in crime by producing *Celebrated Crimes*, an eight-
volume set of true crime tales blended with a dash of fiction.

The Mohicans of Paris, a sensational novel, contains a detective chapter with a shrewd police commissary who believes "a woman must play some part in a mysterious drama," and advises accordingly.

541   Look for the woman!
>   —M. Jackal's axiom, repeated several times,
>   *The Mohicans of Paris,* 1855; English
>   translation, 1859

This famous line—*"Cherchez la femme!"*—is also used in Dumas's stage adaptation.

542   "There is a woman in every case; as soon as a report is made to me, I say: 'Look for the woman!' The woman is sought for, and when she is found . . ."
"Well?"
"The man is soon found."
>   —Exchange between M. Jackal and Mme.
>   Desmarest, *The Mohicans of Paris,* Act
>   III, scene vii, 1864

DAPHNE DU MAURIER 1907–

English romantic suspense novelist, awarded the Grand Master title by Mystery Writers of America in 1977.

543   Last night I dreamt I went to Manderley again.
>   —One of the most famous opening lines in
>   fiction, *Rebecca,* 1938

FRIEDRICH DÜRRENMATT 1921–

Swiss playwright and detective novelist; creator of Kommissar Hans Barlach, self-described as "a big black old tomcat that likes to catch mice."

544   Justice is not a mincing machine but a compromise.
>   —*The Marriage of Mr. Mississippi,* Act I,
>   1952; English translation by Michael
>   Bullock, 1959

545   Forgetfulness—the only grace that can sooth a heart consumed by an angry fire.
>   —*The Judge and His Hangman,* 1952;
>   English translation by Therese Pol, 1955

546   Nothing makes man as evil as suspicion.
—Hans Barlach, *The Quarry*, 1959; English
translation by Eva H. Morreale, 1962

547   A criminologist has the obligation to question reality.
—Hans Barlach, ibid.

548   In the realm of science there is nothing more repugnant than a miracle.
—Johann Wilhelm Möbius, *The Physicists*,
Act I, 1962; English translation by James
Kirkup, 1964

549   What once was thought can never be undone.
—Johann Whilhelm Möbius, ibid., Act II

WESSEL EBERSOHN 1940–

South African-born novelist and mystery writer whose works are banned in his own country; creator of Yudel Gordon, a South African police psychiatrist.

550   Theft was a great crime to those who possessed much. . . . It was a far lesser crime to those who possessed little. . . . It was no crime at all for those who were hungry and owned nothing.
—Reflections of Yudel Gordon, *Divide the
Night*, 1981

UMBERTO ECO 1932–

The Name of the Rose is the first novel by the Italian historian and specialist in semiotics. Against a rich background of mystery, theology, history, and murder, William of Baskerville attempts to live up to the inquisitor's code that he hates.

551   The first duty of a good inquisitor is to suspect especially those who seem sincere.
—Brother William, *The Name of the Rose*,
1980; English translation by William
Weaver, 1983

552   The only truth lies in learning to free ourselves from insane passion for truth.
—Brother William, ibid.

553 I have never doubted the truth of signs . . . they are the only things man has with which to orient himself in the world. What I did not understand was the relation among signs. . . . I behaved stubbornly, pursuing a semblance of order, when I should have known well that there is no order in the universe.

—A dismayed Brother William, when he
solves the mystery as much by accident
as by reasoning, ibid.

JAN EKSTRÖM 1923–

Swedish detective novelist, often called Sweden's John Dickson Carr.

554 That's life—you can't help stepping on everyone else's toes when you're all dancing around the golden calf.

—Martin Bernheim, *Deadly Reunion*, 1975;
English translation by Joan Tate, 1983

T. S. ELIOT 1888–1965

American-born modern poet and playwright who lived most of his life in England. Eliot loved the Sherlock Holmes stories, which he read aloud to his wife while she mended socks. His play, *Murder in the Cathedral*, made use of lines from Conan Doyle's "The Musgrave Ritual"; other works also showed his familiarity with the genre.

555 Any man might do a girl in.

—Sweeney, *Sweeney Agonistes*, 1926

But not any man would keep the body in the bath with a gallon of Lysol.

556 He always has an alibi and one or two to spare.

—"Macavity: The Mystery Cat," *Old
Possum's Book of Practical Cats*, 1939

STANLEY ELLIN 1916–1986

American suspense and private eye novelist, three-time Edgar winner, twice for short stories, and once for best novel, *The Eighth Circle*; awarded the Grand Master title by Mystery Writers of America in 1981.

557 It's funny how many people there are in the world that you should like more than you do.
—Junie, *The Key to Nicholas Street*, 1952

558 If you're paid well enough for lifting a rock you don't get too queasy at the sight of whatever is crawling underneath it.
—*The Eighth Circle*, 1958

559 Any good, capable masochist could make a sadist out of a saint.
—Murray Kirk, ibid.

560 There's no place in this world for well-meaning fools. It's tough enough when you've got brains and know how to use them.
—Murray Kirk, ibid.

RALPH WALDO EMERSON 1803–1882

American poet, essayist, and philosopher.

561 Commit a crime, and the world is made of glass.
—"Compensation," *Essays: First Series*, 1841

HOWARD ENGLE 1931–

Canadian radio producer and detective novelist; creator of Benny Cooperman, private detective making a modest living in Grantham, Ontario.

562 If you find kittens in the doghouse are they puppies?
—Benny Cooperman, *Murder Sees the Light*, 1985

LOREN D. ESTLEMAN 1952–

American writer of westerns and detective novels; creator of Detroit private eye Amos Walker, known as a man who "keeps his mouth shut, even at the dentist's," and in another series, Peter Macklin, mob hitman.

563 The road to hell is smooth as glass.
—John Alderdyce to Amos Walker, *Angel Eyes*, 1981

564 A private eye with a code may be nothing more than a pebble on the beach, but at least he stands out from the grains of sand.
—Amos Walker, ibid.

565   Everytime I take on a job I mortgage a piece of myself to my clients and I can't get it back until it's paid off.
—Amos Walker, ibid.

566   I felt like Macbeth's maid.
—Amos Walker, scrubbing the blood away,
The Midnight Man, 1982

567   "It's just the lady or the tiger with you mob guys, isn't it?"
"More like the tiger or the tiger."
—Exchange between Inspector George
Pontier and Charles Maggiore, *Any Man's
Death*, 1986

The allusion is to "The Lady or the Tiger," by Frank Stockton (q.v.).

HELEN EUSTIS 1916–

Edgar-winning American mystery novelist and translator, whose high reputation rests on her first detective novel, *The Horizontal Man*, though she has written well-regarded short stories, and *The Fool Killer*, a mystery novel for children.

568   Eustis has said:
"When I feel stuck in my own life, I read mysteries. I know that in mysteries everything will move along and not stand still, and that eventually everything will be solved."
—"Talk with Helen Eustis," Lewis Nichols,
New York Times Book Review, 1954

569   What you were yesterday is fixed for always, making its mark on what you are today, what you will be tomorrow.
—*The Horizontal Man*, 1946

570   I have no faith in the use of the academic intellect for practical purposes.
—Professor George Hungerford, ibid.

571   The Lord made cats for killing mice, mice for gnawing stores, stores for feeding folks, and the Fool Killer for killing fools.
—Dirty Jim Jelliman, *The Fool Killer*, 1954

A. A. FAIR. *See* Erle Stanley Gardner.

RUNA FAIRLEIGH

A pseudonym; the author's one book, appropriately titled *An Old-Fashioned Mystery*, was introduced and edited by L. A. Morse.

572   It's far, far better to be lucky than to be good.
                              —Sebastian Cornichon, *An Old-Fashioned Mystery*, 1983

573   You really can't say that old Runa didn't play Fairleigh.
                              —Sebastian Cornichon, ibid.

Some people don't like puns, but it could have been Morse.

WILLIAM FAULKNER 1897–1962

American Nobel Prize–winning novelist; creator of Gavin Stevens, the shrewd attorney of Yoknapatawpha County, featured in *Intruder in the Dust* and in *Knight's Gambit*, a Queen's Quorum selection.

574   In my time I have seen truth that was anything under the sun but just, and I have seen justice using tools and instruments I wouldn't want to touch with a ten-foot fence rail.
                              —Gavin Stevens, "An Error in Chemistry," *Knight's Gambit*, 1949

KENNETH FEARING 1902–1961

American poet and crime novelist whose major work, *The Big Clock*, is one of the classic suspense tales.

575   The big clock was running as usual. . . . Sometimes the hands of the clock actually raced, and at other times they hardly moved at all. But that made no difference to the big clock. The hands could move backward, and the time it told would be right just the same. It would still be running as usual, because all other watches have to be set by the big one.
                              —*The Big Clock*, 1946

CHARLES FELIX

Pseudonymous English author who wrote *The Notting Hill Mystery*, one of the earliest detective novels; creator of insurance investigator Ralph Henderson. The novel includes a floor plan, a copy of a marriage certificate, and a fragment of writing torn from a letter.

576   Those whose lives have been passed in the deception of others, not unfrequently end by deceiving themselves.
—Ralph Henderson, *The Notting Hill Mystery*, 1862

577   The most fatal enemy of crime is over-precaution.
—Ralph Henderson, ibid.

JOY FIELDING 1945–

Canadian suspense novelist, who examines the lives of women under great stress.

578   Don't put the blame where it belongs; put it where it's easiest to disregard.
—Gail Walton, *Life Penalty*, 1984

CORTLAND FITZSIMMONS 1893–1949

American author of well over a dozen mysteries; creator of Ethel Thomas, self-styled old maid and direct literary descendant of Anna Katharine Green's Amelia Butterworth.

579   I think it is a mistake to relieve a man of a sense of responsibility if he has one.
—Ethel Thomas, *The Whispering Window*, 1936

580   A murder, to me, is like a good fire—if they must happen I want to be where I can see them and be a part of the activity.
—Ethel Thomas, *The Moving Finger*, 1937

IAN FLEMING 1908–1964

English spy novelist; creator of Agent 007, James Bond—whom he referred to as that "cardboard booby."

581   John le Carré's evaluation was even less polite:
"The really interesting thing about Bond is that he would be what I call the ideal defector. Because if the money was better, the booze freer and women easier over there in Moscow, he'd be off like a shot. Bond, you see, is the ultimate prostitute."
—Quoted by Donald McCormick, *Who's Who in Spy Fiction*, 1977

582   At gambling, the deadly sin is to mistake bad play for bad luck.
> —*Casino Royale*, 1953

583   It's not difficult to get a Double 0 number if you're prepared to kill people. . . . It's nothing to be particularly proud of.
> —James Bond, ibid.

584   Surround yourself with human beings. . . . They are easier to fight for than principles.
> —Mathis to James Bond, ibid.

585   They have a saying in Chicago: "Once is happenstance. Twice is coincidence. The third time it's enemy action."
> —Goldfinger to James Bond, *Goldfinger*, 1959

586   A personable man and a baronet to boot—if that was what one did to a baronet.
> —James Bond's private joke, *On Her Majesty's Secret Service*, 1963

587   The only kind of money to have—not quite enough.
> —James Bond, turning down a generous gift from Marc-Auge, ibid.

J. S. FLETCHER 1863–1935

English detective novelist Joseph Smith Fletcher, whose output in the 1920s and 1930s rivaled that of Edgar Wallace (q.v.). He published over ninety detective novels in forty-eight years.

588   It's a murder case. I feel it. Instinct perhaps. I'm going to ferret out the truth.
> —Frank Spargo, *The Middle Temple Murder*, 1918

589   Chinamen have long arms! I've heard of them stretching all the way from Peking to Piccadilly—and getting a tight hold at the end of the stretch.
> —Edward Cherry of the CID, New Scotland Yard, *The Kang-He Vase*, 1924

LUCILLE FLETCHER 1912–

American suspense novelist, whose plots usually provide an unpredictable double twist; awarded a Raven by Mystery Writers of America for her screenplay *Sorry, Wrong Number*.

590   Murder is always good copy, particularly when it happens to the rich and venal.
—*Eighty Dollars to Stamford*, 1975

RAE FOLEY 1900–1978

Pseudonym of American Elinore Denniston, who also wrote as Dennis Allan. As Foley, prolific writer of romantic suspense and detective novels; creator of Hiram Potter, amateur sleuth.

591   Every murder strikes at the heart of civilization; it is an attack on all mankind.
—Hiram Potter, *Fatal Lady*, 1964

592   Sooner or later, we come face to face with ourselves; we fall flat on our faces because of some choice we made.
—*Suffer a Witch*, 1965

ANDREW FORRESTER, JR.

Apart from the fact that his name is found on the title pages of five books, little is known about the author. His most important work, *The Female Detective*, presents the adventures of the first professional female detective in fiction, Mrs. G—— of the Metropolitan London Police.

593   Examine most of the great detected cases on record, and you will find a little accident has generally been the clue to success.
—Mrs. G——, "The Unknown Weapon," *The Female Detective*, 1864

594   In the history of crime and its detection chance plays the chief character.
—Mrs. G——, ibid.

FREDERICK FORSYTH 1938–

English writer of suspense thrillers; his first novel, *The Day of the Jackal*, won an Edgar.

595   Everyone seems to remember with great clarity what he was doing on November 22, 1963, at the precise moment he heard President Kennedy was dead.
—*The Odessa File*, 1972

DICK FRANCIS 1920–

English champion steeplechase jockey, racing correspondent, and crime and suspense novelist. *Forfeit* won an Edgar, *Whip Hand* won an Edgar and a Golden Dagger.

596 If one stripped oneself continuously of all human dignity would one in the end be unaware of its absence?
—Daniel Roke, *For Kicks*, 1965

597 One more day, I thought in the end. Anyone could manage just one more day.
—Gene Hawkins, *Blood Sport*, 1967

598 It's only five miles to the top of Everest, and everyone can walk five miles, can't they?
—Walt Prensela, ibid.

599 Facts are not judgments, and judgments are not facts.
—Charles Todd, *In the Frame*, 1976

600 Emotion is a rotten base for politics.
—Charles Todd, ibid.

601 Envy is the root of all evil.
—Charles Todd, ibid.

602 The most damaging lies are told by those who believe they're true.
—Charles Todd, ibid.

603 The abstract isn't always the same as the particular.
—Philip Nore, *Reflex*, 1980

604 Everything ends.
—Philip Nore, ibid.

605 Not even a saint could sit on a goldmine and be too lazy to pick up the nuggets.
—Cassie Morris, *Twice Shy*, 1981

GILBERT FRANKAU 1884–1952

English novelist, whose output included two espionage novels and several detective short stories.

606 Celia's gone to powder her nose. The number of times that girl powders her nose is simply remarkable. I believe it's all due to war strain.
—*Winter of Discontent*, 1941

NICHOLAS FREELING 1927–

English crime and detective novelist, who now lives in Strasbourg; winner of a Gold Dagger for *Gun before Butter* and an Edgar for *King of the Rainy Country*; creator of the Dutch detective Inspector Van der Valk and his wife, Arlette, and Henri Castang, each featured in a series of novels.

607   One only needs a big enough bribe to give in like a lamb.
—Lucienne Englebert, *Gun before Butter*, 1963

608   If we had less morality we might have more justice.
—Mr. Samson, *Criminal Conversation*, 1965

609   Even intelligent people succumb to their own propaganda.
—"Writer's Foreword," *The Dresden Green*, 1966

610   If it comes from the right pretend you're going to hit it: if it comes from the left disregard it. If it's in front pass it and if it's behind the hell with it.
—Very simple driving system, ibid.

611   There are always so many stupid little details to take one's mind off a larger problem.
—*A Dressing of Diamond*, 1974

612   Life is splitting ideals into compromises.
—Henri Castang, *Castang's City*, 1980

613   They say murder is grave because irrevocable, because you can't bring life back. Are the crimes not graver when, and because, life goes on? When the consequences continue to ripple steadily outward . . . distorting and destroying?
—*Arlette*, 1981

MARY E. WILKINS FREEMAN 1852–1930

American short story writer and novelist.

614   Crime detection is not a secret art; anybody can do it if he has the wits, and the time, and patience to get at all the facts, and if he knows enough of the ways of men and women.
—"The Long Arm," *American Detective Stories*, 1927

R. AUSTIN FREEMAN 1862–1943

English physician, detective novelist, and inventor of the "inverted" detective story; creator of the premier scientific detective, Dr. John Evelyn Thorndyke, barrister-at-law of Inner Temple and Professor of Medical Jurisprudence at St. Margaret's Hospital.

615   A collection of his inverted tales was published in *The Singing Bone*, which made him one of the recognized masters of the detective story. Later Freeman wrote:
"Some years ago I devised, as an experiment, an inverted detective story in two parts. The first part was a minute and detailed description of a crime, setting forth the antecedents, motives, and all attendant circumstances. The reader had seen the crime committed, knew all about the criminal, and was in possession of all the facts. It would have seemed that there was nothing left to tell, but I calculated that the reader would be so occupied with the crime that he would overlook the evidence. And so it turned out. The second part, which described the investigation of the crime, had to most readers, the effect of new matter. All the facts were known; but their evidential quality had not been recognized."
—"The Art of the Detective Story," 1924

616   A sound thinker gives equal consideration to the probable and the improbable.
—Dr. John Thorndyke, *The Red Thumb Mark*, 1907

617   Nobody but an utter fool arrives at a conclusion without data.
—Dr. John Thorndyke, ibid.

618   A fortunate guess often brings more credit than a sound piece of reasoning with a less striking result.
—Dr. John Thorndyke, ibid.

619   Life is made up of strange coincidences. Nobody but a reviewer of novels is ever really surprised by a coincidence.
—Dr. John Thorndyke, *The Eye of Osiris*, 1911

620   The one salient biological truth is the paramount importance of sex.
—Dr. John Thorndyke, ibid.

621   A particularly hardy conscience may be quite easy under the most unfavourable conditions.
—"The Case of Oscar Brodsky," *The Singing Bone*, 1912

622   The evidential value of any fact is an unknown quantity until the fact has been examined.
—Dr. John Thorndyke, "The Old Lag," ibid.

623   By lovers of paradox we are assured that it is the unexpected that always happens. But this is, to put it mildly, an exaggeration. Even the expected happens sometimes.
—*The Stoneware Monkey*, 1938

624   To me an anomalous fact—a fact which appears unconnected, or even discordant with the body of known facts—is precisely the one on which attention should be focussed.
—Dr. John Thorndyke, ibid.

625   A man's wealth can be estimated in terms of what he can do without.
—*The Jacob Street Mystery*, 1942

CELIA FREMLIN 1914–

English mystery and suspense novelist, who won an Edgar for *Uncle Paul*.

626   Infatuation means "A love that it is inconvenient to go on with."
—*Uncle Paul*, 1959

627   The only really satisfactory confidante for your troubles is someone who enjoys them, and this inevitably cuts out anyone who actually loves you.
—*The Spider-Orchid*, 1977

628   Hope lights up our darkness.
—*With No Crying*, 1980

DAVID FROME 1898–1983

Pseudonym of Zenith Brown, an American who also wrote mysteries as Leslie Ford. As Frome, creator of Mr. Pinkerton and Major Lewis.

629   Murder is an awfully bad thing for anyone to get away with, even once.
—*The Strange Death of Martin Green*, 1931

JOHN FULLER 1937–

English poet and Fellow of Magdalen College at Oxford, whose first novel, *Flying to Nowhere*, is a gothic mystery set in the Middle Ages on a remote Welsh island.

630 Which of us can distinguish the savour of Life from the savour of corruption?
>—The Abbot, *Flying to Nowhere*, 1984

JACQUES FUTRELLE 1875–1912

American journalist and writer of detective stories; creator of Professor Augustus S.F.X. Van Dusen, better known as the Thinking Machine. Futrelle and his wife were aboard the *Titanic* on its first and only voyage. Sometime during the night of April 14–15, 1912, he pushed his wife into a lifeboat, but refused to get in himself. The last four Thinking Machine stories were saved only because he had left them behind in London.

631 Two and two always equal four, except in unusual cases, where they equal three or five.
>—Professor Augustus S.F.X. Van Dusen,
>"The Problem of Cell 13," *The Thinking Machine*, 1907

632 Nothing is impossible. The mind is master of all things. When science fully recognizes that fact a great advance will have been made.
>—Professor Augustus S.F.X. Van Dusen, ibid.

633 Lock me in a cell in any prison anywhere at any time, wearing only what is necessary, and I'll escape in a week.
>—Professor Augustus S.F.X. Van Dusen, issuing his famous challenge, ibid.

634 The subtler murders—that is, the ones which are most attractive as problems—are nearly always the work of a cunning woman. I know nothing about women myself.
>—Professor Augustus S.F.X. Van Dusen,
>"The Scarlet Thread," ibid.

635   You are not a man; you are a brain—a machine—a thinking machine.

> —The Russian chess champion to Professor
> Augustus S.F.X. Van Dusen, who has
> just beaten him in a game, "The Thinking
> Machine," *The Thinking Machine on the
> Case*, 1908

636   I wouldn't convict a dog of stealing jam on circumstantial evidence alone, even if he had jam all over his nose. . . . Well behaved dogs don't eat jam.

> —Professor Augustus S.F.X. Van Dusen,
> "The Motor Boat," ibid.

637   The way I reached my conclusions? Logic—just simple deductions from known facts. As simple as that two and two make four—not sometimes but all the time.

> —Professor Augustus S.F.X. Van Dusen,
> "The Case of the Mysterious Weapon,"
> *Ellery Queen's Mystery Magazine*, 1950

ÉMILE GABORIAU 1833–1873

French writer who admired Baudelaire's translations of Poe, and was inspired to write detective novels; creator of Monsieur Lecoq, the professional policeman, and Père Tabaret, the amateur detective.

638   Give me the hunting of a man! *That* calls the faculties into play, and the victory is not inglorious! . . . Ah! if people knew the excitement of these parties of hide and seek which are played between the criminal and the detective, everybody would be wanting employment at the bureau of secret police.

> —Père Tabaret, *The Widow Lerouge*, 1866;
> first English translation, 1873

639   Not an *alibi*, nothing? . . . No explanations? The idea! It is inconceivable. Not an *alibi?* We must be mistaken: he is certainly not the criminal.

> —Père Tabaret, ibid.

640   A man can shine in the second rank, who would be totally eclipsed in the first.

> —Monsieur Lecoq to Fanferlot, *File No. 113*,
> 1867; first English translation, 1875

641 Vengeance is a delicious fruit, that must ripen in order that
we may fully enjoy it.
—M. Verduret, ibid.

Burton E. Stevenson (q.v.), in *Stevenson's Home Book
of Quotations*, gives the line a different translation:
"Revenge is a luscious fruit that you must leave to
ripen."

642 When one has your disposition, and is poor, one will either
become a famous thief or a great detective. Choose.
—Baron Moser to Lecoq, his too-clever
employee, *Monsieur Lecoq*, 1868; first
English translation, 1880

643 Always distrust appearances; believe precisely the contrary of
what appears to be true, or even probable.
—Monsieur Lecoq's axiom, ibid.

644 Regard with distrust all circumstances which seem to favor
our secret desires.
—Monsieur Lecoq's axiom, enriched, ibid.

GABRIEL GARCÍA MÁRQUEZ 1928–

South American writer, recipient of the 1982 Nobel Prize for
Literature, whose works often deal with the consequences of crime.
Chronicle of a Death Foretold is a classic inverted detective novel.

645 Give me a prejudice and I will move the world.
—Examining magistrate, *Chronicle of a
Death Foretold*, 1981; English translation
by Gregory Rabassa, 1983

ERLE STANLEY GARDNER 1889–1970

American lawyer and crime fiction novelist, awarded the Grand
Master title by Mystery Writers of America in 1961; creator of
lawyer sleuth Perry Mason. He used other pseudonyms, with A. A.
Fair being the best known. As Gardner, one of the century's most
popular authors.

646 One of Gardner's favorite remarks:
"We build castles in the air, and sometimes we put
foundations under them."
—Quoted by Dorothy B. Hughes, *The Case
of the Real Perry Mason*, 1978

647   I'm a paid gladiator. I fight for my clients. Most clients aren't square shooters. That's why they're clients. They've got themselves into trouble. It's up to me to get them out. I have to shoot square with them. I can't always expect them to shoot square with me.
—Perry Mason to Della Street, *The Case of the Velvet Claws*, 1933

648   It's sort of an obsession with me to do the best I can for a client. My clients aren't blameless. Many of them are crooks. Probably a lot of them are guilty. That's not for me to determine. That's for a jury to determine.
—Perry Mason, ibid.

649   I wouldn't want to live unless I could work for a living.
—Della Street, *The Case of the Stuttering Bishop*, 1936

650   I never take a case unless I am convinced my client was incapable of committing the crime charged.
—Perry Mason, *The Case of the Perjured Parrot*, 1939

651   If you've followed my cases, you'll note that most of them have been cleared up in the courtroom. I can suspect the guilty, but about the only way I can really prove my point is by cross-examining witnesses.
—Perry Mason to client Charles Sabin, ibid.

652   If we can dish it out, we should be able to take it.
—*The D.A. Goes to Trial*, 1940

653   Once milk becomes sour, it cannot be made sweet again.
—E. P. Grolley, *The D.A. Cooks a Goose*, 1942

654   The real way to a man's stomach is through his heart.
—Nell Simms, *The Case of the Drowsy Mosquito*, 1943

655   Food preservation is the first law of nature.
—Nell Simms, ibid.

656   Never explain. A friend who needs explanation isn't worth keeping.
—Harvey Brady to Perry Mason, ibid.

657   I'd rather have my hand cut off than betray the interests of a
            client.
                                        —Perry Mason, *The Case of the Singing
                                            Skirt*, 1959

Writing as **A. A. FAIR**, creator of Bertha Cool, "profane, massive,
belligerent, and bulldog," and her partner, disbarred lawyer Donald
Lam.

658   Loyalty is a fine thing, but self-preservation is the first law of
            nature.
                                        —Donald Lam, realizing the truth of the old
                                            adage, *Top of the Heap*, 1952

JOHN GARDNER 1926–

English spy novelist, commissioned to write new James Bond
adventures eighteen years after the death of Ian Fleming (q.v.);
creator of Boysie Oakes, cowardly secret agent.

659   There's no such thing as a goodie or a baddie any more. Just
            people . . . standing in the dusk of history.
                                        —Mostyn to Boysie Oakes, *Amber Nine*,
                                            1966

BRIAN GARFIELD 1939–

American writer of westerns, crime novels, and espionage thrillers,
who writes under many different names. *Hopscotch* won an Edgar.

660   The system thinks a lot about the rules of the game but never
            asks whether the game itself has any meaning.
                                        —Simon Crane, *The Hit*, 1970

661   The hunting way of life is the only one natural to man.
                                        —Mikhail Yaskov, *Hopscotch*, 1975

ANDREW GARVE 1908–

Pseudonym used by English journalist Paul Winterton, who has
also written as Roger Bax and Paul Somers. As Garve, author of
over forty mystery novels and thrillers of surprising variety and very
considerable proficiency.

662   Men'll kiss their wives goodbye in the mornin' even though
            they 'ates the sight of 'em. 'Abit, that's what it is—just 'abit.
                                        —Mrs. Biggs, *No Tears for Hilda*, 1950

663   What I can never understand is why men have to *murder* their wives just because they prefer somebody else.
—Inspector Haines, ibid.

664   An unrepentant sinner can expect little sympathy—a defiant one even less.
—Mr. Perkins, ibid.

665   Eccentricity is one of the hallmarks of strong characters and original minds.
—*The Cuckoo Line Affair*, 1953

666   Authors rarely welcome even the most constructive advice.
—*Home to Roost*, 1976

Writing as **ROGER BAX**.

667   Watch the goat from the front, the horse from behind, and the bad man from all sides.
—*Two if by Sea*, 1949

JONATHAN GASH 1933–

Pseudonym of English bacteriologist John Grant. As Gash, creator of Lovejoy, antiques dealer willing to bend (or break) the law anytime for a pair of dueling pistols, a Chippendale table, or whatever.

668   A tin can is a tin can is a tin can, but a tin can made with loving hands glows like the Holy Grail.
—Lovejoy's Law of Loving, *Gold from Gemini*, 1978

669   Antiques, women and survival are my only interests. It sounds simple, but you just try putting them in the right order.
—Lovejoy, *The Grail Tree*, 1979

670   Don't you try telling me that virtue is or has its own reward because it's not and it hasn't.
—Lovejoy, ibid.

671   A bad forgery's the ultimate insult.
—Lovejoy, *The Vatican Rip*, 1981

672   Antiques are everything. First, last, every single thing. Forever and ever.
—Lovejoy, *The Gondola Scam*, 1983

WILLIAM CAMPBELL GAULT 1910–

American private eye novelist; creator of Brock ("The Rock") Callahan. *Don't Cry for Me* won an Edgar, as did *The Cana Diversion*, and in 1984, Private Eye Writers of America gave him their Life Achievement award.

673   Being depressed by the poor isn't much worse than being bored by the rich.
—Brock Callahan, *The Bad Samaritan*, 1982

674   Dirty jobs are bound to soil the men who work at them.
—Brock Callahan, *The Cana Diversion*, 1982

WALTER B. GIBSON 1897–1985

American novelist and magician; writing as Maxwell Grant, creator of The Shadow.

675   Who knows what evil lurks in the hearts of men? The Shadow knows!
—One of the most famous lines in the history of radio and detective fiction.

676   We all know it's pulp. Now let's treat it as if it were a masterpiece.
—John Cole, director of the radio program during its Blue Coal peak; quoted in *Murderess Ink*, 1977

677   Crime was coming back and the Shadow recognized it; therefore he needed a few examples to prove properly that crime did not pay.
—*Murder by Magic*, 1945

678   All for one and nothing for anybody else.
—Demo Sharpe's motto, ibid.

MICHAEL GILBERT 1912–

English solicitor and crime fiction novelist, awarded the Grand Master title by Mystery Writers of America in 1987. His work falls into many categories—the puzzle, the romantic thriller, the police procedural, the espionage tale.

679   You can't go out shooting without ammunition.
—Macrea, *Death Has Deep Roots*, 1951

680   Real, deliberate, unprovoked rudeness can be quite as shocking as physical violence.
—*Fear to Tread*, 1953

681   All lawyers are the natural enemies of the police.
—Superintendent Haxtell, *Blood and Judgment*, 1959

682   Mistaken generosity rarely paid dividends.
—Mr. Morgan's reflection, *The Crack in the Teacup*, 1966

683   In this job, there is neither right nor wrong. Only expediency.
—Mr. Behrens, a quiet and effective spy, "Cross-Over," *Game without Rules*, 1967

684   People speak lightly of starving who have never tried it.
—Annunziata Zecchi, *The Etruscan Net*, 1969

SIR WILLIAM S. GILBERT 1836–1911

English playwright who worked with the composer Sir Arthur Sullivan to create comic operas. Some of Gilbert's best-known lines suit a criminous context.

685   It is most distressing to us to be the agents whereby our erring fellow-creatures are deprived of that liberty which is so dear to all—but we should have thought of that before we joined the force.
—Sergeant of Police, *The Pirates of Penzance*, Act II, 1880

686   A policeman's lot is not a happy one.
—Sergeant of Police, ibid.

This line is often quoted or paraphrased in mysteries, detective stories, and police procedurals. Clayton Rawson (q.v.) has a particularly appropriate rewording in *No Coffin for the Corpse*.

687   My object all sublime
I shall achieve in time—
To let the punishment fit the crime.
—*The Mikado*, Act II, 1885

B. M. GILL 1921–

Pseudonym of English author Barbara Margaret Trimble. As Gill, writer of crime fiction; *The Twelfth Juror* won a Gold Dagger.

688   Who makes the rules in this less than perfect world?
—George Webber, *Victims*, 1981

BARTHOLOMEW GILL 1943–

Pseudonym of Irish-American author Mark McGarrity. As Gill, creator of Inspector Peter McGarr, who first appeared in *McGarr and the Politician's Wife* in 1977.

689   Life is too short to go through it like a drudge.
—Inspector Peter McGarr, *McGarr and the Sienese Conspiracy*, 1977

690   Little of what we do or cause others to do can be explained reasonably.
—Inspector Peter McGarr, *McGarr and the P.M. of Belgrave Square*, 1983

691   How the past can tyrannize, delimiting our scope of activity—the choices we make, the things that happen to us, what we choose to do.
—Inspector Peter McGarr, ibid.

DOROTHY GILMAN 1923–

American suspense novelist; creator of the outrageously inventive and charming Mrs. Emily Polifax, with her penchant for odd hats, growing geraniums, and spying.

692   There *are* no happy endings . . . there are only happy people.
—Mrs. Emily Polifax, *Mrs. Polifax on the China Station*, 1983

JOHN GODEY 1912–

Pseudonym of American Morton Freedgood, who also writes as Stanley Morton. *The Taking of Pelham One Two Three* is his best-known work. As Godey, creator of Jack Albany, a bit-part actor.

693   Swearing, like foreign languages, is best learned at an early age.

> —But the mayor never quit trying, because he regarded it as a social grace, *The Taking of Pelham One Two Three*, 1973

694   Nothing like money, hot naked money, to change the thinking of a lifetime.

> —Ryder, ibid.

WILLIAM GODWIN 1756–1836

William Godwin struck the note of the modern crime novel in *Caleb Williams*, which was originally titled *Things As They Are; or The Adventures of Caleb Williams*, and was intended to point out the corruption inherent in any legal system that gives one man power over another. Godwin wrote it to make a political point, and his viewpoint is the reverse of the Golden Age detective story where virtue triumphs and evil is punished.

695   I did nothing but what the law allows.

> —Tyrrell, *Caleb Williams*, 1794

> The law has allowed Tyrrell to maliciously prosecute his young cousin Emily Melville for debt, an action that led directly to her death in prison, and was illegal in itself, for Emily Melville was a minor and should never have been prosecuted in the first place.

696   Either therefore we all of us deserve the vengeance of the law, or the law is not the proper instrument for correcting the misdeeds of mankind.

> —Mr. Raymond, ibid.

MILDRED GORDON 1912–1979 and GORDON GORDON 1912–

American mystery writers, who tried to write the kind of stories they enjoyed reading; creators of John Ripley, Special Agent of the FBI.

697   You never know what's behind any door.

> —John Ripley's reflection, *Casefile: FBI*, 1953

EDWARD GOREY 1925–

American writer and illustrator, winner of a Raven from the Mystery Writers of America for *Dracula*'s stage set and costumes.

698   Once upon a time there was a baby. It was worse than other
babies. . . . Dangerous objects were left about in the hope
that it would do itself an injury, preferably fatal.
—The Beastly Baby, 1962

699   They spent the better part of the night murdering the child in
various ways.
—The Loathsome Couple, 1977

CHESTER GOULD 1900–1985

American comic strip artist; creator of Dick Tracy, who first
appeared in the *Chicago Tribune* on October 4, 1931. Max Allan
Collins (q.v.) has written the text since 1977. The strip is syndicated
in over five hundred newspapers and read by millions.

The Encyclopedia of Mystery and Detection notes that Dick Tracy
expressed his philosophy in two now-famous phrases:

700   Crime does not pay.
—Dick Tracy

701   Little crimes lead to big crimes.
—Dick Tracy

C. W. GRAFTON 1909–1982

American lawyer, author of three crime novels; creator of Gil
Henry, a young lawyer with "more curiosity than an old maid."

702   You have to take life as you find it, don't you? Dealer's choice
is fair enough, even when you aren't the dealer.
—Marty Sothern to her brother, Jess
London, *Beyond a Reasonable Doubt*,
1950

SAMUEL GRAFTON 1907–

American newspaperman and writer of one crime novel.

703   An occupational cripple is any man who has held one job for
more than five years.
—A. Thomas, *A Most Contagious Game*,
1955

SUE GRAFTON 1940–

American detective novelist and screenwriter; creator of private eye
Kinsey Milhone, who first appeared in *"A" Is for Alibi*, which the
author dedicated to her father, C. W. Grafton (q.v.).

704   Too much virtue has a corrupting effect.
—Kinsey Milhone, *"A" Is for Alibi*, 1982

WINSTON GRAHAM 1910–

English historical and mystery novelist; his detectives are often amateurs, suspects themselves, or emotionally involved with the suspect.

705   To be honest around a central lie is like building a house with the foundations unlevel.
—*After the Act*, 1965

ANNA KATHARINE GREEN 1846–1935

American writer who figures importantly in the history of the genre as one of the first women detective story novelists. Her first and best novel was *The Leavenworth Case*; creator of Mr. Ebenezer Gryce, a competent, hardworking New York policeman, and Miss Amelia Butterworth, called "a meddlesome old maid."

706   It is not for me to suspect, but to detect.
—Mr. Ebenezer Gryce, *The Leavenworth Case*, 1878

707   Now it is a principle which every detective recognizes, that if of a hundred leading circumstances connected with a crime, ninety-nine of these are acts pointing to the suspected party with unerring certainty, but the hundredth equally important act one which that person could not have performed, the whole fabric of suspicion is destroyed.
—Mr. Ebenezer Gryce, ibid.

708   It would never do for me to lose my wits in the presence of a man who had none too many of his own.
—Miss Amelia Butterworth, overcoming a faint spell when she views her first body, *That Affair Next Door*, 1897

709   When a man cares for nothing or nobody, it is useless to curse him.
—John Poindexter, *The Circular Study*, 1900

F. L. GREEN 1902–1953

Anglo-Irish writer of a dozen suspense novels. *Odd Man Out*, a novel of political murder and betrayal, remains one of the finest works set against the conflict in Northern Ireland.

710 Dreamin' is fine, but the real thing is at a price.
        —Jimmy Prescot, *Odd Man Out*, 1947

711 Hide things from people, and they will be wanting to know
        the why and the wherefore.
        —*Mist on the Water*, 1948

GRAHAM GREENE 1904–

English writer, awarded the Grand Master title by Mystery Writers
of America in 1976. He has called his thrillers and crime novels
"entertainments," and his serious works "novels." Over time, the
distinction has blurred, and categories shifted.

712 One of the things which danger does to you after a time is—,
        well, to kill emotion. I don't think I shall ever feel anything
        again except fear. None of us can hate anymore—or love.
        —D., *The Confidential Agent*, 1939

713 It is impossible to go through life without trust; that is to be
        imprisoned in the worst cell of all, oneself.
        —*The Ministry of Fear*, 1943

714 In human relations kindness and lies are worth a thousand
        truths.
        —Scobie, *The Heart of the Matter*, 1948

715 Despair is the price one pays for setting oneself an impossible
        aim.
        —Ibid.

716 Any victim demands allegiance.
        —Scobie, ibid.

717 Reality in our century is not something to be faced.
        —Dr. Hasselbacher, *Our Man in Havana*,
        1958

718 Beware of formulas. If there's a God, he's not a God of
        formulas.
        —Beatrice Severn, ibid.

STEPHEN GREENLEAF 1942–

American private eye novelist; creator of John Marshall Tanner,
who calls himself "a nondescript private eye who could stuff all of
his assets into some carry-on luggage if he owned any carry-on
luggage."

719   The investigator's trade is short on glamour and long on moral ambiguity.
—John Marshall Tanner, *Grave Error*, 1979

720   Never is a long time. It usually gives out when you get past forty.
—John Marshall Tanner, ibid.

721   "Do you ever feel that if something good happens to you, then something bad must surely follow?"
"With me it's more than a feeling, it's a law."
—Exchange between Maximilian Kottle and
John Marshall Tanner, *Deathbed*, 1980

722   His suit—gray, herringbone, priceless—fit him as well as disgrace fit Nixon.
—Ibid.

723   I'm not in business to achieve the Humanistic Calculus; I'm in business to serve my client.
—John Marshall Tanner, ibid.

724   Anything can be a job. Sex. Death. God.
—John Marshall Tanner's reflection at his
nephew's funeral, *Fatal Obsession*, 1983

725   If ignorance were a muffler, the world would be as silent as a tomb.
—Professor Grunig, *Beyond Blame*, 1986

JOHN GREENWOOD. *See* John Buxton Hilton.

EDWARD GRIERSON 1914–1975

English solicitor, who used his legal background to good effect in several very fine crime fiction works.

726   The witness box, though frequently a forum for perjuries and evasions, made for justice in the end; it was a sort of truth machine.
—Belief of Sir Evelyn, *Reputation for a
Song*, 1952

727   Though a man may sometimes escape the public consequences of his acts, he cannot escape his own character.
—Ibid.

728   At moments of embarrassment one is capable of any banality.
—*The Second Man*, 1956

FRANK GRUBER 1904–1969

Prolific American detective novelist who used various pseudonyms; creator of Otis Beagle, Johnny Fletcher and Sam Cragg, and Simon Lash.

729   Best thing to melt ice is hot air.
—Johnny Fletcher, *The Hungry Dog*, 1941

730   He may have been the apple of *your* eye, but to me he was only a cinder.
—Race track cop to Sam Cragg, ibid.

731   "You've got more crust—"
"Than a piece of toast?"
—Exchange between Betty Travis and
Johnny Fletcher, *The Navy Colt*, 1941

732   If you hang around money some of it's apt to stick to you.
—Johnny Fletcher to Sam Cragg, *The
Scarlet Feather*, 1948

PHILIP GUEDALLA 1889–1944

English historian, biographer, and essayist.

733   The detective story is the normal recreation of noble minds.
—Quoted by Dorothy L. Sayers, *The
Omnibus of Crime*, 1929

Playwright Anthony Shaffer (q.v.) has some fun with this line.

WILLIAM HAGGARD 1907–

Pseudonym of English army officer and civil servant Richard Henry Michael Clayton. As Haggard, espionage and international intrigue novelist; creator of Colonel Charles Russell of the Security Executive.

734   Charles Russell hadn't expected that his God would be a fool. He'd be a senior administrator, even more potent than Russell himself. He wouldn't hold it against a colleague that he'd simply done his duty.
—*The Doubtful Disciple*, 1969

BRETT HALLIDAY 1904–1977

Best-known pseudonym of American writer Davis Dresser. As Halliday, creator of red-haired, two-fisted, Martell-drinking Mike Shayne.

735   All murders have the tang of melodrama somewhere along the line.
> —Mike Shayne to Inspector Quinlan, *Michael Shayne's Long Chance*, 1944

736   He poured himself a drink and counted the money. It came to ten thousand even, mostly in fifties and twenty-fives.
> —Mike Shayne, getting ready to foil a political blackmailer, *The Violent World of Michael Shayne*, 1965

HARLAN PAGE HALSEY 1839?–1898

American writer who used various pseudonyms for his dime novels; his Old Sleuth became one of the first series detectives.

737   Never fail.
> —Flyaway Ned's motto, *The Old Detective's Pupil*, 1895

DONALD HAMILTON 1916–

Swedish-born American espionage novelist; creator of Matt Helm, counterspy who operates under the code name "Eric."

738   What we were, never was. What we did, never happened.
> —Mac, the supersecret counterintelligence group chief, to Matt Helm at the end of the war, *Death of a Citizen*, 1960

739   I don't trust anybody under thirty. But then I don't trust anybody over thirty either.
> —Matt Helm, *The Interlopers*, 1969

DASHIELL HAMMETT 1894–1961

American Pinkerton agent who became one of the most popular *Black Mask* writers and a master of the American hard-boiled school. As Raymond Chandler (q.v.) pointed out, Hammett gave murder back to the kind of people who commit it. He put them into his detective stories and novels, letting them talk, act, and think as such people did; creator of the Continental Op, Sam Spade, Ned Beaumont, and Nick and Nora Charles.

740 From any crime to its author there is a trail. It may be . . . obscure; but, since matter cannot move without disturbing other matter along its path, there always is—there must be—a trail of some sort. And finding and following such trails is what a detective is paid to do.
—"House Dick," *Dead Yellow Women*, 1947

741 You think I'm a man and you're a woman. That's wrong. I'm a manhunter and you're something that has been running in front of me.
—The Op to Princess Zhukovski, "The Gutting of Couffignal," 1925

742 She looked as if she were telling the truth, though with women, especially blue-eyed women, that doesn't always mean anything.
—The Op, *Red Harvest*, 1929

743 I don't mind a reasonable amount of trouble.
—Sam Spade, *The Maltese Falcon*, 1930

744 He adjusted himself to beams falling, and then no more of them fell, and he adjusted himself to them not falling.
—Said of Flitcraft, ibid.

745 The cheaper the crook, the gaudier the patter.
—Sam Spade, ibid.

746 Everybody has something to conceal.
—Sam Spade, ibid.

747 Once a chump, always a chump.
—Sam Spade, ibid.

748 I won't play the sap for you.
—Sam Spade to Bridgid O'Shaughnessy, ibid.

749 When a man's partner is killed he's supposed to do something about it.
—Sam Spade, ibid.

750 I'm a detective and expecting me to run criminals down and then let them go free is like asking a dog to catch a rabbit and

let it go. It can be done, all right, and sometimes it is done, but it's not the natural thing.
—Sam Spade, ibid.

751 Don't be too sure I'm as crooked as I'm supposed to be. That kind of reputation might be good business—bringing in high-priced jobs and making it easier to deal with the enemy.
—Sam Spade to Bridgid O'Shaughnessy, ibid.

752 I can stand anything I've got to stand.
—Ned Beaumont, *The Glass Key*, 1931

753 I'd rather lie to him than have him think I'm lying.
—Nick Charles, *The Thin Man*, 1934

754 I don't like crooks, and even if I did, I wouldn't like crooks that are stool-pigeons, and if I liked crooks that are stool-pigeons, I still wouldn't like you.
—Miriam Nunheim to her husband, ibid.

JOSEPH HANSEN 1923–

American novelist who has also used the pseudonyms Rose Brock and James Colton. As Hansen, creator of David Brandstetter, homosexual investigator of insurance death claims.

755 Hansen has said:
"Homosexuals have commonly been treated shabbily in detective fiction—vilified, pitied, at best patronized. This was neither fair nor honest. When I sat down to write *Fadeout* in 1967 I wanted to write a good, compelling whodunit, but I also wanted to right some wrongs."
—*Twentieth-Century Crime and Mystery Writers*, 2nd ed., 1985

756 The trouble with life was, nobody ever got enough rehearsal.
—David Brandstetter's observation, *Skinflick*, 1979

757 Beauty is so often mankind's undoing.
—Luther Prentice, *Nightwork*, 1984

THOMAS W. HANSHEW 1857–1914

American dime novelist; creator of Hamilton Cleek, the "Vanishing Cracksman" who has an amazing ability for disguising himself. And then, as Barzun and Taylor punned: "His enemies couldn't tell a hawk from a Hanshew."

758   I have lived a life of crime from my very boyhood because I couldn't help it, because it appealed to me, because I glory in risks and revel in dangers. I never knew where it would lead me—I never thought, never cared.
>—Hamilton Cleek, about to convert his "useless life into a useful one," for love of a good woman, *Cleek, the Man of the Forty Faces*, 1913

759   A positively infallible recipe for the invasion of England: Wait until the Channel freezes and then skate over.
>—Hamilton Cleek to Count von Hetzler, ibid.

760   Who feeds on hope alone makes but a sorry banquet.
>—Ibid.

CYRIL HARE 1900–1958

Pseudonym of Alfred Alexander Gordon Clark, English barrister and later county circuit judge in Surrey; creator of Francis Pettigrew. Hare's own favorite among his novels was *Tragedy at Law*, which many English barristers consider to be the classic detective story with a legal background.

761   The police nearly always pick on the obvious person. And it is distressing to observe that they are nearly always right.
>—Francis Pettigrew, *With a Bare Bodkin*, 1946

762   Before you start a search, it's a good thing to have some idea of what you're looking for.
>—Inspector John Mallett, ibid.

763   A lying witness is not necessarily a guilty one.
>—Mr. MacWilliam, *That Yew Tree's Shade*, 1954

TIMOTHY HARRIS 1946–

American film writer and detective novelist; creator of Thomas Kyd, Los Angeles private eye.

764   The crime of beating a man nearly to death doesn't lie in the pain you inflict; it's that you have created a *beaten* man.
>—Thomas Kyd, *Goodnight and Good-bye*, 1979

RAY HARRISON 1928–

English writer of detective novels set in the Victorian period; creator of Sergeant Joseph Bragg and Constable James Morton.

765   Not everyone with a motive stoops to crime.
—Chief Inspector Forbes, *French Ordinary Murder*, 1983

FRANCES NOYES HART 1890–1943

American detective novelist, whose first book, *The Bellamy Trial*, was also her best. Her second, *Hide in the Dark*, popularized the parlor game "Murder."

766   It's the greatest murder trial of the century—about every two years another one of 'em comes along.
—The Reporter, *The Bellamy Trial*, 1927

SIMON HARVESTER 1910–1975

Pseudonym of English writer Henry St. John Clair Rumbold-Gibbs, who also wrote as Henry Gibbs. As Harvester, noted for the timeliness of his espionage novels; creator of Dorian Silk, featured in the "Road" novels.

767   "I figure you imagine yourself a John Buchan hero maybe. Was it Richard Hanoi and the thirty-eight steps?"
"Hannay, colonel, not Hanoi. And one more step."
—Exchange between Russian agent and Dorian Silk, *Zion Road*, 1968

S. T. HAYMON

English historical novelist, biographer, and detective novelist; creator of Detective-Inspector Ben Jurnet. *Ritual Murder* won a Silver Dagger in 1982.

768   Murders are about love. . . . If you were a cynic you might even say they are the purest expression of it. Love—for a man or a woman, for money, revenge, religion, or even love of one's self. One way or another, all murders are crimes of passion.
—Detective-Inspector Ben Jurnet, *Stately Homicide*, 1984

769   Time. . . . Do you really believe the past arranges itself for
our convenience into those paltry little squares they print on
calendars?
—Elena Appleyard, ibid.

MATTHEW HEAD 1907–1985

Pseudonym of John Edwin Canaday, art critic and food writer. As
Head, detective novelist; creator of Dr. Mary Finney, best doctor
within two hundred miles of the equator, and her associate
missionary friend, Emily Collins.

770   There's more ways to kill a cat than throwing the grand piano
at it.
—Moore, *The Smell of Money*, 1943

771   Death makes a kind of frame for life. . . . The minute
you're dead, the minute the whole thing is finished and over
with, you're a complete person for the first time.
—Dr. Mary Finney, in one of her rare
philosophical moments, *The Congo Venus*,
1950

EUGENE P. HEALY

American detective novelist; creator of Paul Craine, would-be
writer of mysteries featured in two novels.

772   One man's mate is another man's passion.
—Betty Burchell to Paul Craine, *Mr.
Sandeman Loses His Life*, 1940

773   A fate worse than debt.
—Ibid.

H. F. HEARD 1889–1971

English social historian and religious author, as well as detective
novelist; creator of Mr. Mycroft, who first appeared in *A Taste for
Honey*, now regarded as a minor classic with Holmesian overtones.

774   A trained mind is one which never bores unintentionally.
—Mr. Mycroft, claiming to quote a silly
remark of Mr. Wilde, *A Taste for Honey*,
1941

775 The absolute desert is simply untidiness extended to lunatic lengths and breadths.
—Sydney Silchester, *Reply Paid*, 1942

MARK HEBDEN 1916–

Pseudonym of English adventure novelist John Harris, who also writes as Max Hennessy. As Hebden, creator of Inspector Clovis Pel.

776 When nothing normally happens, you know if a sparrow falls.
—Madame Fabre, *Pel and the Staghound*, 1982

M.V. HEBERDEN 1906–

Mary Violet Heberden was one of the first women to write in the private eye tradition of the American hard-boiled school (use of her initials disguised her sex from her readers for some time); she also wrote as Charles L. Leonard. James Sandoe included her under both names in his annotated list, *The Hard-Boiled Dick* (1952), and Jacques Barzun included her on a list of his favorite women writers. As Heberden, creator of Rick Vanner and Desmond Shannon.

777 The less explaining you do the less people speculate.
—Desmond Shannon, *Aces, Eights, and Murder*, 1941

778 One law for the rich and one for the poor, that's what there is.
—*The Lobster Pick Murder*, 1941

779 God preserve me from idiots and men in love, which is the same thing.
—Ibid.

780 'Tis better to make a good run than a bad stand.
—*Murder Goes Astray*, 1943

781 They that take the sword shall perish by the sword. Ditto for machine guns.
—Ibid.

782 One seldom loves people for their virtues.
—Justine Trinquard, *Engaged to Murder*, 1949

783   You can't run other people's lives for them. They have to
          make or mar on their own.
                    —Rick Vanner's thought, ibid.

Writing as **CHARLES L. LEONARD**, creator of Paul Kilgerrin, a
private investigator called in on espionage cases.

784   We-disown-you-if-you-fail.
                    —Paul Kilgerrin's description of an
                      assignment, *Expert in Murder*, 1945

O. HENRY 1862–1910

Pseudonym of American William Sidney Porter, prolific short story
writer whose speciality was the twist at the end; creator of partners
Jeff Peters and Andy Tucker, who con their way through the stories
in *The Gentle Grafter*, a Queen's Quorum selection.

785   Whenever he saw a dollar in another man's hands he took it
          as a personal grudge, if he couldn't take it any other way.
                    —Jeff Peters, of Andy Tucker, "The Octopus
                      Marooned," *The Gentle Grafter*, 1908

786   It was beautiful and simple as all truly great swindles are.
                    —Jeff Peters, ibid.

787   There are two times when you never can tell what is going to
          happen. One is when a man takes his first drink; and the
          other is when a woman takes her latest.
                    —Jeff Peters, ibid.

788   Cases were decided in the chambers of a six-shooter instead
          of a supreme court.
                    —"Law and Order," 1911

GEORGETTE HEYER 1902–1974

English author of regency and historical romances, and a dozen
well-constructed suspense and detective novels, noted for playing
fair with her readers; creator of Superintendent Hannasyde and
Sergeant (later Inspector) Hemingway.

789   When fate's got it in for you there's no limit to what you may
          have to put up with.
                    —Sergeant Hemingway, *A Blunt Instrument*,
                      1938

GEORGE V. HIGGINS 1939–

American crime novelist and former assistant U.S. attorney for the District of Massachusetts, noted for his realistic portrayal of the Boston underworld.

790   This life's hard, but it's harder if you're stupid,
—Jackie Brown, *The Friends of Eddie Coyle*, 1972

JACK HIGGINS 1929–

Pseudonym of Henry Patterson, English suspense and international intrigue novelist, who has also written under other names. After the success of *The Eagle Has Landed*, which was published under the Jack Higgins pseudonym, many of his earlier novels have been reprinted under that name.

791   Liberal principles are all very fine as long as they leave you with something to have principles about.
—Superintendent Miller, *A Prayer for the Dying*, 1973

792   When a man knows he'll die if he stays where he is, it concentrates his mind wonderfully on moving somewhere else.
—Kurt Steiner, *The Eagle Has Landed*, 1975

PATRICIA HIGHSMITH 1921–

American crime novelist who has lived in Europe since 1963. She considers criminals "dramatically interesting, because for a time at least they are active, free in spirit, and they do not knuckle down to anyone"; creator of Tom Ripley.

793   Highsmith has said:
"I find the public passion for justice quite boring and artificial, for neither life nor nature cares if justice is ever done or not."
—Quoted by Julian Symons, *Bloody Murder*, 1972

794   Every man is his own law court and punishes himself enough.
—*Strangers on a Train*, 1950

R. LANCE HILL 1943–

Canadian suspense novelist and screenplay writer.

795   Giving the devil his due will always jostle the angels.
—Isabelle Lomolin, *The Evil That Men Do*,
1978

REGINALD HILL 1936–

English detective and crime novelist, who also writes using the
names Dick Morland, Patrick Ruell, and Charles Underhill. As
Hill, creator of Superintendent Andrew Dalziel and Detective
Inspector Peter Pascoe.

796   Elimination is the better part of detection.
—Superintendent Andrew Dalziel, *An
Advancement of Learning*, 1971

797   If anyone grabs you from behind, don't think, give 'em the
heel and the elbow.
—Superintendent Andrew Dalziel's dictum,
Ruling Passion, 1973

798   How can you have scandal in an age which has abolished
responsibility?
—Miss Annabelle Andover, *A Pinch of Snuff*,
1978

799   Life's a downhill run. Hard to stop.
—Molly Keatley, *The Spy's Wife*, 1980

800   The family that spies together, sties together.
—Old Cockney Russian Proverb, ibid.

801   Everybody needs a little improbability in their life.
—Patrick Alderman, *Deadheads*, 1983

JAMES HILTON 1900–1954

English writer who wrote only one detective novel, the thoroughly
satisfying *Murder at School*, published under the pseudonym Glen
Trevor. Hilton himself never thought very highly of the book.

802   No one, however clever, should expect to get away with more
than one murder.
—*Murder at School*, 1931

803   Don't take gin for breakfast if you want to live to a decent old
age.
—Ibid.

JOHN BUXTON HILTON 1921–1986

English author of a large number of suspense novels, who also wrote as John Greenwood; creator of Victorian era Detective Inspector Brunt.

804   Hilton said:
"I suppose I am less interested in puzzles—and certainly less in violence—than in character, local colour, folk-lore, social history, and historical influences, most of which loom large in most of my books."
— *Twentieth-Century Crime and Mystery Writers*, 2nd ed., 1985

805   There might even be circumstances under which they could be tolerant of what they do not understand.
— Sergeant Brunt, doubtfully, of the men of Margreave, *Dead-Nettle*, 1977

806   Where there is smoke, something must be smoldering.
— Author's Note, *The Quiet Stranger*, 1985

Writing as **JOHN GREENWOOD**, creator of Mr. Mosley.

807   Unilateral friendship is an uphill furrow.
— Donald Thwaites, *Murder, Mr. Mosley*, 1983

CHESTER HIMES 1909–1984

American novelist, who began writing while serving a seven-year sentence in the Ohio State Penitentiary. He was one of the first black writers to follow in the Hammett-Chandler tradition; creator of Grave Digger Jones and Coffin Ed Johnson.

808   Himes, who felt himself a stranger in every white country he'd ever been in, said:
"I only felt at home in my detective stories."
— *My Life of Absurdity: The Autobiography of Chester Himes*, vol. II, 1976

809   This is Harlem, where anything can happen.
— Grave Digger Jones, *The Crazy Kill*, 1959

810   Money—the one lubrication for love.
— *All Shot Up*, 1960

811   Every time I see you two big fellows I think of two hog
           farmers lost in the city.
                        —Detective Haggerty to Coffin Ed Johnson
                        and Grave Digger Jones, ibid.

812   Is everybody crooked on this mother-raping earth?
                        —Grave Digger Jones, *The Heat's On*, 1966

813   "Blink once and you're dead."
           "Blink twice and you're buried."
                        —Coffin Ed Johnson and Grave Digger
                        Jones, ibid.

CORNELIUS HIRSCHBERG 1901–

American jeweler who won an Edgar for his only crime novel,
Florentine Finish.

814   What you can have if you have what it takes!
                        —Saul Handy, *Florentine Finish*, 1963

815   It was time to go home; a destination I had failed to provide.
                        —Saul Handy, ibid.

TIMOTHY HOLME 1928–

English actor, journalist, and detective novelist; creator of Commis-
sario Achille Peroni, "the Rudolf Valentino of the Italian police."

816   People who only work in one genre are nothing but piffling
           amateurs.
                        —Dame Iolanthe Higgens, a crime novelist
                        who also writes novels, criticism,
                        biography, history, drama, and poetry,
                        The Assisi Murders, 1985

817   A mystery is something dark in itself which sheds light on
           everything around it.
                        —Ibid.

SAMUEL HOLT. *See* Donald Westlake.

LEONARD HOLTON 1915–1983

Pseudonym of Irish-American Leonard Wibberley, newspaperman
and novelist. As Holton, creator of Father Joseph Bredder, a
policeman of God, concerned with the soul of a criminal.

818   Your profession is based on faith. Mine, on doubt.
                            —Inspector Minardi to Father Bredder, *The
                            Saint Maker*, 1959

819   Justice is stupid. Death is blind.
                            —Ben, the ship's cook, *A Touch of Jonah*,
                            1968

820   I have to work from what I call spiritual fingerprints, which I
            find are just as useful in identifying people as physical
            fingerprints.
                            —Father Bredder, *A Corner of Paradise*,
                            1977

KENNETH HOPKINS 1914–

Pseudonym of English novelist Christopher Adams. As Hopkins,
detective novelist, creator of Dr. Blow and Professor Manciple.

821   When reading cannot be indulged in only conversation
            remains.
                            —*Dead Against My Principles*, 1960

822   Misdirected enthusiasm is worse than apathy.
                            —Professor Gideon Manciple, *Body Blow*,
                            1962

GEORGE HOPLEY. *See* Cornell Woolrich.

E. W. HORNUNG 1866–1921

English writer Ernest William Hornung; creator of Raffles, one of
the first great cracksmen. Hornung referred to Raffles as "a villain,"
and thought it was no service to his memory to gloss over the fact.
He dedicated the first collected edition of Raffles stories to his
brother-in-law, Arthur Conan Doyle, with the words: "To A.C.D.
This Form of Flattery." However he might flatter, he was less than
reverent about Conan Doyle's great detective, coining the great
double pun: "Though he might be more humble, there's no police
like Holmes."

823   Why should I work when I could steal? Why settle down to
            some humdrum uncongenial billet when excitement, ro-
            mance, danger, and a decent living were all going begging

together? Of course, it's very wrong, but we can't all be moralists, and the distribution of wealth is very wrong to begin with.
—Raffles, "The Ides of March," *The Amateur Cracksman*, 1899

824 What's the satisfaction of taking a man's wicket when you want his spoons? Still, if you can bowl a bit your low cunning won't get rusty, and always looking for the weak spot's just the kind of mental exercise one wants.
—Raffles, "Gentlemen and Players," ibid.

S. B. HOUGH 1917–

English crime and science fiction novelist Stanley Bennett Hough, who also writes as Bennett Stanley and Rex Gordon. He referred to his novel *Sweet Sister Seduced* as a "did-he-do-it?"

825 In Hough's opinion:
"Much of the literature of our time is formless and shapeless; the detective story on the other hand can and frequently does have a form as demanding as that of a Mozart symphony, while, at the same time, offering the literary artist a medium of inquiry into human folly and psychology and the life of his times."
—*Twentieth-Century Crime and Mystery Writers*, 1980

826 Who studies human character as a whole? We leave it to the novelists and playwrights.
—David Feltham, *Dear Daughter Dead*, 1965

GEOFFREY HOUSEHOLD 1900–

English suspense and adventure novelist, who has said that his goal is to "give the reader fear." In his best works, such as *Rogue Male*, *Watcher in the Shadows*, and *Dance of the Dwarfs*, he succeeds.

827 One should never allow one's illusion of woman to be destroyed by a mere accident.
—Claudio Howard-Wolferstan, *Fellow Passenger*, 1955

828 One must sometimes live up to a false reputation in order to be trusted.
—Owen Dawnay, *Dance of the Dwarfs*, 1968

829   Sheer, sober, human idiocy is the commonest thing in the world.
—Eudora Hilliard, *Red Anger*, 1975

HARTLEY HOWARD. *See* Harry Carmichael.

EDITH HOWIE

American short story writer and author of some half-dozen feminine murder mysteries published in the 1940s and early 1950s.

830   You think you've got something by the tail, but don't forget the man and the bear.
—*Murder's So Permanent*, 1942

P. M. HUBBARD 1910–1980

Englishman Philip Maitland Hubbard served in the Indian Civil Service until 1947, and then worked mostly as a free-lance writer. His first novels were traditional mysteries, his later ones suspense novels, evoking a sense of isolation, with the natural surroundings playing a role as important as that of the human participants.

831   To do the right thing for an even doubtful motive is seldom wholly satisfactory.
—Mr. Claydon, the vicar, *Flush As May*, 1963

832   No paradise is complete without its snake.
—*High Tide*, 1970

DOROTHY B. HUGHES 1904–

American writer of stylish thrillers and mysteries, awarded an Edgar for mystery criticism in 1950, and the Grand Master title in 1977.

833   A watched phone never rang.
—*The Bamboo Blonde*, 1941

834   When a world is crazed with war, many sparrows fall.
—Toni Donne, *The Fallen Sparrow*, 1942

835   When man wants an evil, he'll always find someone evil to supply him.
—Marshal Hackaberry, *The Expendable Man*, 1963

VICTOR HUGO 1802–1885

French novelist, poet, and playwright, whose *Les Miserables* was a Haycraft-Queen Cornerstone Library selection.

836   It is nothing to die, but it is frightful not to live.
> —Jean Valjean, *Les Miserables*, 1862;
> English translation by Lascelles Wraxall,
> 1862

RICHARD HULL 1896–1973

Pseudonym of Richard Henry Sampson, English chartered accountant. As Hull, a major practitioner of the inverted school.

837   In the cause of art, one must be prepared to make sacrifices. And I intend that my conduct, till this matter is over, shall be thoroughly artistic.
> —Edward, *The Murder of My Aunt*, 1934

FERGUS HUME 1859–1932

English writer, today remembered as the author of *The Mystery of a Hansom Cab*, though he wrote almost one hundred fifty other mystery novels and stories. This novel was his first, and came out shortly before Arthur Conan Doyle's A *Study in Scarlet*.

838   Eve only ate the apple because she didn't like to see such a lot of good fruit go to waste.
> —Felix Rolleston, *The Mystery of a Hansom Cab*, 1886

839   The illusions of youth are mostly due to the want of experience.
> —Ibid.

840   The world winked at secret vices as long as there was an attempt at concealment, though it was cruelly severe on those which were brought to light.
> —Ibid.

841   People's blame is always genuine, their praise rarely so.
> —*Madam Midas*, 1888

842   Jokes can be sanctified by time quite as much as creeds.
> —Mr. Calton, ibid.

E. HOWARD HUNT 1918–

American political figure (who became famous for his role in the Watergate scandal) and writer of hard-boiled novels and spy thrillers under various pseudonyms; writing as Robert Dietrich, creator of Steve Bentley, a Washington, D.C., accountant.

843   All you need is money, endurance, and powerful friends. And the more money the better.

> —To make it in our nation's capital, as
> Steve Bentley knew, *Mistress to Murder*,
> 1960

844   Don't think I can't smell a cover-up.

> —Steve Bentley, in a novel written *before*
> Watergate, *Angel Eyes*, 1961

HORACE GORDON HUTCHINSON 1859–1932

English writer of mystery and detective novels.

845   But he was, as my uncle said, a bit of a bounder, or at least on the boundary line.

> —Said of Dr. Pratt, *The Mystery of the*
> *Summer House*, 1919

ALDOUS HUXLEY 1894–1963

English writer and novelist, whose one crime story, "The Gioconda Smile," is a skillful tale of adultery and murder.

846   In married life three is often better company than two.

> —Mr. Hutton, "The Gioconda Smile," *Mortal*
> *Coils*, 1922

FRANCIS ILES. *See* Anthony Berkeley.

RACHEL INGALLS

American writer, who has lived in England since 1964. Her third novel, *Mrs. Caliban*, makes use of the conventions of the murder mystery, suspense, and science fiction genres.

847   Sweep everything under the rug for long enough, and you have to move right out of the house.

> —*Mrs. Caliban*, 1983

MICHAEL INNES 1906–

Pseudonym of English novelist and Oxford don J.I.M. Stewart. As Innes, creator of Inspector John Appleby, that "damned academic policeman."

848   You can never tell . . . what will come of an idea.
                        —Horace Cudbird, *There Came Both Mist
                            and Snow*, 1940

849   I don't much believe in justice. So often we must punish in one man the deed that is born in another man's thought.
                        —Arthur Ferryman to John Appleby, ibid.

850   Consulting doctors is either a waste of money or a forlorn hope.
                        —Clement Cotton, ibid.

851   Ordinary people ought to be able to mind their own business, even if a policeman can't.
                        —Joan Cavenett, *The Weight of the
                            Evidence*, 1943

852   Nothing is more infallibly indicative of bad morals than bad champagne.
                        —Lady Clancarron to Lady Appleby, *A
                            Private View*, 1952

853   Always go on till you're stopped.
                        —Appleby's principle, *Silence Observed*,
                            1961

WILLIAM IRISH. *See* Cornell Woolrich.

P. D. JAMES 1920–

English detective novelist Phyllis Dorothy James, who has said that if mystery writers (and she might well have added, mystery readers) share a common bond, it is that many of them are lovers of order— social, literary, moral, and psychological; creator of Chief Superintendent Adam Dalgliesh and Cordelia Gray.

854   James has said:
           "The mystery's very much the modern morality play. You have an almost ritual killing and a victim, you have a murderer who in some sense represents the forces of evil, you

have your detective coming in—very likely to avenge the
death—who represents justice, retribution. And in the end
you restore order out of disorder."

—Quoted in an interview, *New York Times
Book Review*, October 10, 1982

855   Detection requires a patient persistence which amounts to
obstinacy.

—Chief Superintendent Adam Dalgliesh, *An
Unsuitable Job for a Woman*, 1972

856   They'll tell you that the most destructive force in the world is
hate. Don't you believe it, lad. It's love. And if you want to
make a detective you'd better learn to recognize it when you
meet it.

—Chief Superintendent Adam Dalgleish,
quoting old Greenall, the first
detective-sergeant he had worked under,
Death of an Expert Witness, 1977

857   A murderer sets himself aside from the whole of humanity
forever.

—Dr. Kerrison, ibid.

SEBASTIEN JAPRISOT 1931–

Pseudonym of Jean-Baptiste Rossi, award-winning French suspense
novelist and scriptwriter.

858   Pain is not black, it is not red. It is a well of blinding light
that exists only in your mind. But you fall into it all the
same.

—*The Lady in the Car with Glasses and a
Gun*, 1966; English translation by Helen
Weaver, 1967

F. TENNYSON JESSE 1888–1958

English mystery novelist, playwright, and criminologist, who
coined the word "murderee" to refer to victims who unconsciously
cooperate with their murderers; creator of Solange Fontaine, a
young Frenchwoman gifted by nature with an extra spiritual sense
that warns her of evil.

859   It has been observed, with some truth, that everyone loves a
good murder.

—*Murder and Its Motives*, 1924

860   You will never find a true murderer—that is, one who kills
not for rage in the heat of the moment, which is another
thing altogether—but a man who deliberately kills—who is
not a colossal egoist.
> —Ibid.

861   The fun of anything consists in its limitations. . . . the
framework of the rules saying what we can't do.
> —Introduction, *The Solange Stories*, 1931

862   Of all the emotions pure naked terror is the most demoraliz-
ing save jealousy.
> —"The Pedlar," ibid.

863   The best clues to a crime were in the characters of the people
connected with it, and were worth all the burnt matches,
footprints, or even fingerprints in the world.
> —Solange Fontaine's favorite axiom, "The
> Canary," ibid.

THOMAS JOB 1900–1947

Welsh-born American dramatist and professor of literature, author
of the mystery play *Uncle Harry*.

864   Murderers, like artists, must be hung to be appreciated.
> —Uncle Harry's opinion, *Uncle Harry*, Act I,
> scene i, 1942

ROMILLY JOHN 1906– and KATHERINE JOHN d. 1984

English poet and his wife, a noted translator of Scandinavian
literature, who wrote one Golden Age mystery together.

865   There's no lunacy like regarding any woman as exceptional.
> —Matthew Barry, *Death by Request*, 1933

DIANE JOHNSON 1934–

American essayist and novelist, biographer of Dashiell Hammett
(q.v.), and author of two psychological suspense novels, *The
Shadow Knows* and *Lying Low*.

866   Men are generally more law-abiding than women. Women
have a feeling that since they didn't make the rules, the rules
have nothing to do with them.
> —Theo Waits, *Lying Low*, 1978

LUCILLE KALLEN

American television scriptwriter and detective novelist; creator of Maggie Rome and C. B. Greenfield.

867 Monstrous behavior is the order of the day. I'll tell you when to be shocked. When something human and decent happens!
—C. B. Greenfield to Maggie Rome,
Introducing C. B. Greenfield, 1979

868 A lawyer's relationship to justice and wisdom . . . is on par with a piano tuner's relationship to a concert. He neither composes the music, nor interprets it—he merely keeps the machinery running.
—Ibid.

869 Crime detection is largely a matter of combining physical activity with the intelligent and informed application of life experience.
—C. B. Greenfield, *The Tanglewood Murder*,
1980

870 There are two actions that are almost equally reprehensible to me. One is the act of beginning a sentence and then refusing to finish it. The other is murder.
—C. B. Greenfield to Maggie Rome, ibid.

871 There comes a time when consistency runs a poor second to hedonism.
—C. B. Greenfield, *A Little Madness*, 1986

STUART M. KAMINSKY 1934–

American historian, film critic, and detective novelist; creator of Toby Peters, a Hollywood private eye of the 1940s.

872 Some Californians mark their lives by the earthquakes and tremors they experience.
—Toby Peters, *Murder on the Yellow Brick
Road*, 1977

873 Truth has a way of shoving itself in your face and making your life more difficult.
—Toby Peters, *High Midnight*, 1981

874   Half the fun of being alive is not knowing what tomorrow will bring. The other half comes by pretending that you don't care.

—Toby Peters, *Catch a Falling Clown*, 1981

875   There are coincidences in the world and there is magic. I believe in both, but only after all other explanations have been exhausted.

—Toby Peters, *He Done Her Wrong*, 1983

ZOË KAMITSES 1941–

American actress and suspense novelist.

876   Whores and New York City look better at night.

—*Moondreamer*, 1983

HENRY KANE 1918–

Prolific American novelist of the hard-boiled school; creator of private dick Peter Chambers, who sometimes calls himself a "Private Richard."

877   Put that down as rule one. A guy with a heater that likes to talk, that guy can be taken.

—Peter Chambers, *A Halo for Nobody*, 1947

HARRY KEMELMAN 1908–

American detective novelist, whose first novel, *Friday the Rabbi Slept Late*, won an Edgar; creator of Rabbi David Small.

878   Misfortune can happen to anyone. Only the dead are safe from it.

—Rabbi David Small, *Friday the Rabbi Slept Late*, 1964

879   A nine mile walk is no joke, especially in the rain.

—The sentence that sets Nick Welt off on a logical train of thought in the title story of the collection, *The Nine Mile Walk*, 1967

BAYNARD H. KENDRICK 1894–1977

American detective novelist, first president of Mystery Writers of America, made Grand Master in 1966; creator of Miles Standish

Rice ("The Hungry"), a Florida deputy game and fishing commissioner and deputy sheriff, and in another series, blind Captain Duncan Maclain, who has cultivated an ability to shoot at sounds.

880 I would love to have a murder. . . . A murder is practically an exigent need for a de-tecka-tive. To hell with accidents.
> —Miles Standish Rice, *The Iron Spiders*, 1936

881 Murder builds you a paper house and you must keep adding to its foundations.
> —Captain Duncan Maclain, *Blind Man's Bluff*, 1943

882 I have no eyes to deceive me.
> —Captain Duncan Maclain, *Out of Control*, 1945

883 Lots of people have heard I'm blind. . . . As a matter of fact, I am—although I see a lot of things that might be better hidden.
> —Captain Duncan Maclain, *Blind Allies*, 1954

MILWARD KENNEDY 1894–1968

Pseudonym of English civil servant Milward Rodon Kennedy Burge, who also wrote under other names. As Kennedy, Golden Age detective novelist, and for many years mystery critic for London's *Sunday Times*. His novel *Half-Mast Murder* was the first mystery to be called a "who-dun-it," in a review published in *American News of Books*, July 1930.

884 If you are found with your throat cut, no one will suspect your wife or the bishop, but all will account it suicide.
> —To a "Dear Friend," *Poison in the Parish*, 1935

WILLIAM KENNEDY 1928–

American newspaperman and Pulitzer Prize–winning novelist, author of the Albany Cycle, a series of novels exploring the Albany underworld of the 1930s. Jack "Legs" Diamond, the gangster "for whom violence and death were well-oiled tools of the trade," is the protagonist of *Legs*, the first novel in the series.

885   "What are your feelings about wilful murder?"
            "I try to avoid it."
                              —Exchange between Weissberg and Jack
                              "Legs" Diamond, *Legs*, 1975

886   Jack could tie both his shoes at once.
                              —Said of Jack "Legs" Diamond, ibid.

887   A sucker don't get even till he gets to heaven.
                              —Doc Fay, *Billy Phelan's Greatest Game*,
                              1978

GERALD KERSH 1911–1968

English-born, naturalized American who was once declared dead
and was revived dramatically, and during the Blitz was buried alive
three times and survived. His mysteries tend to the bizarre.

888   Circumstances being favourable, any man can get hold of
            any child and do whatever he likes, and go home and have a
            cup of tea and get away with it.
                              —Detective-Inspector Turpin, *Prelude to a
                              Certain Midnight*, 1947

889   It takes a broad back to take the weight of a woman's trust.
                              —"Thicker Than Water," *Guttersnipe: Little
                              Novels*, 1954

890   There are idiots, and idiots; but there is no idiot quite so
            idiotic as your class-conscious idiot.
                              —"Guttersnipe," ibid.

JOSEPH KESSELRING 1902–1967

American playwright and professor of music, author of the macabre
comic play *Arsenic and Old Lace*.

891   One of our gentlemen found time to say, "How delicious!"
                              —Aunt Abby, *Arsenic and Old Lace*, Act I,
                              1941

892   Insanity runs in my family. It practically *gallops!*
                              —Mortimer Brewster, trying to explain why
                              he can't marry, ibid., Act II

DOUGLAS KIKER 1930–

American television news correspondent and novelist; creator of Mac McFarland, a newspaperman down on his luck, who turns amateur detective when his dog discovers the body of a murdered woman.

893   Peel away the layers, and most prayers ultimately are selfish.
—Mac McFarland, *Murder on Clam Pond*, 1986

C. DALY KING 1895–1963

American detective novelist and psychologist, who coined the word "obelist" (which he sometimes defined as a person of little importance, and at other times as one who views with suspicion); creator of Michael Lord and Dr. Trevis Tarrant.

894   When there is only one possibility, it can't be wrong.
—Dr. Trevis Tarrant, "The Episode of the Headless Horrors," *The Curious Mr. Tarrant*, 1935

895   Holding a lottery ticket does at least expose one to luck.
—Captain Michael Lord, *Obelists Fly High*, 1935

RUFUS KING 1895–1966

American detective novelist, whose *Murder by the Clock* is on the Haycraft-Queen Cornerstone Library list; creator of Lieutenant Valcour of the New York Police.

896   It was forever astonishing him: the specious arguments or violent flares of emotion by which so many people would arrive at murder, would seize it as a solution to their special problem. And it never was.
—Lieutenant Valcour's reflection, *Murder in the Willett Family*, 1931

RUDYARD KIPLING 1865–1936

English Nobel Prize–winning poet, short story writer, and novelist, whose *Kim* is a classic tale of secret agents and adventure. Spying is the Great Game to which Kim aspires.

897   Education is greatest blessing if of best sorts. Otherwise, no earthly use.
—Teshoo Lama, *Kim*, 1901

898   There was a mystery somewhere. . . . Here was a man after his own heart—a tortuous and indirect person playing a hidden game.
—Kim, of Colonel Creighton, ibid.

899   When he comes to the Great Game he must go alone— alone and at peril of his head.
—Mahbub Ali, ibid.

900   We of the Game are beyond protection. If we die, we die. Our names are blotted from the book. That is all.
—"The Maharatta," secret agent E.23, ibid.

C.H.B. KITCHIN 1895–1967

English barrister, novelist, and detective story writer Clifford Henry Benn Kitchin; creator of Malcolm Warren, a young stockbroker forced to turn sleuth.

901   The consciousness of innocence is a great comfort.
—Malcolm Warren, *Death of My Aunt*, 1929

902   A historian of the future will probably turn, not to blue books or statistics, but to detective stories if he wishes to study the manners of our age.
—Malcolm Warren, *Death of His Uncle*, 1939

CLIFFORD KNIGHT 1886–

American newspaperman and mystery novelist; creator of Professor Huntoon Rogers, English teacher and amateur criminologist.

903   He's been dragging red herrings around this house until it smells like Fisherman's Wharf.
—Kelly Reevers, *The Affair of the Fainting Butler*, 1943

KATHLEEN MOORE KNIGHT

American novelist who also wrote as Alan Amos. As Knight, author of dozens of mystery and detective novels published between 1935 and 1960; creator of Margot Blair and Elisha Macomber, each featured in a series of novels.

904   No man is qualified to remove the skeleton from his own closet.
—Felix Norman to Margot Blair, *Rendezvous with the Past*, 1940

FREDERICK KNOTT 1918–

Anglo-American mystery and suspense playwright, who was awarded special Edgars for *Dial "M" for Murder* and *Write Me a Murder*.

905   Fear—jealousy—money—revenge—and protecting someone you love.

> —Max Halliday, listing the five important
> motives for murder, *Dial "M" for Murder*,
> Act I, 1952

RONALD A. KNOX 1888–1957

English detective story writer and Catholic theologian, most
remembered today for his "Detective Story Decalogue," which
nicely established the rules the Golden Age lived by. He was also
one of the first Sherlock Holmes scholars; creator of Miles Bredon,
ace investigator for the Indescribable Insurance Company.

906   It is impossible . . . not to make inferences; the mistake is
to depend on them. . . . In detection one should take no
chances, give no one the benefit of the doubt.

> —Reeves, *The Viaduct Murder*, 1925

907   There's a curious sort of statute of limitations in the learned
world which makes it impossible to call a man a liar if he has
gone on lying successfully for fifty years.

> —Ibid.

908   Murder isn't sticking to the rules; it's an unfair solution.

> —Angela Bredon, *The Footsteps at the Lock*,
> 1928

909   These people play tennis instead of cricket. . . . It isn't that
I mind tennis, but it hasn't got the tradition value of cricket.
Who ever heard of somebody refusing to do a shady thing on
the ground that it wasn't tennis?

> —Miles Bredon, *The Body in the Silo*, 1933

910   It is the ambition of the Scot to be respected in death as it is
the illusion of the Englishman that he is loved.

> —*Double Cross Purposes*, 1937

911   Nothing lends such a zest to life as the thought of the other
things one ought to be doing.

> —Vernon Lethaby, ibid.

JOSEPH WOOD KRUTCH 1893–1970

American professor of English at Columbia University, who was on the editorial staff of *The Nation*, and a defender of the mystery genre.

912   "Only a detective story" is now an apologetic and depreciatory phrase which has taken the place of that "only a novel" which once moved Jane Austen to unaccustomed indignation.

— "Only a Detective Story," *The Nation*,
November 25, 1944

JEAN DE LA BRUYÈRE 1645–1696

French writer and moralist.

913   If poverty is the mother of all crimes, lack of intelligence is their father.

— *Characters*, 1688; English translation by
Henri Van Laun, 1885

EMMA LATHEN

Joint pseudonym of American economist Mary J. Latsis, 1927?–, and corporate financier Martha Henisart, 1929?–. As Lathen, award-winning detective novelists; creators of John Putnam Thatcher, senior vice president of Wall Street's Sloan Guaranty Trust.

914   Wall Street is, at bottom, a collection of endearingly childlike innocents, always expecting the good, the beautiful, the true, and the profitable.

— *Pick Up Sticks*, 1970

JONATHAN LATIMER 1906–1983

American private eye novelist; creator of Bill Crane, committed to an asylum in his first novel, *Murder in the Madhouse*.

915   I am a Doctor of Deduction. I am interested in everything.

— Bill Crane, *Murder in the Madhouse*, 1935

916   Genius is an infinite capacity for not being satisfied.

— Bill Crane, *Headed for a Hearse*, 1935

917   In two days we start a fight in a taxi-dance joint, find a murdered guy and don't tell the police, crash in on Braymer

and his dope mob, bust in on a party, kidnap a gal, steal a car and rob a graveyard. The only thing we ain't done is to park in a no-parking zone.
> —Tom O'Malley, reviewing events
> *three-quarters* through the book, *The Lady
> in the Morgue*, 1936

918 I'm going to get so drunk you'll be able to bottle me.
> —Bill Crane, ibid.

HILDA LAWRENCE 1906–

American mystery novelist; creator of private eye Mark East, and Beulah Pond and Bessy Petty, New England spinsters with a talent for sleuthing. Lawrence, an addict of mystery fiction, took to writing it because she couldn't find enough to read.

919 Let sleeping dogs lie is an excellent maxim, unless you are stronger than the dog.
> —Max Herald, *The Pavilion*, 1946

MAURICE LEBLANC 1864–1941

French crime writer; creator of one of the great crooks of literature, Arsène Lupin, known as "the prince of thieves."

920 Arsène Lupin, gentleman-burglar, will return when the furniture is genuine.
> —Note left at the residence of Baron
> Schormann, "The Arrest of Arsène Lupin,"
> *Arsène Lupin: Gentleman-Burglar*, 1907;
> English translation by George Morehead,
> 1910

921 A little advertising never does any harm.
> —"The Queen's Necklace," ibid.

922 The most diverse effects often proceed from the same cause.
> —Jean Daspry, "The Seven of Hearts," ibid.

923 Where force fails, cunning prevails.
> —Arsène Lupin's advice, "Madame Imbert's
> Safe," ibid.

JOHN LE CARRÉ 1931–

Pseudonym of English espionage novelist David John Moore Cornwell, awarded the Grand Master title by Mystery Writers of America in 1984; creator of George Smiley, reflective spymaster of the intelligence agency known as "the Circus."

924   Smiley himself was one of those solitaries who seem to have come into the world fully educated at the age of eighteen. Obscurity was his nature, as well as his profession. . . . A man who, like Smiley, has lived and worked for years among his country's enemies learns only one prayer: that he may never, never be noticed.
—A Murder of Quality, 1962

925   What is important is seldom urgent. Urgent equals ephemeral, and ephemeral equals unimportant.
—Ibid.

926   There is no true thing on earth. There is no constant, no dependable point, not even in the purest logic or the most obscure mysticism; least of all in the motives of men when they are moved to act violently.
—Smiley, reflecting on the obscurity of motive in human behavior, ibid.

927   We just don't know what people are like, we can never tell; there isn't any truth about human beings, no formula that meets each one of us.
—Smiley, ibid.

928   Intelligence work has one moral law—it is justified by results.
—The Spy Who Came in from the Cold, 1963

929   We do disagreeable things so that ordinary people here and elsewhere can sleep safely in their beds at night.
—Control to Leamas, ibid.

930   We have to live without sympathy, don't we? That's impossible of course. We act it to one another, all this hardness; but we aren't like that really. I mean . . . one can't be out in the cold all the time; one has to come in from the cold . . . do you see what I mean?
—Control to Leamas, ibid.

931   It's easy to forget what intelligence consists of: luck and speculation.
—Leclerc, *The Looking-Glass War*, 1965

932   Do you know what love is? . . . It is whatever you can still betray.
—Adrian Haldane, ibid.

933   To be inhuman in defence of our humanity, harsh in our defence of compassion. To be single-minded in defence of our disparity.

> —Smiley's dilemma, *The Honourable Schoolboy*, 1977

934   In every operation there is an above the line and a below the line. Above the line is what you do by the book. Below the line is how you do the job.

> —*A Perfect Spy*, 1986

GYPSY ROSE LEE 1914–1970

One would like to think the famous American stripper really wrote *The G-String Murders*. Alas, it was ghostwritten by Craig Rice (q.v.), but there is no reason why that should spoil the fun.

935   American columnist Henry V. Wade once wrote: "Gypsy Rose Lee, the strip-tease artist, has arrived in Hollywood with twelve empty trunks."

> —Quoted by Colin Dexter, *Last Seen Wearing*, 1976

936   Full-length, hand-tinted pictures of girls in various forms of undress graced the walls. The one of me, wearing a sunbonnet and holding a bouquet of flowers just large enough to bring the customers in and keep the police out, was third from the left.

> —Gypsy Rose Lee, *The G-String Murders*, 1941

937   You either bury that body in the woods tonight or you finish your honeymoon without your mother.

> —Gypsy Rose Lee's mother, *Mother Finds a Body*, 1942

STANISLAW LEM 1921–

Noted Polish science fiction author who writes an occasional detective novel.

938   The secret of growing old is having lots of experience you can no longer use.

> —An old lady who goes on to remark on the *fundamental* difference between being seventy years old and being ninety years old, *The Chain of Chance*, 1975; English translation by Louis Iribarne, 1978

CHARLES L. LEONARD. *See* M. V. Heberden.

ELMORE LEONARD 1925–

American crime and suspense novelist, winner of an Edgar for *La Brava*. With *Glitz*, he made the best-seller list and the cover of *Newsweek*.

939   Referring to his writing, Leonard has said: "I try to leave out the parts that people skip."
                    —Quoted in *The Writer's Book of Quotations*, 1985

940   No one ever got in trouble keeping his mouth shut.
                    —Jim O'Boyle, *52 Pick-up*, 1974

941   If work was a good thing the rich would have it all and not let you do it.
                    —Louverture Damien's wife, *Split Images*, 1981

942   A prompt man is a lonely man.
                    —Bryan Hurd, ibid.

943   A good rule was, whenever you were with people whose intentions were in doubt, the first thing you did was look for a way out or something to hit them with.
                    —Jack Delaney, *Bandits*, 1987

944   "I read in the paper that in the U.S., I think it was just this country, a woman is beaten or physically abused something like every eighteen seconds."
        "You don't tell me."
        "Somebody made a study."
        "You wouldn't think that many women would get out of line would you?"
                    —Exchange between Jack Delaney and Roy Hicks, ibid.

NATHAN LEOPOLD 1904–1971

American, convicted in the Leopold-Loeb murder trial, paroled in 1958.

945   What a rotten writer of detective stories life is!
                    —*Life Plus 99 Years*, 1958

GASTON LEROUX 1868–1927

French author famous for his many sensational novels, but especially for his first detective novel, *The Mystery of the Yellow Room*, and for *The Phantom of the Opera*.

946   It's dangerous, very dangerous . . . to go from a preconceived idea to find the proofs to fit it.
> —Joseph Rouletabille, *The Mystery of the Yellow Room*, 1907; English translation, 1908

947   Coincidences are the worst enemies to truth.
> —Joseph Rouletabille, ibid.

GEORGE HENRY LEWES 1817–1878

English dramatist, literary critic, and social commentator.

948   Murder, like talent, seems occasionally to run in families.
> —*The Physiology of Common Life*, 1859–60

949   We must never assume that which is incapable of proof.
> —Ibid.

MICHAEL Z. LEWIN 1942–

American detective novelist; creator of private eye Albert Samson and Lt. Leroy Powder of the Indianapolis police, each featured in his own series.

950   It's hard to live a reputation down. Especially when your actions live up to it.
> —Albert Samson, *The Enemies Within*, 1974

951   If you didn't have no temptation, then you'd never have the chance to feel real virtuous.
> —Canteen supervisor to Lt. Powder, who thinks it should be against the law to sell cakes and pies, *Hard Line*, 1982

952   If you hoe where there are no weeds there will be no weeds.
> —Lt. Leroy Powder's gardening philosophy, ibid.

FRANCES LOCKRIDGE 1896–1963 and RICHARD LOCK-RIDGE 1898–1982

American husband-and-wife writing team; creators of Pam and Jerry North and their cats.

953   Nobody is going to go to that much trouble to *get* murdered. But if you are going to murder somebody, you expect to go to a lot of trouble. I would.
—Pam North to Lieutenant Weigand, *The Norths Meet Murder*, 1940

954   Complications may trap you—leave booby traps, intricate time tables, alibis—to the writers of mysteries. Waylay, strike, and walk away.
—Advice to would-be murderers, *Murder within Murder*, 1946

955   Hating is a *complete* emotion.
—Peggy Mott, *Murder Is Served*, 1948

956   "It's convincing that two and two make four. It's neat—simple. Also, they do."
        "People aren't like arithmetic. You can't add up people. There wouldn't be any—well any *fun* left."
—Exchange between Jerry and Pam North, ibid.

957   Unlikely melodrama is the likeliest to happen of anything in the world.
—Pam North, *Death Has a Small Voice*, 1953

PETER LOVESEY 1936–

English detective novelist who has turned his interest in history and sports to good account in a series of Victorian police detective novels. *Waxwork* won a Silver Dagger, and *The False Inspector Dew* won a Gold Dagger; creator of Constable Thackeray and Sergeant Cribb.

958   Lovesey has said:
        "Our world of social welfare and easier divorce and psychiatric care has removed many of the bad old reasons for murder."
—"The Historian," *Murder Ink*, 1977

959   Killing two men in cold blood like that! The calculation in it—it's horrible. Most murders you can understand, even if you don't altogether agree with the outcome. Jealous husbands, neglected wives, sons and daughters wanting to inherit—murder's a family thing, as often as not. But killing strangers as a way to pass the time on a river trip isn't nice, not nice at all.
> —Constable Thackeray, *Swing Swing Together*, 1976

960   In the art of seduction, the motor car is an unreliable accessory.
> —Johnny Finch, *The False Inspector Dew*, 1982

MARIE BELLOC LOWNDES 1868–1947

English author of crime fiction and historical romances; her most famous work, *The Lodger*, reworks the Jack-the-Ripper theme.

961   What to me is very startling and terrible, is that the intelligent criminal has nothing in his appearance, manner or, I fear, nature, making him any different from those about him. To me, with regard to murder, the word that should be used is not "Who?" but "Why?"
> —November 29, 1912, *Diaries and Letters of Marie Belloc Lowndes*, 1971

JOHN LUTZ 1939–

American short story crime writer and detective novelist, who also writes under other names. As Lutz, creator of Alo Nudger, ex-cop turned private eye.

962   If she keeps practicing, someday she'll be mediocre.
> —Fat Jack McGee, of a would-be blues singer, *The Right to Sing the Blues*, 1986

FRANCIS LYNDE 1856–1930

American novelist and detective story writer; creator of Scientific Sprague, government chemist who is sent West to test soils but becomes involved in solving railroad mysteries.

963 Reason, and the proper emphasis to be placed upon each fact as it comes to bat, are the only two needful qualities in any problem solving—and about the only two.
> —Scientific Sprague, "High Finance in
> Cromarty Gulch," *Scientific Sprague*, 1912

964 I had it all figured out to the tenth decimal place, *and I didn't put in the factor of chance!*
> —Scientific Sprague, "The Cloud-Bursters,"
> ibid.

ARTHUR LYONS 1946–

American detective novelist; creator of half-Jewish private eye Jacob Asch, who views all life as "an underwater bicycle race."

965 Stereotypes are the basis of all bigotry.
> —Jacob Asch, *Dead Ringer*, 1977

966 We're all entitled to a dream, even if it will never come true.
> —Jacob Asch, ibid.

967 The heavy-breathing, leggy blondes all went to Spade and Marlowe; I wound up with the refugees from Barnum and Bailey.
> —Jacob Asch, *Hard Trade*, 1981

R. A. MACAVOY 1949–

American science fiction novelist whose books blend adventure, fantasy, mystery, and detection.

968 Godlike objectivity, even if possible, was far too much trouble.
> —Detective-Sergeant Anderson's opinion,
> *Twisting the Rope*, 1986

969 Great sorrow drives out lesser.
> —Ibid.

ED McBAIN 1926–

Most successful of the pseudonyms used by American police procedural novelist Evan Hunter. As McBain, awarded the Grand Master title by Mystery Writers of America in 1986; creator of Steve Carella and the other officers of the 87th Precinct.

970 It was the belief of every detective on the 87th Squad that the real motive behind half the crimes being committed in the city was *enjoyment* pure and simple—the *fun* of playing Cops and Robbers.
—*Jigsaw*, 1970

971 If you can't do the time, don't do the crime.
—*Heat*, 1981

972 It was easy to allow this precinct to burn you out. . . . When you realized it was a *war* you were fighting . . . good guys versus the bad guys, and in a war you got tired, man, in a war you burned out.
—Detective Steve Carella, *Ice*, 1983

973 In *my* book, *anybody* who kills anybody is a crazy.
—Lieutenant Peter Byrnes, ibid.

974 A bad situation can only get worse.
—An adage of police work, *Lightning*, 1984

CHARLES McCARRY 1930–

American espionage novelist; creator of Paul Christopher, spy and poet.

975 You think that truth and reality are the same thing. In this world, *lies* are the reality. People can't live without them.
—Wolkowicz to Paul Christopher, *The Last Supper*, 1983

976 Do you know what makes a man a genius? The ability to see the obvious.
—Wolkowicz to Paul Christopher, ibid.

HELEN McCLOY 1904–

American author of mystery and detective novels and short stories, winner of an Edgar for mystery criticism; creator of Dr. Basil Willing, psychiatrist-detective.

977 Every criminal leaves psychic fingerprints. And he can't wear gloves to hide them.
—Dr. Basil Willing, *Dance of Death*, 1938

978 Psychic clues have to be studied and sifted like physical clues.
—Dr. Basil Willing, ibid.

979   Nothing is more likely to cause a blunder than a lie.
                        —Dr. Basil Willing, ibid.

980   No human being can ever perform any act without a motive,
           conscious or unconscious. The unmotivated act was a myth
           like the unicorn or the sea serpent.
                        —Dr. Basil Willing's belief, *Cue for Murder*,
                        1942

981   Habit is far stronger than the lessons of experience.
                        —Dr. Basil Willing, ibid.

982   The folly of the officious is proverbial: don't rush in where
           angels fear to tread. Let well enough alone. Let sleeping dogs
           lie. Do not monkey with the buzz-saw. Do not disturb!
                        —*Do Not Disturb*, 1943

983   The true Golden Rule is minding your own business in all
           circumstances.
                        —Ibid.

984   In a city you thought of all life as human life. You had to live
           in the heart of the woods to realize that humanity was a slight
           ripple on the surface of a flood of life that seeped into every
           vacant crack, flowed into every biological vacuum the
           moment it occurred.
                        —*Panic*, 1944

985   Who said the middle years of life are always a parody of the
           youthful dreams?
                        —*Better Off Dead*, 1951

986   Today a plot is indecent anywhere outside a mystery, the last
           refuge of the conservative writer.
                        —Emmett Avery, *Two-thirds of a Ghost*,
                        1956

JAMES McCLURE 1939–

South African-born police procedural novelist who now lives in
England. His first novel, *The Steam Pig*, won a Golden Dagger, and
his nonseries espionage thriller *Rogue Eagle*, a Silver Dagger;
creator of Lieutenant Tromp Kramer and his Bantu Detective
Sergeant Mickey Zondi of the Trekkersburg Murder and Robbery
Squad.

987   Nobody is quite the individual he believes himself to be.
　　　　　—*The Gooseberry Fool*, 1974

988   A coincidence is the first thing most people dismiss.
　　　　　—*The Sunday Hangman*, 1977

HORACE McCOY 1897–1955

American scriptwriter and suspense novelist, one of the leaders of the hard-boiled school, though he deeply resented the classification.

989   Why are these high-powered scientists always screwing around trying to prolong life instead of finding pleasant ways to end it?
　　　　　—Gloria to Robert, *They Shoot Horses, Don't They?*, 1935

990   I think your whole future is mapped out from the day you're born, from the day you're even conceived, and that no matter what you do, you can't beat it. There's no escape.
　　　　　—Mona, *I Should Have Stayed Home*, 1938

JOHN D. MacDONALD 1916–1986

American writer of crime fiction and private eye novels with seventy-seven books—often published as paperback originals—to his credit, awarded the Grand Master title by Mystery Writers of America in 1971; creator of Travis McGee, "creaking knight errant, yawning at the thought of the next dragon."

991   MacDonald said:
　　　　　"I want story, wit, music, wryness, color, and a sense of reality in what I read, and I try to get it in what I write."
　　　　　—Introduction, *The Good Old Stuff*, 1982

992   Life is random. Luck is the factor. The good and the evil are struck down, and there is no cause to look for reasons. There is a divine plan, but it is not so minute and selective that it deals with individuals on the basis of their merit. Were that so, all men would be good, out of fear if nothing else. Those unholy four could have gathered up a tart in front of a bar. They happened to take Helen. It was chance. No blame can be assessed.
　　　　　—A father's thoughts after his daughter is slain by a quartet of casual young killers, *The End of the Night*, 1960

993   Life is the process of finding out, too late, everything that should have been obvious to you at the time.
—*The Only Girl in the Game*, 1960

994   There is almost no useful thing the human animal will not in his eternal perversity misuse, whether it be alcohol, gasoline, gunpowder, aspirin, chocolate fudge, mescaline, or LSD.
—Travis McGee, *One Fearful Yellow Eye*, 1966

995   People spend so much time fretting about what they did yesterday and dreading what might happen tomorrow, they miss out on all of their todays.
—Ibid.

996   Pride of any kind is a high place, and any fall can kill.
—Travis McGee, *The Girl in the Plain Brown Wrapper*, 1968

997   It is humiliating, when you should know better, to become victim of the timeless story of the little brown dog running across the freight yard, crossing all the railroad tracks until a switch engine nipped off the end of his tail between wheel and rail. The little dog yelped, and he spun so quickly to check himself out that the next wheel chopped through his little brown neck. The moral is, of course, never lose your head over a piece of tail.
—*The Scarlet Ruse*, 1973

998   A bore is a person who deprives you of solitude without providing you company.
—Meyer, *The Turquoise Lament*, 1973

999   Integrity is not a conditional word.
—Travis McGee, ibid.

1000   There are no hundred percent heroes.
—Travis McGee, *Cinnamon Skin*, 1982

1001   The most deadly commitment of all is to be committed only to one's self.
—Travis McGee, *The Lonely Silver Rain*, 1985

1002   Self-delusion is one of the essentials of life.
—Travis McGee, ibid.

1003 Muscle stuff is pointless, especially when there are so many more satisfying ways to make a man sorry he's alive.
—Tucker Loomis, *Barrier Island*, 1986

PHILIP MacDONALD 1899–1981

Anglo-American detective novelist, who also wrote under other names. MacDonald considered the ideal detective story to be "a sort of competition between author and reader"; creator of Colonel Anthony Gethryn, described as "a man of action who dreamed while he acted; a dreamer who acted while he dreamed."

1004 If at first you don't succeed . . . pry, pry again!
—Colonel Anthony Gethryn to Superintendent Arnold Pike, *The Nursemaid Who Disappeared*, 1938

1005 Are these men living at these addresses?
—Adrian Messenger's question, *The List of Adrian Messenger*, 1959

ROSS MACDONALD 1915–1983

Pseudonym of Canadian-American writer Kenneth Millar, husband of Margaret Millar (q.v.), who also wrote using the names John Macdonald and John Ross Macdonald, so some confusion with John D. MacDonald is inevitable; creator of Lew Archer, observer of the seamier side of Southern California. Mystery Writers of America awarded him the Grand Master title in 1973, and in 1982, when he was already fatally ill, the Private Eye Writers of America awarded him their first Life Achievement Award.

1006 You can't blame money for what it does to people. The evil is in the people, and money is the peg they hang it on. They go wild for money when they've lost their other values.
—Lew Archer, *The Moving Target*, 1949

1007 Sex and money: the forked root of evil.
—Lew Archer, *The Drowning Pool*, 1950

1008 Nothing wrong with Southern California that a rise in the ocean wouldn't cure.
—Ibid.

1009 Never sleep with anyone whose troubles are worse than your own.
—Advice given to Lew Archer, *Black Money*, 1966

1010 What you do to other people you do to yourself—that's the converse of the Golden Rule.
—Lew Archer, ibid.

1011 I have a secret passion for mercy. But justice is what keeps happening to people.
—Lew Archer, *The Goodbye Look*, 1969

1012 Money costs too much.
—Lew Archer, ibid.

1013 We gave her everything. But it wasn't what she wanted.
—Mrs. Crandall, referring to her daughter Susan, *The Underground Man*, 1971

1014 "Am I supposed to know you? I have a terrible memory for faces."
"I have a terrible face for memories."
—Exchange between a woman and Lew Archer, "The Suicide," *Lew Archer, Private Investigator*, 1977

First published in *Manhunt*, October 1953, as "The Beat-Up Sister."

PATRICK McGINLEY 1937–

Irish author of suspense novels. In *Bogmail*, his first novel, the murder weapon is a volume of the 1911 *Encyclopaedia Britannica*.

1015 Imagination is what a policeman needs, not logic. A born policeman has a criminal imagination. The only difference between him and a criminal is that he uses his imagination to solve rather than commit crime.
—Sergeant McGing, *Bogmail*, 1978

JILL McGOWAN 1947–

Scottish suspense and mystery novelist.

1016 A trouble shared was a trouble exacerbated.
—Donald Mitchell, *A Perfect Match*, 1983

PAUL McGUIRE 1903–1978

Australian diplomat, writer, and poet; author of many mystery novels published between 1931 and 1940. *Burial Service* is his finest novel.

1017   I sincerely hope that sailors at sea are praying for those in peril on the shore.
> —Hope of the battered hero, *7:30 Victoria*, 1935

1018   Confidence is a good thing . . . but conceit is a mortal poison.
> —George Buchanan, *Burial Service*, 1938

1019   I have considerable respect for the Official Mind when it is accompanied by an Official Conscience.
> —Tony Grant, who knows that an Official Conscience can k.o. an Official Sense of Discretion, *The Spanish Steps*, 1940

WILLIAM MacHARG 1863–1947

American writer; with Edwin Balmer (q.v.), creator of Luther Trant, one of the first fictional detectives to make use of psychology. On his own, creator of O'Malley, smartest of all "dump cops."

1020   "Cherchez la femme."
"Not at all; what we got to do is look for the woman."
> —Exchange between the narrator and O'Malley, "The Scotty Dog," *The Affairs of O'Malley*, 1940

1021   Maybe instead of a cop I ought to be a crook, but I figure a crook works harder than a cop, and I ain't that fond of working.
> —O'Malley, "The Checkered Suit," ibid.

1022   If a guy slips a cop a ten-dollar bill they call it a bribe, but a waiter just takes it and says, "Thank you."
> —O'Malley, "Broadway Murder," ibid.

WILLIAM McILVANNEY 1936–

Scottish schoolteacher, writer, and police procedural novelist; creator of Detective Inspector Jack Laidlaw of the Glasgow police department. His first detective novel, *Laidlaw*, won a Silver Dagger, as did his second, *The Papers of Tony Vetch*.

1023   People often choose the guilts they can handle. It's a way of hiding from the truth.
> —*Laidlaw*, 1977

1024 You know who casts the first stone? The guiltiest bastard in
the crowd.

> —Detective Inspector Jack Laidlaw, *The
> Papers of Tony Vetch*, 1983

HELEN MacINNES 1907–1985

American thriller and suspense novelist whose books, often best-
sellers, dealt with political threats and international situations.

1025 God made the country, man made the town. Pity men
couldn't learn better.

> —Frances Myles, *Above Suspicion*, 1941

1026 Expect the worst, and you won't be disappointed.

> —Ibid.

MARY McMULLEN 1920–1986

Pseudonym of American crime and suspense novelist Mary Reilly
Wilson, whose first mystery, *Stranglehold*, won an Edgar in 1952.
Her second novel was not published until 1974, but then a new
book appeared almost every year until her death.

1027 Sanity is sometimes a matter of going on, outwardly, as if
everything is all right.

> —*Prudence Be Damned*, 1978

1028 Take the goods the gods provide, and don't stand and sulk
when they are snatched away.

> —*Something of the Night*, 1980

H. C. McNEILE 1888–1937

English soldier and author of military adventure stories; using the
pseudonym Sapper, creator of Captain Hugh "Bull-dog"
Drummond.

1029 Demobilised officer, finding peace incredibly tedious, would
welcome diversion. Legitimate, if possible; but crime, if of a
comparatively humourous description, no objection. Excitement essential. Would be prepared to consider permanent
job if suitably impressed by applicant for his services. Reply
at once Box X10.

> —Captain Hugh Drummond's advertisement
> in the Personal columns of *The Times*,
> *Bull-Dog Drummond*, 1920

1030 I shall only undertake murder in exceptional cases.
—Captain Hugh Drummond, reassuring his
housekeeper, ibid.

1031 There must be compensations in respectability, otherwise so
many people wouldn't be respectable.
—Carl Peterson, using an alias, of course,
The Third Round, 1924

JOHN MALCOLM 1936–

Pseudonym of English antiquarian John Malcolm Andrews. As
Malcolm, detective novelist; creator of Tim Simpson, art expert and
investment consultant.

1032 There's an old saying about a consultant being a man who
borrows your watch to tell you the time.
—Tim Simpson, *A Back Room in Somers
Town*, 1984

1033 When a crocodile sees an inexperienced land animal
entering the water it can't help itself assuming that dinner has
arrived.
—Tim Simpson, *The Gwen John Sculpture*,
1985

JOHN P. MARQUAND 1893–1960

Pulitzer Prize–winning American novelist and detective story
writer; creator of Mr. Moto, the popular Japanese secret agent.

1034 Referring to his creation, Marquand said:
"Mr. Moto was my literary disgrace. I wrote about him to get
shoes for the baby."
—*New York Times*, August 3, 1958

1035 You may be an officer, but you're only a gentleman by act of
Congress.
—Casey Lee to Jim Driscoll, *No Hero*, 1935

1036 Undue exertion of nearly any form leads to difficult conse-
quences, and at any rate is undignified.
—Tom Nelson's reflection, *Thank You, Mr.
Moto*, 1936

1037 I can do many, many things. I can mix drinks and wait on
tables and I am a very good valet. I can navigate and manage

small boats. I have studied at two foreign universities. I also know carpentry and surveying and five Chinese dialects. So very many things come in useful.

—Mr. Moto, *Think Fast, Mr. Moto*, 1937

NGAIO MARSH 1899–1982

New Zealand–born theater director and detective novelist, awarded the Grand Master title by Mystery Writers of America in 1977; creator of Superintendent Roderick Alleyn. Inability to pronounce her name (ny'o, a Maori name for a local flowering tree), has not kept anyone from enjoying her novels.

1038   "So you imagine—?" Nigel began.
         "I do not imagine; detectives aren't allowed to imagine. They note probabilities."

—Inspector Roderick Alleyn, *A Man Lay Dead*, 1934

1039   Custom makes monsters of us all.

—Inspector Roderick Alleyn, *Death in Ecstacy*, 1936

1040   I am not what you describe as artsy-craftsy.

—Mrs. Bünz, drawing her handwoven cloak about her, *Death of a Fool*, 1956

WILLIAM MARSHALL 1944–

Australian police procedural novelist; creator of the Yellowthread Street Police Station, Hong Bay District of Hong Kong, and Detective Chief Inspector Harry Feiffer.

1041   The temptation to say something is well nigh irresistible.

—Dirty Elmo Fan, *Thin Air*, 1977

1042   Chance discoveries favour those with a prepared mind.

—Dr. Curry, ibid.

1043   When everything possible has been eliminated, the solution has to be the *impossible*.

—Detective Inspector John Phillip Auden, *Skulduggery*, 1979

1044   When all the possible answers have been eliminated, whatever remains, however impossible, is the solution.

—Detective Inspector Bill Spencer, bitterly, when he finds himself the last human being functioning in a world taken over by machines, *Sci Fi*, 1981

A.E.W. MASON 1865–1948

English detective novelist Alfred Edward Woodley Mason, who tried to "combine the crime story which produces a shiver with the detective story which aims at a surprise"; creator of Inspector Gabriel Hanaud, who first appeared in *At the Villa Rose*, and then in other novels and several short stories.

1045 It is a great advantage to be intelligent and not to look it.
>—Inspector Gabriel Hanaud, *At the Villa Rose*, 1910

1046 It's not my business to hold opinions . . . my business is to make sure.
>—Inspector Gabriel Hanaud, ibid.

1047 A heavy, clever, middle-aged man, liable to become a little gutter-boy at a moment's notice.
>—Mr. Ricardo's description of Inspector Gabriel Hanaud, ibid.

1048 We are the servants of Chance, the very best of us. Our skill is to seize quickly the hem of her skirt, when it flashes for the fraction of a second before our eyes.
>—Inspector Gabriel Hanaud, *The House of the Arrow*, 1924

1049 People without brains are always dangerous.
>—Inspector Gabriel Hanaud, ibid.

1050 There are two parties to a crime: The criminal and the victim.
>—Commissaire Herbesthal, *The Prisoner in the Opal*, 1928

1051 Suspense is worse than the worst of news.
>—Diana Tasborough, ibid.

1052 He is locking the stable after the horse has stolen the oats.
>—Mr. Richards, indignantly repeating one of Inspector Gabriel Hanaud's fractured idioms, ibid.

1053 Chance was the most willing of goddesses, but the most jealous. She demanded a swift mind and a deadly hand. She showed her face for the fraction of a second, just the time to breathe her message, and the clouds closed again. It was your fault if your ears were not quick to catch the words.
>—Inspector Gabriel Hanaud's old doctrine, ibid.

1054 More and more clearly do I observe that the chief of our success we owe to chance and the mistakes of the other man.
> —Inspector Gabriel Hanaud, ibid.

1055 Mademoiselle, I have served.
> —Inspector Gabriel Hanaud, with great
> simplicity, ibid.

J. C. MASTERMAN 1891–1977

Oxford don, writer of mysteries, and real-life wartime master game player who directed and manipulated double agents to Great Britain's advantage; creator of Ernst Brendel, "the lawyer who knows all about crime." Masterman also wrote *The Double-Cross System* (a secret report completed in 1945, published as a book in 1971), which has been called the best document describing double agents and deception.

1056 When the only alternatives are the improbable and the wildly improbable, it is wiser to concentrate on the former.
> —Ernst Brendel, *An Oxford Tragedy*, 1933

1057 Breaking the rules is fun, and the middle-aged and respectable have in this regard a capacity for innocent enjoyment at least as great as that of the youthful and rebellious.
> —Introduction, *Fate Cannot Harm Me*, 1935

WHIT MASTERSON

Joint pseudonym of Americans Robert Wade, 1920–, and Bill Miller, 1920–1961; creators of Mort Hagen, divorce detective, or as it said on his card, "Domestic Investigator."

1058 I asked an attorney once what are good grounds for divorce in California. What do you think he said? Marriage!
> —Mort Hagen, *Dead, She Was Beautiful*,
> 1955

HAROLD Q. MASUR 1909–

American lawyer and detective novelist; creator of Scott Jordan, a lawyer who turns detective to protect his clients, and sometimes, himself.

1059 She was *Vogue* on the outside and vague on the inside.
> —Scott Jordan, of the ex-Mrs. Dan Varney,
> *Send Another Hearse*, 1960

EDWARD MATHIS 1927–

American detective novelist; creator of private eye Dan Roman.

1060   We are seldom more than we consider ourselves to be.
—Mrs. Boggs, *From a High Place*, 1985

BRANDER MATTHEWS 1852–1929

Early critic and novelist, possibly the first to introduce the concept that the writer should play fair with the reader.

1061   Consider how frequently Fortuné du Boisgobey failed to play fair.
—"Poe and the Detective Story," *Scribner's Magazine*, 1907

W. SOMERSET MAUGHAM 1874–1965

English playwright, novelist, and short story writer, author of *Ashenden; or, The British Agent*, now regarded as one of the first realistic novels dealing with the life of the secret agent.

1062   Maugham said of the genre:
"It may well be that when the historians of literature come to discourse upon the fiction produced by the English-speaking peoples in the first half of the twentieth century, they will pass somewhat lightly over the compositions of the 'serious' novelists and turn their attention to the immense and varied achievement of the detective writers."
—Quoted by John Ball, "Murder at Large," *The Mystery Story*, 1976

1063   There will always be men who from malice or for money will betray their kith and kin and there will always be men who, from love of adventure or a sense of duty, will risk a shameful death to secure information valuable to their country.
—Preface, *Ashenden; or, The British Agent*, 1928

1064   If you do well you'll get no thanks and if you get into trouble you'll get no help.
—R.'s warning, ibid.

1065   It was Ashenden's principle . . . to tell as much of the truth as he conveniently could.
—Ibid.

A. E. MAXWELL

Joint pseudonym of American writers Ann Elizabeth Maxwell, 1944–, and Evan Maxwell; creators of Fiddler and his still-loved ex-wife, Fiora.

1066   Interfering in other people's business can be hazardous to your health.
> —Fiddler, *Just Another Day in Paradise*, 1985

1067   Society can make a union legal or illegal, but it can't do a damn thing about unruly hearts.
> —Fiddler, *The Frog and the Scorpion*, 1986

1068   The trouble was as complex as a good Chardonnay, as hidden as the roots of the silent vines, and as deadly as steel sliding between living ribs.
> —*Gatsby's Vineyard*, 1987

L. T. MEADE 1854–1914

Irish author Lillie Thomas Meade, who wrote girls' books, and mystery and detective fiction, often in collaboration with another author, most notably with Robert Eustace, who also collaborated with Dorothy L. Sayers (q.v.).

1069   Men do curious things for money in this world.
> —"Madam Sara," *The Sorceress of the Strand*, 1903

MARGARET MILLAR 1915–

Canadian-American mystery novelist, wife of Ross Macdonald (q.v.), winner of an Edgar for *Beast in View*, awarded the Grand Master title by Mystery Writers of America in 1983; creator of Dr. Paul Prye, a consulting psychiatrist who calls himself a "cosmopolitan quack."

1070   Most conversations are simply monologues delivered in the presence of a witness.
> —Dr. Paul Prye, *The Weak-Eyed Bat*, 1942

1071   Look like the innocent flower, but be the serpent under it.
> —Ibid.

1072 When you're counting alibis and not apples, one plus one equals none.
—Dr. Paul Prye, ibid.

1073 You'll always be cheated if you put your value on the wrong things.
—Paul Blackshear, *Beast in View*, 1955

1074 Private problems don't constitute an excuse for bad manners.
—Mrs. Fielding, *A Stranger in My Grave*, 1960

1075 Perfect young men don't get murdered, they don't even get born.
—Franklin Ford, *Beyond This Point Are Monsters*, 1970

1076 If you go around looking for accidents, asking for them, they can't be called accidents any more.
—Estivar, ibid.

1077 Life is something that happens to you while you're making other plans.
—Estivar, ibid.

This line, with a slight difference in wording, is associated with John Lennon of the Beatles.

A. A. MILNE 1882–1956

English author of children's literature and creator of the immortal Winnie-the-Pooh, verse, plays, novels, and mysteries, best remembered by mystery fans for *The Red House Mystery*.

1078 Milne commented:
"It is, to me, a distressing thought that in nine-tenths of the detective stories of the world murderers are continually effecting egresses when they might just as easily go out."
—Introduction, *The Red House Mystery*, 1922

1079 And added:
"The detective must have no more special knowledge than the average reader. The reader must be made to feel that, if he too had used the light of cool inductive reasoning and the logic of stern remorseless facts then he too would have fixed the guilt."
—Ibid.

1080   Instinct always gets the better of reason.
—Susan Cunningham, *The Perfect Alibi: A Detective Story in Three Acts*, Act III, scene ii, *Four Plays*, 1932

GLADYS MITCHELL 1901–1983

English detective novelist, who also wrote under other names. As Mitchell, creator of Dame Beatrice Lestrange Bradley, sometimes called Mrs. Croc (for crocodile), because she is "definitely saurian in type."

1081   Killing is not a sane reaction to the circumstances of life.
—Dame Beatrice Lestrange Bradley, *The Rising of the Moon*, 1945

1082   All detective work is sneaking. That's why only gentlemen and cads can do it.
—Keith Innes, ibid.

CLEVELAND MOFFETT 1863–1926

American author, who frequently used Paris as the setting for his works. *Through the Wall* was selected for the Haycraft-Queen Cornerstone Library by Ellery Queen, who called it a neglected high spot in detective fiction.

1083   A good detective *knows* certain things before he can prove them and acts on his knowledge. That is what distinguishes him from an ordinary detective.
—Paul Coquenil, *Through the Wall*, 1909

1084   Half the charm of life is in suspense.
—Paul Coquenil, ibid.

1085   A great detective must have infinite patience. That is, the quality next to imagination that will serve him best. Indeed, without patience, his imagination will serve him but indifferently.
—Ibid.

HUBERT MONTEILHET 1928–

French professor of history, and author of witty psychological suspense novels.

1086 Monteilhet has said:
"As I understand it, the 'detective' novel is for the modern public what the tragedy was for contemporaries of Pericles or Louis XIV."
—*Twentieth-Century Crime and Mystery Writers*, 2nd ed., 1985

1087 The worst blessing can always give way to a lesser evil.
—*Murder at Leisure*, 1969; English translation by W. W. Halsey II, 1971

1088 Sometimes an excess of tact can be more dangerous than a little boorishness.
—Ibid.

MICHAEL MORGAN

Joint pseudonym of American detective writers C. E. Carle and Dean M. Dorn, Hollywood publicists; creators of Bill Ryan, Hollywood stuntman.

1089 Never do a stunt you don't know all about before you do it.
—Old stuntman's advice to Bill Ryan, *Nine More Lives*, 1947

1090 Don't tell me you carry a heater in your girdle, Madam!
—Bill Ryan, *Decoy*, 1953

1091 I sat beside her in the Traxton's Parisian Room and let the edges of my eyes siphon up the pleasure of her tall, slender figure in a blue evening gown which made a low-bridged criss-cross right above where the meat on a chicken is the whitest.
—Bill Ryan, ibid.

NIGEL MORLAND 1905–1986

English newspaperman and detective novelist, who has used other names as well. As Morland, creator of "Plain Palmyra Pym."

1092 Every woman from a daily help to the Queen of England can gauge a man quicker than a flea can hop.
—Palmyra Pym, *A Rope for the Hanging*, 1938

1093 The older they are, the harder they fall.
—Speaking of women and movie actors, *A Gun for a God*, 1940

1094   I've got a good memory and I play hunches because women
work that way—it's the same as logic, but it's quicker.
—Palmyra Pym, "Cyanide City," *Mrs. Pym
and Other Stories*, 1976

CHRISTOPHER MORLEY 1890–1957

American bookseller and mystery author; creator of Roger Mifflin,
whose pleasure is "bibliotherapy," the prescribing of the right book
for the reader.

1095   There is no one so grateful as the man to whom you have
given just the book his soul needed.
—Roger Mifflin, *The Haunted Bookshop*,
1919

1096   The world has been printing books for 450 years and yet
gunpowder still has a wider circulation.
—Roger Mifflin's lament, ibid.

ARTHUR MORRISON 1863–1945

English social historian and detective story writer; creator of Martin
Hewitt, the first popular detective after Sherlock Holmes.

1097   Some curiosity has been expressed as to Mr. Martin Hewitt's
system . . . he himself always consistently maintains that
he has no system beyond a judicious use of ordinary
faculties.
—"The Lenton Croft Robberies," *Martin
Hewitt, Investigator*, 1894

1098   A collector has no conscience in the matter of his own
particular hobby.
—Mr. Martin Hewitt, "The Stanway Cameo
Mystery," ibid.

1099   One must disregard nothing but the impossible.
—Mr. Martin Hewitt, ibid.

1100   Clues lie where least expected.
—Mr. Martin Hewitt, "The Nicobar Bullion
Case," *The Chronicles of Martin Hewitt*,
1885

1101   There is nothing in this world that is at all possible that has
not happened or is not happening in London.
—Mr. Martin Hewitt's aphorism, "The Case
of the Missing Hand," ibid.

JOHN MORTIMER 1923–

English barrister and writer, who also writes as Geoffrey Lincoln. As Mortimer, detective novelist and story writer; creator of Horace Rumpole, barrister at law, who says that "being a lawyer's got almost nothing to do with knowing the law."

1102   A person who is tired of crime is tired of life.
> —Horace Rumpole, "Rumpole and the
> Younger Generation," *Rumpole of the
> Bailey*, 1978

1103   A little silence can come as something of a relief. In the wear and tear of married life.
> —Horace Rumpole, "Rumpole and the
> Married Lady," ibid.

1104   Never plead guilty!
> —Rumpole's motto, which he believes should
> be written up in Chambers in letters a
> foot high, "Rumpole and the Learned
> Friends," ibid.

1105   I soon found it's crime which not only pays moderately well, but which is by far the greatest fun.
> —Horace Rumpole, "Rumpole and the Man
> of God," *The Trials of Rumpole*, 1979

1106   Marriage is like pleading guilty to an indefinite sentence. Without parole.
> —Horace Rumpole, ibid.

1107   Simple faith is far more important than the constant scramble after unimportant facts.
> —The Reverend Mordred Skinner, ibid.

PATRICIA MOYES 1923–

English detective novelist whose work, though begun in 1959, recalls the Golden Age; creator of Detective Chief Inspector Henry Tibbett.

1108   My nose tells me we're on the wrong lines.
> —Detective Chief Inspector Henry Tibbett,
> *Dead Men Don't Ski*, 1959

1109   My motto is—if there's a guilty secret, the more people who
know about it the better.
> —Sammy Smith, *Johnny Under Ground*,
> 1965

1110   Tibbett, Tibbett, hang him from a gibbet.
> —Aunt Dora's mnemonic, which made
> Tibbett's aura turn distinctly hostile, *Murder
> Fantastical*, 1967

MAX MURRAY 1901–1956

Australian-born newspaperman and mystery novelist who worked in
Australia, England, and the United States; author of twelve
"Corpse" books.

1111   No dear, there's no tramp. There never is. The tramp is
always a pious hope.
> —Firth Prentice to Celia Sim, who would like
> to believe that a tramp killed Angela
> Pewsey, *The Voice of the Corpse*, 1948

1112   Death is not necessarily the heaviest sentence that can be
imposed on man. There are times when it can seem the
lightest.
> —The Reverend Henry Holland, ibid.

WILLIAM MURRAY 1926–

American magazine writer and novelist; creator of Shifty Anderson,
a close-up magician turned sleuth.

1113   A cliché is a truth repeating itself.
> —Sam Vespucci, *Tip on a Dead Crab*, 1984

MYSTERY 1981

A publishing oddity, one of four "generic" books published that
year.

1114   That's when I got lazy, which for a private eye, is spelled
s-m-a-r-t.
> —The nameless narrator, *Mystery; No-Frills
> Book*, 1981

MAGDALEN NABB 1947–

English detective novelist who lives in Florence, a city lovingly portrayed in her work; creator of Marshal Guarnaccia of the Carabinieri.

1115   Never get so fascinated by the extraordinary that you miss the ordinary.
—Professor Forli, *Death of a Dutchman*, 1983

FREDERICK NEBEL 1903–1967

American writer of the hard-boiled school, creator of private eye "Tough Dick" Donahue, who "could take it."

1116   I've been up against crooks, guns, and I've double-crossed them to get what I wanted. That's what my game is. It's not a polite business of questions-and-answers bunk. You work against crooks and you've got to beat them at their own game.
—Dick Donahue, "Rough Justice," *Black Mask*, November 1930

1117   When I take on a client, I expect a break. I expect the truth. If it is the truth, I'm just as liable to risk my neck for the guy as not. I'm a nice guy ordinarily. But when a man two-times on me, I'm a louse—the lousiest kind of louse you ever ran across.
—Dick Donahue, "Spare the Rod," *Black Mask*, August 1931

1118   Broads. They trick us, cheat us, and try to murder us . . . and when they get it in the neck, we—get a touch of heart.
—Dick Donahue, "Get a Load of This," *Black Mask*, February 1933

ANTHONY OLCOTT 1950–

American Slavic scholar and detective novelist; creator of Ivan Duvakin.

1119   Life came in three basic styles: better, worse, and the same.
—*Murder at the Red October*, 1981

1120   Rights exist only if you take them.
—*May Day in Magadan*, 1983

1121 When you are a little fish, the waters are always deep.
—Ibid.

ANTHONY OLIVER 1923–

English antiquarian and detective novelist; creator of Mrs. Lizzie Thomas and retired Detective Inspector John Webber.

1122 You should never presume to offer advice in a kitchen.
—Mrs. Thomas, *The Elberg Collection*, 1985

1123 Of all the attributes granted to detectives in fiction, omniscience was the one which made him angrier than any other.
—Retired Detective Inspector John Webber's reflection, ibid.

1124 There are few things more tiresome than being rescued by friends.
—Rudyard Smith, ibid.

1125 Common sense of course is a poor card in a court of law.
—Rudyard Smith, ibid.

AUSTIN O'MALLEY 1858–1932

American aphorist, with a string of academic letters after his name: M.D., Ph.D., L.L.D.

1126 God is not a police-magistrate.
—*Keystones of Thought*, 1914

1127 The reason there are so many imbeciles among imprisoned criminals is that an imbecile is so foolish even a detective can detect him.
—Ibid.

SISTER CAROL ANNE O'MARIE 1933–

American Catholic nun and detective novelist; creator of Sister Mary Helen.

1128 "Spiritual reading, huh?"
        "St. P. D. James."
—Exchange between young Sister Anne and seventy-five-year-old Sister Mary Helen, who disguises her mystery-reading with a prayer book cover, *A Novena for Murder*, 1984

1129 People ought to retire at forty when they feel overused and go back to work at sixty-five when they feel useless.
>—Sister Mary Helen, *Advent of Dying*, 1986

OLIVER ONIONS 1873–1961

English writer of ghost stories and crime novels.

1130 A man with a grudge against the world will be very likely indeed to take that grudge out of the nearest person.
>—James Jeffries's reflection, *In Accordance with the Evidence*, 1911

1131 *Crime* . . . has suffered more at the hands of criminals than it has at the hands of justice. There are few perfect crimes. Most of them are accidental, the mere explosion of momentary passion. And that is well, for the world wants few masterpieces in that sort.
>—James Jeffries, ibid.

EDWARD PHILLIPS OPPENHEIM 1866–1946

English author of countless espionage and adventure novels, called "The Prince of Storytellers." *The Great Impersonation* is his best known work.

1132 The world is full of liars.
>—Everard Dominey, *The Great Impersonation*, 1920

1133 Men are more lovable for the bad qualities they don't possess than for the good ones they do.
>—Eileen Bates, *Simple Peter Cradd*, 1931

1134 Aren't we all fools . . . in one or two things? . . . All the same, even a fool, though, can sometimes give good advice.
>—Martin Campbell Brockenhurst, *The Man Who Changed His Plea*, 1942

BARONESS EMMA ORCZY 1865–1947

Hungarian baroness, English by adoption; creator of the Scarlet Pimpernel, Lady Molly of Scotland Yard, Patrick Mulligan, and the Old Man in the Corner, the first and most famous of the armchair detectives.

1135 We seek him here, we seek him there,
The Frenchies seek him everywhere.
Is he in heaven?—Is he in hell?
That demmed, elusive Pimpernel?
—*The Scarlet Pimpernel*, 1903

These lines were actually written by Orczy's husband, Montagu Barstow, who collaborated with her in writing the play. They also appear in the novel *The Scarlet Pimpernel*, which was written first, but did not find a publisher until the play was successful.

1136 There is no such thing as a mystery in connection with any crime, provided intelligence is brought to bear upon its investigation.
—The Old Man in the Corner, "The Fenchurch Street Mystery," *The Old Man in the Corner*, 1909

1137 Don't tell me that women have not ten times as much intuition as the blundering and sterner sex; my firm belief is that we shouldn't have half so many undetected crimes if some of the so-called mysteries were put to the test of feminine investigation.
—Mary Granard of the Female Department, "The Ninescore Mystery," *Lady Molly of Scotland Yard*, 1910

JOE ORTON 1933–1967

English playwright who wrote black humor mystery plays. Orton himself was brutally murdered at the age of thirty-four.

1138 "The British police force used to be run by men of integrity."
"That is a mistake which has been rectified."
—Fay to Truscott, *Loot*, Act II, 1966

1139 God is a gentleman. He prefers blondes.
—Hal, ibid.

1140 You're guilty. You don't have to explain. Only the innocent do that.
—Nick Beckett, *What the Butler Saw*, Act II, 1969

1141 You can't be a rationalist in an irrational world. It isn't
rational.
—Dr. Rance, ibid.

1142 All classes are criminal today. We live in an age of equality.
—McCorquodale, *Funeral Games*, Part I,
scene ii, 1970

THE OXFORD ENGLISH DICTIONARY

The English Philological Society began work on A *New English
Dictionary on Historical Principles* in 1857, with volunteer readers
collecting citations from works old and new. The result of their
efforts became *The Oxford English Dictionary*, a monumental work
intended to show historical usage of each word. "Detective" was one
of the newer words, with the first citation dated in 1843; the
following citations illustrate early usage.

1143 Intelligent men have been recently selected to form a body
called the "detective police." . . . at times the detective
policeman attires himself in the dress of ordinary individuals.
—*Chambers's Journal of Popular Literature*,
XII.54, citation dated 1843

The Detective Department, with two inspectors and
six sergeants, was established in 1842

1144 Some London detectives were dispatched, to give their keen
wits to the search.
—*Annual Register 185*, 1856

1145 The criminal turned detective is wonderfully suspicious and
cautious.
—*The Dialogues of Plato*; English translation
by Benjamin Jowett, vol. III, 1875

MARCO PAGE 1909–1968

Pseudonym of American screenwriter Henry Kurnitz, one of the
writers who adapted Agatha Christie's play *Witness for the Prosecution* for the screen. As Page, author of mystery novels.

1146 An alibi tighter than a Scotch auditor.
—*Fast Company*, 1938

MARTIN PAGE 1938–

English journalist and author; *The Pilate Plot* was chosen Best First Novel by the British Arts Council in 1978.

1147   Blessed are the ugly and determined, for they acquire the wealth and power to command the handsome and clever.
>—John Pierpont Morgan's reflection, *Set a Thief*, 1984

STUART PALMER 1905–1968

American detective novelist; creator of Miss Hildegarde Withers, who can hurl a monkey wrench into the machine, as her old friend and rival, Inspector Oscar Piper, would say.

1148   A detective has no beliefs. He either suspects or he knows.
>—Inspector Oscar Piper, *The Penguin Pool Murder*, 1931

1149   Sometimes a detective has to make two and two into six, at the very least.
>—Miss Hildegarde Withers, *The Puzzle of the Silver Persian*, 1934

1150   She's just a meddlesome old battle-ax who happens to be the smartest sleuth I know.
>—Inspector Oscar Piper of Miss Hildegarde Withers, *The Puzzle of the Red Stallion*, 1935

ORANIA PAPAZOGLOU 1951–

American mystery novelist, wife of William DeAndrea (q.v.); creator of Patience Campbell McKenna, known as "Pay" or "McKenna."

1151   Logic is a wonderful invention. It is so wonderful, people often mistake it for reason. Reason, however, requires sense. Logic requires only consistency.
>—Pay McKenna, *Sweet, Savage Death*, 1984

1152   If there is no way out, the best course of action is to find a way further in.
>—Pay McKenna, *Wicked, Loving Murder*, 1985

1153   If you don't burn the candle at both ends, what's the candle got two ends *for?*

> —Radd Stassen, *Death's Savage Passion*,
> 1986

SARA PARETSKY 1947–

American detective novelist and insurance company executive; creator of V. I. Warshawski, a Chicago private eye who specializes in corporate crime, often confounding her male peers.

1154   Rule number something or other—never tell anybody anything unless you're going to get something better in return.

> —V. I. Warshawski, *Deadlock*, 1984

ROBERT B. PARKER 1932–

American detective novelist, winner of an Edgar for *Promised Land;* creator of Boston private eye Spenser, no first name given, and with an *s* like the poet Edmund Spenser.

1155   Parker has said:
"Honor is indefinable, but easily recognized."

> —"Marxism and the Mystery," *Murder Ink*,
> 1977

1156   I take hold of one end of the thread and I keep pulling it till it's all unraveled.

> —Spenser's method, *The Godwulf*
> *Manuscript*, 1973

1157   Everyone gets scared when they are overmatched in the dark; it's not something to be ashamed of.

> —Spenser, ibid.

1158   I care about promises and I don't want to make one I can't be sure I'll keep.

> —Spenser, *Mortal Stakes*, 1975

1159   When in doubt, cook something and eat it.

> —Spenser's Rule, ibid.

1160   Two moral imperatives in your system are never to allow innocents to be victimized and never to kill people except involuntarily. . . . You will live a little diminished, won't you?

> —Susan Silverman to Spenser, ibid.

1161 How'd you get shot, Spenser? Well, it's this way, Saint Pete, I was staked out in a hotel corridor but my hand went to sleep. Then after a while my whole body nodded off. Did Bogey's hand ever go to sleep, Spenser? Did Kerry Drake's? No, sir. I don't think we can admit you here to Private-Eye Heaven, Spenser.
—*The Judas Goat*, 1978

1162 I say I gonna do something, I do it. It gets done. I hire on for something, I stay hired. I do what I take the bread for.
—Hawk, ibid.

1163 The sun is shining its ass off.
—Typical Spenser remark, *Looking for Rachel Wallace*, 1980

1164 You don't have much hope of getting the truth, if you think you know in advance what the truth ought to be.
—Spenser, *Pale Kings and Princes*, 1987

1165 Coincidence exists, but believing in it never did me any good.
—Spenser, ibid.

1166 Your work is mortal, your mistakes will be too.
—Susan Silverman to Spenser, ibid.

FRANK PARRISH 1929–

One of several pseudonyms used by Scottish novelist Roger Longrigg. As Parrish, creator of Dan Mallett, good-hearted poacher often suspected of crimes he must solve to clear himself.

1167 Combinin' duty wi' pleasure is a mark o' the superior mind.
—Sergeant Hallam, *Sting of the Honeybee*, 1978

RICHARD NORTH PATTERSON 1947–

American mystery and suspense novelist; *The Lasko Tangent* won an Edgar for best first mystery of the year.

1168 It's good to be alone without being lonely.
—Mary Carelli, *The Lasko Tangent*, 1979

1169 The idea of death was ugly and enormous, like infinity made personal.
—Christopher Paget's reflection, ibid.

1170   Reasons are invention of the mind, to justify the wishes of the heart.
> —John Joseph Englehardt, *Escape the Night*, 1983

BARBARA PAUL 1931–

American science fiction, mystery, and detective novelist, who sometimes uses historical personages in a fictional setting.

1171   Do they have a pill that can change the past?
> —Giacomo Puccini to Enrico Caruso, *A Cadenza for Caruso*, 1984

ELLIOT PAUL 1891–1958

American newspaperman, boogie-woogie pianist, writer of detective novels and nonfiction works; creator of Homer Evans, an American in Paris.

1172   In America, in 1913, an income tax law was passed and the rich have been devising tax dodging rackets ever since.
> —Homer Evans, *The Mysterious Mickey Finn*, 1939

1173   Fortune is blind but not invisible.
> —Chief Frémont, *Mayhem in B-Flat*, 1940

1174   One cannot, as the Americans say, play every instrument in the band.
> —Monsieur Delafon, ibid.

1175   Once the truth is known, it becomes easier to prove it. In other words, the solution leads back to the problem.
> —Homer Evans, *Murder on the Left Bank*, 1951

RAYMOND PAUL 1940–

American college teacher and writer of historical detective novels; creator of Lon Quinncannon.

1176   Paul has said:
"I believe that an excellent way to discover the prevailing attitudes of any era—social, moral, political—is to study its major public trials."
> —*Contemporary Authors*, vol. 106, 1982

1177   No physical exertion is more fatiguing than an unsuccessful
effort to sleep.
—The Tragedy at Tiverton, 1984

1178   Gratitude is what a man gives you when he doesn't want to be
bothered to return the favor.
—Lon Quinncannon, ibid.

DON PENDLETON 1927–

American who also writes as Dan Britain and Stephan Gregory. As
Pendleton, creator of Mack Bolan, the Executioner, whose motto is
"Live large and stay hard."

1179   I can only die one death at a time.
—Mack Bolan, *Vegas Vendetta*, 1971

1180   To know the truth is to be responsible for it. God help me. I
knew too much, too young.
—Mack Bolan, *Thermal Thursday*, 1979

1181   A man is not truly alive until he has found something worth
dying for.
—Mack Bolan, ibid.

1182   It does life good to have the devil in it, so long as you keep
your foot planted firmly on his neck.
—Buddy to Mack Bolan, *Council of Kings*,
1985

ANNE PERRY 1938–

English author of Victorian mysteries; creator of Inspector Thomas
Pitt and his wife Charlotte.

1183   A man should at least have the courage of his sins.
—Albie Frobisher's opinion, *Bluegate Fields*,
1984

1184   Do you suppose God has a sense of humor? Or would that be
blasphemous?
—Emily Ashworth, *Death in Devil's Acre*,
1985

THOMAS PERRY 1947–

American crime and suspense novelist; winner of an Edgar for *The
Butcher's Boy*.

1185 Once upon a time there was a helicopter pilot in Viet Nam who got a bit off course and got shot down. As he climbed from the wreckage he said, "What a break! Now we know where the bastards were hiding."
—Kepler, *Metzger's Dog*, 1983

1186 God, in his bounty and generosity, always creates more horses' asses than there are horses to attach them to.
—Immelmann, ibid.

ELIZABETH PETERS 1927–

Pseudonym of American Egyptologist Barbara Mertz, who also writes romantic suspense as Barbara Michaels. As Peters, mystery and detective novelist, winner of the first Anthony Grand Master award; creator of Jacqueline Kirby and Amelia Peabody Emerson, each featured in her own series.

1187 Why should any independent, intelligent female choose to subject herself to the whims and tyrannies of a husband?
—Miss Amelia Peabody, *Crocodile on the Sandbank*, 1975

1188 There are always exceptions to every rule, but only if you really know what you're doing.
—*Die for Love*, 1984

1189 Marriage, in my view, should be a balanced stalemate between equal adversaries.
—Amelia Peabody Emerson, *The Mummy Case*, 1985

1190 If someone lies down and invites you to trample him, you are a remarkable person if you decline the invitation.
—Amelia Peabody Emerson, *The Lion in the Valley*, 1986

ELLIS PETERS 1913–

Pseudonym of Edith Pargeter, English author of historical novels and a translator of Czech poetry and prose. As Peters, creator of the Felse family, and, in another series, Brother Cadfael, a twelfth-century detective-monk. *Death and the Joyful Woman* won an Edgar, *Monk's Hood*, a Silver Dagger.

1191 You'll never get to be a saint if you deny the bit of the devil in you.
> —Brother Cadfael's advice to Brother Mark,
> *Monk's Hood*, 1980

1192 Despair is deadly sin, but worse, it is mortal folly.
> —Brother Cadfael, *The Devil's Novice*, 1983

EDEN PHILLPOTTS 1862–1960

English novelist, poet, and playwright, who also wrote as Harrington Hext. As Phillpotts, author of some two dozen crime tales.

1193 Reason is with us to save us from too much evidence of our senses—often false.
> —Peter Ganns, *The Red Redmaynes*, 1922

1194 The biggest fool may come out with a bit of sense when you least expect it.
> —*The Marylebone Miser*, 1926

1195 Crime increases as superstition decreases.
> —*"Found Drowned,"* 1931

1196 As for the largest-hearted of us, what is the word we write most often in our chequebooks?—"Self."
> —*A Shadow Passes*, 1933

ALLAN PINKERTON 1819–1884

Scottish-American who resigned from the Chicago Police Department in 1850 to open the Pinkerton National Detective Agency to deal with railway thefts. His trademark was a large, unblinking eye—"The eye that never sleeps." He himself became known as the Eye or the Big Eye, hence the term "private eye." Later he (and others, under his name) wrote up agency archive cases into books which blended fact and fiction in a highly successful sensational manner.

1197 We never sleep.
> —Motto of the Pinkerton men as it appeared
> on the covers of most of the books.

C. L. PIRKIS 1839–1910

English writer of romantic novels and detective stories; creator of Loveday Brooke, one of the earliest fictional female private investigators, a sensible and practical woman, possessed of so much common sense it amounts to genius.

1198   While all people are agreed as to the variety of motives that instigate crime, very few allow sufficient margin for variety of character in the criminal.
> —Loveday Brooke, "The Black Bag Left on a Door-step," *The Experiences of Loveday Brooke, Lady Detective*, 1894

1199   I start on my work without theory of any sort—in fact, I may say, with my mind a perfect blank.
> —Loveday Brooke, "The Murder at Troyte's Hill," ibid.

1200   If you lay it down as a principle that the obvious is to be rejected in favor of the abstruse, you'll soon find yourself launched in the predicament of having to prove that two apples added to two other apples do not make four.
> —Mr. Dyer to Loveday Brooke, "Drawn Daggers," ibid.

EDGAR ALLAN POE 1809–1849

American writer and poet, master of the mysterious and terrifying, who wrote the first well-known detective story, "The Murders in the Rue Morgue." With this story, which he called one of his "tales of ratiocination," he established the form of a new genre; creator of Chevalier C. August Dupin.

1201   Arthur Conan Doyle asked:
"Where was the detective story until Poe breathed the breath of life into it?"
> —Presiding over a celebratory dinner given by the Authors' Club in London for Poe's centenary, 1909

1202   It will be found, in fact, that the ingenious are always fanciful, and the *truly* imaginative never otherwise than analytic.
> —"The Murders in the Rue Morgue," 1841; first collected in *Prose Romances*, 1843, and then in *Tales*, 1845

1203   There is such a thing as being too profound.
> —C. Auguste Dupin, ibid.

1204   Truth is not always in a well. In fact, as regards the more important knowledge, I do believe that she is invariably superficial.
> —C. Auguste Dupin, ibid.

1205 It appears to me that this mystery is considered insoluble, for the very reason which should cause it to be regarded as easy of solution—I mean for the *outré* character of its features.

> —C. Auguste Dupin, laying down one of the great aphorisms of detective fiction, ibid.

1206 My ultimate object is only the truth.

> —C. Auguste Dupin, ibid.

1207 Coincidences, in general, are great stumbling-blocks in the way of that class of thinkers who have been educated to know nothing of the theory of probabilities.

> —C. Auguste Dupin, ibid.

1208 There are few persons, even among the calmest thinkers, who have not occasionally been startled into a vague yet thrilling half-credence in the supernatural, by *coincidences* of so seemingly marvellous a character that, as *mere* coincidences, the intellect has been unable to receive them.

> —"The Mystery of Marie Rogêt," 1842; first collected in *Tales*, 1845

1209 Perverseness is one of the primitive impulses of the human heart.

> —"The Black Cat," 1843; first collected in *Tales*, 1845

1210 Who has not, a hundred times, found himself committing a vile or silly action, for no other reason than because he knows he should *not*?

> —Ibid.

1211 "The fact is, we have all been a good deal puzzled because the affair *is* so simple, and yet baffles us altogether."

"Perhaps it is the very simplicity of the thing which puts you at fault."

> —Monsieur G——, Prefect of the Parisian police, answered by C. Auguste Dupin, "The Purloined Letter," 1844; first collected in *Tales*, 1845

1212 As poet *and* mathematician, he would reason well; as mere mathematician, he could not have reasoned at all.

> —C. Auguste Dupin, ibid.

1213 The wine was *in* and the wit, as a natural consequence, somewhat *out*.

> —"Thou Art the Man," 1844; first collected in *Works*, 1850

1214   This bullet was discovered to have a flaw or seam at right
angles to the usual suture; and upon examination, this seam
corresponded precisely with an accidental ridge or elevation
in a pair of moulds acknowledged by the accused to be his
own property.

—Ibid.

This is an early example of the science now known as
ballistics, but not the first to be found in fiction. In an
American story by William Leggett, "The Rifle,"
published in 1828, an innocent man is cleared of a
murder charge by a demonstration that the fatal bullet
did not fit his gun.

1215   For the love of God, Montresor!

—Fortunato, "The Cask of Amontillado,"
1847; first collected in *Works*, 1850

1216   Poe himself said:
"These tales of ratiocination owe most of their popularity to
being something in a new key. I do not mean to say they are
not ingenious—but people think them more ingenious than
they are—on account of their method and *air* of method. In
the Murders in the Rue Morgue, for instance, where is the
ingenuity in unravelling a web which you yourself have
woven for the express purpose of unravelling? The reader is
made to confound the ingenuity of the supposititious Dupin
with that of the writer of the story."

—Letter to Philip P. Cooke, August 9, 1846;
The Letters of E. A. Poe, 1948

ZELDA POPKIN 1898–1983

American mystery novelist; creator of Mary Carner, an "efficient
department store detective."

1217   There is no privacy for the violently dead.

—*Time Off for Murder*, 1940

1218   Each husband gets the infidelity he deserves.

—Mr. Dengler, *No Crime for a Lady*, 1942

1219   Homicide's the great unveiler. Everything comes to light.

—Mary Carner, ibid.

1220   Crime never pays. Not even life insurance benefits.

—Mr. Murray, ibid.

MELVILLE DAVISSON POST 1869–1930

American lawyer and writer who made important contributions to the detective story; creator of two original and very different detectives: Randolph Mason, the first unscrupulous lawyer who uses his skill to defeat the ends of justice, and Uncle Abner, the stern, upright Virginian, passionately concerned that justice be done.

1221　The great, early judges were of the opinion that the human mind was incapable of fabricating a false consistency of events. At some point there would appear a physical fact to destroy it. This silent witness . . . was always standing in the background to be called by anyone who had the acumen to discover it.

　　　　　　　　　—Foreword, *The Silent Witness*, 1930

1222　Justice cannot reach all wrongs; its hands are tied by the restrictions of the law.

　　　　　　　　　—"The Sheriff of Gullmore," *The Strange Schemes of Randolph Mason*, 1896

1223　No man who has followed my advice has ever committed a crime. Crime is a technical word. It is the law's name for certain acts which it is pleased to define and punish with a penalty. . . . What the law permits is right, else it would prohibit it. What the law prohibits is wrong, because it punishes it.

　　　　　　　　　—Randolph Mason, outlining his cynical code, "The Grazier," *The Man of Last Resort*, 1897

1224　It is a law of the story-teller's art that he does not tell a story. It is the listener who tells it. The story-teller does but provide him with the stimuli.

　　　　　　　　　—"The Doomdorf Mystery," *Uncle Abner, Master of Mysteries*, 1918

1225　It is a world, filled with the mysterious justice of God!

　　　　　　　　　—Uncle Abner, ibid.

1226　Reason is the method by which those who do not know the truth, step by step, finally discover it.

　　　　　　　　　—Uncle Abner, "The Straw Man," ibid.

RAYMOND POSTGATE 1896–1971

English social historian, crime story anthologist, and author of three crime novels. His *Verdict of Twelve* is a Haycraft-Queen Cornerstone Library selection.

1227   Ordinarily kindhearted people will like a child unless it annoys them or causes a great deal of work.
—*Verdict of Twelve*, 1940

1228   There are few people so obstinate as the man who half thinks he is wrong.
—*Somebody at the Door*, 1943

1229   Adultery may or may not be sinful, but is never cheap.
—Ibid.

RICHARD S. PRATHER 1921–

American detective novelist, given the Life Achievement Award by Private Eye Writers of America in 1986, who also writes under other names. As Prather, creator of Shell Scott, Los Angeles private eye who's "handled half the crimes listed in the California Penal Code."

1230   She had a seventy-eight-inch bust, forty-six-inch waist, and seventy-two-inch hips—measurements that were exactly right, I thought, for her height of eleven feet, four inches.
—Shell Scott, viewing a twice-life-sized
statue, *Take a Murder, Darling*, 1958

1231   He was dead, all right. He had been shot, poisoned, stabbed, and strangled. Either somebody had really had it in for him or four people had killed him. Or else it was the cleverest suicide I'd ever heard of.
—Shell Scott, ibid.

1232   The Rand Brothers Mortuary was so beautiful it almost made you want to die.
—Shell Scott, *Dig That Crazy Grave*, 1961

1233   You won't believe this. But that rock just shot me in the ass!
—Hood, shot with a tranquilizer dart by Shell
Scott, who is disguised as a rock, *The
Cockeyed Corpse*, 1964

ANTHONY PRICE 1928–

English newspaper editor and espionage novelist, winner of a Silver Dagger for his first novel, *The Labyrinth Makers*, and a Gold

Dagger for *Other Paths to Glory*; creator of Dr. David Audley, Colonel Jack Butler, and Paul Mitchell.

1234   The best way to kill a food taster is by poisoning his master's dish.
>   —Dr. David Audley, *The Alamut Ambush*,
>   1971

1235   Publicity is like power . . . it's a rare man who isn't corrupted by it.
>   —*Colonel Butler's Wolf*, 1972

1236   Never take anything from a stranger. . . . You never know what he'll want in exchange.
>   —Paul Mitchell, remembering his mother's
>   advice, *Other Paths to Glory*, 1974

1237   It's bloody difficult to *fake* a murder—there are too many things to go wrong once you complicate a basically simple act.
>   —Dr. David Audley, ibid.

1238   In my business one good thumping lie can be worth more than a lot of mundane truth.
>   —Dr. David Audley, ibid.

1239   If there was anything worse than getting what one didn't deserve, it was getting in full what one did deserve.
>   —Corporal Jack Butler, *The '44 Vintage*,
>   1978

1240   Beauty is only skin-deep, but it's only the skin you see.
>   —2nd Lieutenant David Audley, ibid.

1241   It's written down in the Constitution—the Right to Get Shot . . . though they call it the Right to Bear Arms.
>   —Winston Spencer Mulholland, *Sion
>   Crossing*, 1984

1242   Being frightened is an experience you can't buy.
>   —Dr. David Audley, ibid.

MAURICE PROCTOR 1906–1973

English police procedural novelist; creator of Detective Chief Inspector Harry Martineau, who regards being a well-known policeman as a social handicap.

1243   The time to do a job was when you had the time to do it.
—Detective Chief Inspector Harry Martineau,
Death Has a Shadow, 1965

BILL PRONZINI 1943–

American mystery critic, commentator, and detective novelist, who also writes under other names. As Pronzini, creator of Nameless, the Everyman of the private eye world.

1244   There's always some damn fool like me to care about things that don't matter in the long run.
—Nameless, *Bones*, 1985

1245   Antagonizing cops is a stupid thing for anyone to do, and that goes double if you happen to be a private investigator.
—Nameless, ibid.

1246   Sometimes there is justice, yes. But does *that* matter, either, in the larger scheme of things—whatever that scheme may be? Maybe it does. Like love, like compassion and caring and friendship—maybe it does.
—Nameless, ibid.

MARIO PUZO 1920–

American novelist, author of *The Godfather*, which takes its epigraph from Balzac: "Behind every great fortune there is a crime."

1247   He's a businessman. I'll make him an offer he can't refuse.
—Don Corleone, about a Hollywood
producer, *The Godfather*, 1969

1248   A lawyer with his briefcase can steal more than one hundred men with guns.
—Don Corleone, ibid.

ELLERY QUEEN

Shared pseudonym of two cousins, Frederic Dannay, 1905–1982, and Manfred B. Lee, 1905–1971, who also wrote as Barnaby Ross. Ellery Queen is their best-known pseudonym and the name of their most famous detective; founders of *Ellery Queen's Mystery Magazine* in 1941. As novelists, short story editors, bibliographers, critics, and collectors, they had immense influence upon the genre, and were awarded the Grand Master title by Mystery Writers of America in 1960.

1249   Let the reader beware!
> —The last words of their first challenge to
> readers, *The Roman Hat Mystery*, 1929

1250   There's little justice and certainly no mercy in this world.
> —Richard Queen to Ellery Queen, ibid.

1251   My work is done with symbols . . . not with human
beings. . . . I choose to close my mind to the human
elements, and treat it as a problem in mathematics. The fate
of the murderer I leave to those who decide such things.
> —Ellery Queen, *The Spanish Cape Mystery*,
> 1935

But at the end of the same book his mind has been
changed:

1252   I've often boasted that the human equation means nothing to
me. But it does, damn it all. It does!
> —Ellery Queen, ibid.

1253   No riddle is esoteric unless it's the riddle of God; and that's no
riddle—it's a vast blankness.
> —Ellery Queen, "The Lamp of God," *The
> New Adventures of Ellery Queen*, 1940

Writing as **BARNABY ROSS**, creators of Drury Lane, retired
Shakespearean actor.

1254   There are no limits to which the human mind cannot soar in
that unique, god-like instant before the end of life.
> —Drury Lane, introducing the theme of the
> dying message, *The Tragedy of X*, 1932

1255   I have often thought that the entire problem of crime and
punishment would be simplified if human beings, con-
fronted by their potential murderers, could leave a sign, no
matter how obscure, to the identity of their nemesis.
> —Drury Lane, ibid.

JULIAN RATHBONE 1935–

English suspense novelist; creator of Nur Bey and Commissioner
Jan Argand, each featured in his own series.

1256   Reality is never ideal. We patch up as we go on. We do not
create things, they happen, and we *cope* with them.
> —Christian Kratt, *The Euro-Killers*, 1979

1257   The rich have lost what true sense of the beautiful they ever
had: loveliness has been reduced to the irreplaceable.
            —*A Spy of the Old School*, 1982

CLAYTON RAWSON 1906–1971

American magician and detective novelist, who also wrote as Stuart
Towne. As Rawson, creator of the Great Merlini. He worked with
the "impossible situation," very much in the John Dickson Carr
tradition, and wrote two books on magic.

1258   Misdirection, then, is the first fundamental principle of
deception. The other two—and they are all used by
magicians, criminals, and detective story authors alike—are
Imitation and Concealment. Understand how these principles operate, and you should be able to solve any trick,
crime, or detective story.
            —Great Merlini, *Death from a Top Hat*, 1938

1259   Misdirection is nothing more than psychology turned upside
down and inside out. The Principles of Deception . . . are
only the orthodox, textbook psychological Laws of Attention,
Observation, and Thought working in reverse.
            —Great Merlini, *The Footprints on the
            Ceiling*, 1939

1260   The guy who cracked that honesty was the best policy was a
dope.
            —*No Coffin for the Corpse*, 1942

1261   A policeman's lot is not so hot.
            —Ibid.

ARTHUR B. REEVE 1880–1936

American writer of detective stories, who was, for a while, one of
the most popular detective writers in America, and the first
American to have a wide following in England; creator of Professor
Craig Kennedy, one of the earliest scientific detectives.

1262   There is a distinct place for science in the detection of crime.
            —Professor Craig Kennedy's theory, *The
            Silent Bullet*, 1912

ROBERT REEVES 1912?–1945

American detective novelist and short story writer; creator of Cellini
Smith, who takes on one job for truly munificent compensation:

$26.94. It seemed, at the time, a fitting epitaph for his bankrupt career as a private operative.

1263   Go and sin with the archangels.
—Monk's send-off for murdered hobo Danny
Meade, *Cellini Smith: Detective*, 1943

1264   "This is my religion."
"In rod we trust."
—Exchange between Dado, patting his
shoulder holster, and Vanzy, ibid.

ROBERT REEVES 1951–

American literary critic and detective novelist; creator of English professor Thomas Theron, who attends Boston's Suffolk Downs Racetrack as faithfully as his own classes.

1265   There are few activities so smug as coldblooded self-appraisal.
—Thomas Theron, *Doubting Thomas*, 1985

1266   Avoid the gratuitous lie; be truthful about details; falsify only a crucial fact or two.
—The Liar's Code, ibid.

1267   The variations on vice are infinite, but the basic tune is simple.
—Thomas Theron, ibid.

HELEN REILLY 1891–1962

American detective novelist, who also wrote as Kieran Abbey. As Reilly, author of well-regarded police procedurals; creator of Inspector Christopher McKee, head of the Manhattan Homicide Squad, who has the "fatal gift of being too often in the right." Two of Reilly's four daughters, Ursula Curtiss and Mary McMullen (q.v.), were mystery and suspense novelists.

1268   Do good and throw it in the sea; if God doesn't see it, the fishes will.
—Quoted as a Chinese proverb, *Three
Women in Black*, 1941

RUTH RENDELL 1930–

English detective and crime novelist, who also writes as Edgar-winning Barbara Vine. As Rendell, winner of two Edgars for short stories and a Gold Dagger for *A Demon in My View*; creator of Detective Chief Inspector Reginald Wexford of Kingsmarkham.

1269   Many emotions go under the name of love, and almost any one of them will for a while divert the mind from the real, true, and perfect thing.
—A Demon in My View, 1976

1270   Selfishness is not living as one wishes to live, it is asking others to live as one wishes to live.
—A Judgement in Stone, 1977

1271   Some say life is the thing, but I prefer reading.
—Giles Mont, ibid.

1272   Americans . . . are a nation of salesmen just as the English are a nation of small shopkeepers.
—Put On by Cunning, 1981

1273   Marriage is a funny old carry-on altogether, isn't it?
—Detective Chief Inspector Reginald Wexford, The Speaker of Mandarin, 1983

JOHN RHODE 1884–1965

Pseudonym of Major Cecil John Charles Street, English career army officer, who also wrote as Miles Burton. As Rhode, creator of Dr. Lancelot Priestley, who in his dry, unemotional way, views detective problems as "the very breath of life to me."

1274   A consciousness of innocence is the only support against an unjust accusation.
—The Murders in Praed Street, 1928

1275   A theory, once formed, is apt to dominate the mind, and there is an inevitable tendency to twist fresh facts as they come to light to suit it.
—Dr. Priestley, The Claverton Mystery, 1933

1276   They who hide know where to find.
—In Face of the Verdict, 1936

CRAIG RICE 1908–1957

Best-known pseudonym of American mystery and detective novelist Georgiana Ann Randolph. She ghosted for Gypsy Rose Lee (q.v.) and others. As Craig Rice, the first mystery author to appear on the cover of *Time*; creator of lawyer John J. Malone, who claims "I've never lost a client yet."

1277 Everyone is entitled to one good murder.
—John J. Malone, *The Wrong Murder*, 1940

1278 I'm not an officer of the law. My profession has always put me on the other side of the fence.
—John J. Malone, ibid.

1279 Bad enough to make mistakes, without going ahead and marrying them.
—Dennis Dennis, *My Kingdom for a Hearse*, 1957

ROBERT RICHARDSON

English journalist and mystery author; creator of Augustus Maltravers, acerbic playwright and amateur detective.

1280 It's so pointless, there has to be a point.
—Augustus Maltravers, *The Latimer Mercy*, 1985

MARY ROBERTS RINEHART 1876–1958

American mystery writer who founded the Had-I-But-Known school with *The Circular Staircase*. The Rinehart formula has been used ever since by countless authors, most successfully by Rinehart herself.

1281 Few of us have any conscience regarding institutions or corporations.
—Miss Rachel Innes, *The Circular Staircase*, 1908

1282 The most commonplace incident takes on a new appearance if the attendant circumstances are unusual.
—Miss Rachel Innes, ibid.

1283 If two and two plus *x* makes six, then to discover the unknown quantity is the simplest thing in the world.
—Miss Rachel Innes, ibid.

ABBY ROBINSON 1947–

American photographer and detective novelist; creator of Jane Meyers, freelance photographer and amateur sleuth.

1284   Art needn't imitate life but it should never jeopardize it.
—Jane Meyers, *The Dick and Jane*, 1985

1285   Minor renown takes up major amounts of time.
—Jane Meyers, ibid.

SAMUEL ROGERS 1894–

American suspense novelist with an interest in abnormal psychology; creator of Paul Hatfield, professor of chemistry and amateur ornithologist.

1286   Haven't you sometimes felt, when you've been sick or tired or worried, that sanity was like a tightrope strung across a great gulf, that you have to walk over it and if the slightest little adjustment should go wrong you'd topple off and never stop falling?
—Harold Forster, *Don't Look Behind You!*, 1944

1287   The human mind, once it is ever so slightly thrown off the track, may wander far astray in the dark and dubious regions.
—Professor Paul Hatfield, *You Leave Me Cold*, 1946

SAX ROHMER 1883–1959

Pseudonym of English writer Arthur Henry Sarsfield Ward. As Rohmer, creator of Dr. Fu Manchu and Moris Klaw, each featured in his own series.

1288   Rohmer wrote that just after he had created Fu Manchu, the evil doctor appeared to him in a dream, saying:
"I, the Mandarin Fu Manchu, I shall go on triumphant. It is your boast that you made me. It is mine that I should live when you are smoke."

1289   This man, whether a fanatic or a duly appointed agent, is, unquestionably, the most malign and formidable personality existing in the known world today. He is a linguist who speaks with almost equal facility in any of the civilized languages, and in most of the barbaric. He is an adept in all the arts and sciences which a great university could teach him. He is also an adept in certain obscure arts and sciences which *no* university of today can teach. He has the brains of any three men of genius.

—Nayland Smith's description of Dr.
Fu Manchu, *The Mystery of Dr.*
Fu Manchu, 1913

1290   Imagine a person, tall, lean and feline, high shouldered, with a brow like Shakespeare and a face like Satan, a close-shaven skull, and long, magnetic eyes of the true cat-green. . . . Imagine that awful being, and you have a mental picture of Dr. Fu Manchu, the yellow peril incarnate in one man.

—Ibid.

1291   Today we may seek for romance and fail to find it: unsought, it lies in wait for us at the most prosaic corners of life's highway.

—Dr. Petrie, ibid.

1292   I am an old fool who sometimes has wise dreams.

—Moris Klaw, "Tragedies in the Greek
Room," *The Dream Detective*, 1920

1293   *Suggestion* is the secret of all so-called occult phenomena!
—Moris Klaw, "The Veil of Isis," ibid.

MIKE ROSCOE

Joint pseudonym of two American real-life private eyes, Michael Ruso, ?–, and John Roscoe, 1921–; creators of Johnny April, tough Kansas City private eye.

1294   There are two times when a man will lie very still.
When he is finished making love with a woman.
When he is finished with life.
The man on the floor lay still with death.

—Opening sentences, *One Tear for My*
Grave, 1955

1295   It is true that death sometimes can appear as a lonely solution but only when a person realizes that his death will not be cried over by at least one person.

—Castleman, ibid.

RICHARD ROSEN 1949–

American detective novelist, winner of an Edgar for his first novel, *Strike Three You're Dead*; creator of Harvey Blissberg, major-league outfielder turned private eye.

1296   "Life is a series of crises separated by brief periods of self-delusion."

"I need a pith helmet to protect me from your sayings."
—Exchange between Mickey Slavin and
Harvey Blissberg, *Fadeaway*, 1986

JOSEPH ROSENBERGER

American novelist; creator of Richard Camellion, the Death Merchant.

1297   The Republicans are thinking of changing the Republican Party emblem from an elephant to a condom, because it stands for inflation, halts production, and gives one a false sense of security while one is being screwed.
—*The Laser War*, 1974

1298   While money doesn't bring happiness, if you have enough of the green stuff you can be unhappy in maximum comfort.
—Attributed to Richard Camellion by
Rosenberger

BARNABY ROSS. *See* Ellery Queen.

JAMES SANDOE 1912–1980

American university professor of English literature and bibliography, compiler of *Murder Plain and Fanciful*, an anthology of true-crime tales, and two-time Edgar winner for mystery criticism. *Sandoe's Reader's Guide to Crime* (1949) is an early and excellent annotated list, as is *The Hard-Boiled Dick* (1952).

1299   Boom-lay, boom-lay, boom-lay-boom.
—Pithy dismissal of Mickey Spillane's first
novel.

However, the sales of *I, The Jury* topped six million copies.

DOROTHY L. SAYERS 1893–1957

English detective novelist, critic, and anthologist; creator of Lord Peter Wimsey. She wrote detective novels about him for nearly fifteen years, and then announced that she would not write any more detective stories. Asked why, she replied, "I wrote the Peter

Wimsey books when I was young and had no money. I made some money and then stopped writing novels and began to write what I had always wanted to write." For the rest of her life she concerned herself with religious literature.

1300 Sayers noted that, fortunately for the mystery monger:
"Whereas, up to the present, there is only one known way of getting born, there are endless ways of getting killed."
—Introduction, *The Omnibus of Crime*, 1929

1301 She warned:
"It is, after all, the reader's job to keep his wits about him, and, like the perfect detective, to suspect *everybody*."
—Ibid.

1302 And claimed:
"Detective authors, by the way, are nearly all as good as gold, because it is part of their job to believe and to maintain that *your sins will find you out*."
—Introduction, *The Third Omnibus of Crime*, 1935

1303 Sex is every man's loco spot . . . he'll take a disappointment, but not a humiliation.
—Lord Peter Wimsey, *Whose Body?*, 1923

1304 He was a respectable scholar in five or six languages, a musician of some skill and more understanding, something of an expert in toxicology, a collector of rare editions, an entertaining man-about-town, and a common sensationalist.
—Description of Lord Peter Wimsey, *Clouds of Witness*, 1926

1305 In detective stories, virtue is always triumphant. They're the purest literature we have.
—Lord Peter Wimsey, *Strong Poison*, 1930

1306 Of course, there is *some* truth in advertising. There's yeast in bread. . . . Truth in advertising is like leaven, which a woman hid in three measures of meal. It provides a suitable quantity of gas, with which to blow out a mass of crude misrepresentation into a form that the public can swallow.
—Lord Peter Wimsey, *Murder Must Advertise*, 1933

1307   A desire to have all the fun is nine-tenths of the law of chivalry.
> —Lord Peter Wimsey to Harriet Vane, *Gaudy Night*, 1935

1308   After *Gaudy Night* was published, Sayers wrote, in an essay that took its title from the novel:
"If the detective story was to live and develop it *must* get back to where it began in the hands of Collins and Le Fanu, and become once more a novel of manners instead of a pure crossword puzzle."
> —"Gaudy Night," Titles to Fame, ed. by Denys K. Roberts, 1937

1309   It is a gentleman's first duty to remember in the morning who it was he took to bed with him.
> —Lord Peter Wimsey, *Busman's Honeymoon*, 1937

1310   If a thing could only have been done one way, and if only one person could have done it that way, then you've got your criminal, motive or no motive.
> —Lord Peter Wimsey, ibid.

1311   Murder for the fun of it breaks all the rules of detective fiction.
> —Harriet Vane, ibid.

1312   Hallering Old Rectory was the kind of house which you might call an off-white elephant.
> —*No Flowers by Request*, 1953

Sayers was one of the various hands who contributed two chapters each to this work, commissioned by the Detection Club in London to fill its depleted treasury. Sayers took time off from translating Dante's *Divine Comedy* to fulfill this duty; it is probably the last detective fiction she wrote.

BENJAMIN M. SCHUTZ 1949–

American clinical psychologist and detective novelist; creator of Leo Haggerty, Washington, D.C., private eye.

1313   All thirty-five-year-olds would make great eighteen-year-olds the second time around.
> —Leo Haggerty, *Embrace the Wolf*, 1985

LEONARDO SCIASCIA 1921–

Italian man of letters, born in Sicily. In the United States, somewhat to his dismay, he is best known as a mystery novelist. He hopes his readers will consider them metaphysical mysteries.

1314   Compared to shame, death is nothing.
—*The Day of the Owl*, 1961; English translation by Archibald Colquhoun and Arthur Oliver, 1964

ANTHONY SHAFFER 1926–

English playwright, author of *Sleuth*; he won an Edgar in 1973 for the screenplay version. He has collaborated with his twin brother, Peter Shaffer, in writing detective novels.

1315   "Tell me, would you agree that the detective story is the normal recreation of noble minds?"
"Who said that?"
"Oh, I'm quoting Philip Guedalla. A biographer of the thirties. The golden age when every cabinet minister had a thriller by his bedside, and all detectives were titled. Before your time, I expect."
"Perhaps it would have been truer to say that noble minds were the normal recreation of detective story writers."
—Exchange between Andrew Wyke and Milo Tindle, *Sleuth*, Act I, 1970

WILLIAM SHAKESPEARE 1564–1616

Greatest of English playwrights, who understood—none better—the impulses and motives that prompt men and women to evil actions. Hundreds of mystery titles have been taken from Shakespeare's works, a major contribution to the genre, since books must have titles, and his are good ones.

1316   How easily murder is discovered!
—Tamora, *Titus Andronicus*, Act II, scene iii, 1593–94

1317   Truth will come to light; murder cannot be hid long.
—Launcelot, *Merchant of Venice*, Act II, scene ii, 1596–97

1318   Murder most foul, as in the best it is.
—Ghost, *Hamlet*, Act I, scene v, 1600–01

Murder Most Foul has been used as a title by at least three mystery writers—Gordon Ashe, Kathleen Buddington Coxe, and Hector Hawton—while Tobias Wells used *Murder Most Fouled Up.*

1319   Murder, though it have no tongue, will speak with most miraculous organ.
>   —Hamlet, ibid., Act II, scene ii

1320   An honorable murderer, if you will,
For naught did I in hate, but all in honor.
>   —Othello to Ludovico, *Othello*, Act V, scene ii, 1602

DELL SHANNON 1921–

Pseudonym of American writer Elizabeth Linington, who also writes under other names. As Shannon, police procedural novelist; creator of Lt. Luis Mendoza and a department of police officers.

1321   We're supposed to be the noblest work of God, but He certainly made a lot of things more beautiful, didn't He?
>   —Matt Piggott, *Spring of Violence*, 1973

GEORGE BERNARD SHAW 1856–1950

Irish critic and playwright, intensely concerned with social conditions.

1322   When we want to read of the deeds that are done for love, whither do we turn? To the murder column; and there we are rarely disappointed.
>   —Preface, *Three Plays for Puritans*, 1901

M. P. SHIEL 1865–1947

English author of a long series of fantastic stories and novels in which detection and mystery play a part; creator of Prince Zaleski, one of the most bizarre detectives in fiction.

1323   Shiel inscribed a first edition of *Prince Zaleski*:
"There is no detective but *the* detective and the father of detectives, the 'Dupin' of Poe, of whom this Zaleski is a legitimate son, and the notorious Holmes a bastard son."
>   —*The Encyclopedia of Mystery and Detection*, 1976

1324 He seemed to me—I say it deliberately and with forethought
—to possess the unparalleled power not merely of disen-
tangling in retrospect but of unravelling in prospect, and I
have known him to relate *coming* events with unimaginable
minuteness of precision. He was nothing if not superlative.

> —Description of Prince Zaleski, "The Stone
> of the Edmundsbury Monks," *Prince
> Zaleski*, 1895

1325 Less death, more disease.

> —"The S. S.," ibid.

GEORGES SIMENON 1903–

Belgian-born writer who has written several hundred novels under
his own name, plus as many more under at least seventeen
pseudonyms; awarded the Grand Master title by Mystery Writers of
America in 1965. As Simenon, creator of Chief Inspector Jules
Maigret, one of the great characters of the literature, who smokes
his pipe and absorbs the atmosphere as he solves crime after crime.

1326 Often asked why he never wrote a big novel, Simenon said:
"My big novel is the mosaic of all my small novels."

> —*Writers at Work*, 1959

1327 In his autobiography Simenon said:
"My very first Maigrets were imbued with the sense, which
has always been with me, of man's irresponsibility. This is
never stated openly in my writings. But Maigret's attitude
towards the criminal makes it quite clear."

> —*When I Was Old*, 1971; English translation
> by Helen Eustis, 1971

1328 I shall know the murderer when I know the victim well.

> —Inspector Jules Maigret, *The Death of
> Monsieur Gallet*, 1931; English translation
> by Margaret Marshall, retitled *Maigret
> Stonewalled*, 1963

1329   "As a policeman, I am bound to draw the logical
conclusion from material evidence."
"And as a man?"
"I want moral proof."

> —Exchange between Inspector Jules Maigret
> and a Ministry of Justice spokesman,
> *Maigret's War of Nerves*, 1940; English
> translation by Geoffrey Sainsbury, 1986

1330   Are not policemen actually repairers of destinies sometimes?
>—Inspector Jules Maigret, *Maigret's First Case*, 1953; English translation by Robert Brain, 1958

1331   Utterly rotten individuals are rare. . . . As for the rest, I tried to prevent them from doing too much harm and to see to it that they paid for the harm they had already done.
>—Inspector Jules Maigret, *Maigret's Memoirs*, 1951; English translation by Jean Stewart, 1963

HELEN SIMPSON 1897–1940

Australian-born English novelist who collaborated with Clemence Dane (q.v.); with Dane, creator of Sir John Saumarez, famous actor-manager and amateur sleuth. On her own, author of one detective novel, *'Vantage Striker*, and other novels and plays.

1332   We could get quite a lot of governing done, if it wasn't for politics.
>—The Prime Minister, *'Vantage Striker*, 1931

1333   Conscience, which makes cowards of us all, can make dyspeptics too.
>—Ibid.

MAJ SJÖWALL 1935– and PER WAHLÖÖ 1926–1975

Swedish husband-and-wife writing team, who chose the crime novel as a form to show the relationship between society and individuals. Their fourth novel, *The Laughing Policeman*, won an Edgar; creators of Martin Beck and his team of professional policemen.

1334   There are lots of good cops around. Dumb guys who are good cops. Inflexible, limited, tough, self-satisfied types who are all good cops. It would be better if there were a few more good guys who were cops.
>—Lennart Kollberg, *The Fire Engine That Disappeared*, 1969; English translation by Joan Tate, 1970

1335   In our profession, we don't usually rely on chance. It so happens that I took note of certain details and then drew certain conclusions.
>—Hjelm of the Forensic Institute, ibid.

1336   A lie doesn't get any nearer the truth by half-repeating it.
> —Gunvald Larsson, ibid.

1337   Police work is built on realism, stubbornness and system. It's
true that a lot of difficult cases are cleared up by coincidence,
but it's equally true that coincidence is an elastic concept that
mustn't be confused with luck or accident. In a criminal
investigation, it's a question of weaving the net of coincidence as fine as possible.
> —*The Abominable Man*, 1971; English
> translation by Thomas Teal, 1972

1338   Intuition has no place in practical police work.
> —Ibid.

JANE SMILEY 1949–

American novelist and university professor. *Duplicate Keys* is her
first murder mystery.

1339   You don't pay for anything by being dead. That's when you
stop paying for it.
> —Susan Gabriel, *Duplicate Keys*, 1984

MARTIN CRUZ SMITH 1942–

American mystery and detective novelist who has published under
the house name Nick Carter, under the pseudonym Simon Quinn,
and under his own name, Martin Smith, to which he added the
middle name Cruz, a name often given to young boys of his
mother's Pueblo Indian tribe.

1340   Once a man indulges himself in murder, in time he thinks
nothing of robbing, and from robbing, he comes next to foul
language and atheism, and from these to opening doors
without knocking.
> —*Gorky Park*, 1981

This is a paraphrase of a famous line by Thomas De
Quincey (q.v.).

1341   Americans, no matter how much money they have, always
find something finally that they can't buy.
> —Ibid.

C. P. SNOW (LORD SNOW) 1905–1980

English senior civil servant, man of letters, and scientist, whose first and last works of fiction, *Death under Sail* and A *Coat of Varnish*, were detective novels.

1342   People talk about material truth and psychological truth as though, if you are interested in the one, you can't be interested in the other. Of course that's nonsense. If I had all the material facts, I shouldn't want any psychological facts. . . . But the point is, one never has *all* the material facts or *all* the psychological facts. One has to do what one can with an incomplete mixture of the two.
—Finbow, *Death under Sail*, 1932

NANCY SPAIN 1917–1964

English mystery and detective novelist; creator of Miriam Birdseye, owner of Birdseye et Cie detective agency.

1343   OUT—GONE TO CRIME.
—Miriam Birdseye's door placard, *Poison for Teacher*, 1949

1344   Novelists, when presented with romantic facts in real life, usually refuse to believe them.
—Ibid.

1345   I never read detective stories. They appear to me to combine all the worst faults of the crossword puzzle and the Grand Guignol, with none of the compensations.
—Philip Lariat, ibid.

ROSS SPENCER 1921–

American private eye novelist; creator of private eye Luke Lassiter, and Chance Purdue, featured in his own series.

1346   My great-grandmother should of been canonized . . . by God she would of been if my great-grandfather could of got hold of a cannon.
—Monroe D. Underwood, *The DADA Caper*, 1978

1347   A gigolo is a man who gets paid for doing what any idiot would be perfeckly willing to do for nothing.
—Monroe D. Underwood, *The Stranger City Caper*, 1980

1348   A small town is where the man what don't drink is a sissy and the man what does is a drunkard.
—Monroe D. Underwood, ibid.

1349   She said if we're successful the Desert Sands might junk their *cause célèbre* and stop trying to start their *d'état*.
I said yeah well those foreign cars have always been a big pain in the ass.
—Chance Purdue, *The Abu Wahab Caper*, 1980

1350   I was the guy who went to lock the barn after the horse had been stolen. And found the barn missing.
—Chance Purdue, *The Radish River Caper*, 1981

1351   The telephone jingled and I pounced on it like a skinny cat pounces on a fat canary. Hangover or no hangover, no one should underestimate the reflexes of a Chicago private detective two months in arrears on his office rent.
—Luke Lassiter, *Monastery Nightmare*, 1986

1352   Fools rush in and come out on stretchers.
—Luke Lassiter's reflection, ibid.

MICKEY SPILLANE 1918–

American private eye novelist, who has said he prefers to read royalty checks rather than critical reviews, given a Lifetime Achievement Award by Private Eye Writers of America in 1984; creator of Mike Hammer.

1353   Commenting on the popularity of his books, Spillane said: "Those big-shot writers . . . could never dig the fact that there are more peanuts consumed than caviar."
—*New York Herald Tribune*, August 18, 1961

1354   The law is fine. But this time I'm the law and I'm not going to be cold and impartial.
—Mike Hammer, *I, The Jury*, 1947

1355   Jack, you're dead now. You can't hear me any more. Maybe you can. I hope so. I want you to hear what I'm about to say. You've known me a long time, Jack. My word is good just as long as I live. I'm going to get the louse that killed you. He

won't sit in the chair. He won't hang. He will die exactly as you died, with a .45 slug in the gut, just a little below the belly button. No matter who it is, Jack, I'll get the one. Remember, no matter who it is, I promise.
—Mike Hammer, ibid.

1356 When you're right you're a hero. When you're wrong you're kill-happy.
—Mike Hammer, *One Lonely Night*, 1951

1357 Why do I have to be the one to pull the trigger and have my soul torn apart afterwards?
—Mike Hammer, ibid.

1358 I lived only to kill the scum and the lice that wanted to kill themselves. I lived to kill so that others could live. I lived to kill because my soul was a hardened thing that reveled in the thought of taking the blood of the bastards who made murder their business. I lived because I could laugh it off and others couldn't. I was the evil that opposed other evil, leaving the good and the meek in the middle to live and inherit the earth!
—Mike Hammer, ibid.

1359 You're the guy things happen to. Some people are accident prone. You're coincidence prone.
—Pat Chambers to Mike Hammer, *Kiss Me, Deadly*, 1952

RICHARD STARK. *See* Donald Westlake.

REED STEPHENS 1947–

Pseudonym of American science fiction novelist Stephen R. Donaldson. As Stephens, private eye novelist; creator of Mick Axbrewder, nicknamed "Brew."

1360 Accidents happen by themselves—crimes have a way of tieing themselves together.
—"Brew" Axbrewder, *The Man Who Killed His Brother*, 1980

1361 I'm not a puzzle solver. . . . My brain doesn't work that way. I get where I'm going—wherever that is—by intuition and information.
—"Brew" Axbrewder, ibid.

1362   Eventually it came to an end, the way everything does (which is probably the nicest thing God has ever done for us).
—"Brew" Axbrewder, *The Man Who Risked His Partner*, 1984

THOMAS STERLING 1921–

American mystery and suspense novelist, who has lived in Italy. His best novel, *The Evil of the Day*, is a modern retelling of Ben Jonson's play *Volpone*.

1363   Money, after all, is only worth what it can buy.
—Hanna Carpenter, *The House without a Door*, 1950

1364   The penalty for pleasing one's self is pleasing no one else.
—Ibid.

1365   It's not bad growing old if you got something somebody else can inherit. You get treated right.
—The gondolier, *The Evil of the Day*, 1955

1366   The police are very adept at detecting man-made plans. Chance is a mystery to everyone.
—Henry Voltor, ibid.

1367   People liked to play fair in order to be able to laugh louder when they won.
—Celia John's reflection, ibid.

BURTON E. STEVENSON 1872–1962

American librarian, compiler of massive reference works, including *Stevenson's Home Book of Quotations*, and mystery novelist.

1368   I think we're too apt to overlook the simple explanations, which are, after all, nearly always the true ones.
—Mr. Godfrey, *The Holladay Case*, 1903

JOHN STEVENSON

American novelist, who has published under his own name and a variety of pseudonyms, including the Nick Carter house name.

1369   "I hope I wasn't interrupting a romantic interlude?"
"Sir?"
"I just wondered. Your zipper is still open."
—Exchange between Hawk and Nick Carter, *The Day of the Dingo*, 1980

ROBERT LOUIS STEVENSON 1850–1894

English poet, story writer, and novelist. Many of his works come close to the mystery-suspense field, and some firmly belong there.

1370 The devil, depend upon it, can sometimes do a very gentlemanly thing.

> —Prince Florizel, "The Young Man With the Cream Tarts," "The Suicide Club," *New Arabian Nights*, 1882

1371 Life is only a stage to play the fool upon as long as the part amuses us.

> —Ibid.

1372 Is there anything in life so disenchanting as attainment?

> —"The Adventure of the Hansom Cab," ibid.

1373 I incline to Cain's heresy. I let my brother go to the devil in his own way.

> —Mr. Utterson, *The Strange Case of Dr. Jekyll and Mr. Hyde*, 1882

Maurice Richardson has said that *The Strange Case of Dr. Jekyll and Mr. Hyde* is "the only detective-crime story in which the solution is more terrifying than the problem."

1374 What hangs people . . . is the unfortunate circumstance of guilt.

> —Michael Finsbury, *The Wrong Box*, 1889; written in collaboration with Lloyd Osbourne

1375 Nothing like a little judicious levity.

> —Michael Finsbury, ibid.

1376 It is the difficulty of the police romance, that the reader is always a man of such vastly greater ingenuity than the writer.

> —Ibid.

1377 I have sometimes thought I should like to try to behave like a gentleman myself; only it's such a one-sided business, with the world and the legal profession as they are.

> —Michael Finsbury, ibid.

1373 Every man has a sane spot somewhere.

> —*The Wrecker*, 1892; written in collaboration with Lloyd Osbourne

FRANK R. STOCKTON 1834–1902

American editor, humorist, and short story writer, author of a famous tale of pure suspense.

1379 And so I leave it with all of you:
Which came out of the opened door,—the lady, or the tiger?
—Title story of the collection, *The Lady or the Tiger*, 1884

BRAM STOKER 1847–1912

Irish theatrical manager and writer of *Dracula*, the classic vampire novel, and many other novels of horror and the supernatural.

1380 How well the man reasoned; lunatics always do within their own scope.
—Mina Murray, of Renfield, *Dracula*, 1897

REX STOUT 1886–1975

One of the most famous American detective novelists, awarded the Grand Master title by Mystery Writers of America in 1958; creator of Nero Wolfe and Archie Goodwin and a Manhattan brownstone somewhere on West 35th Street. Stout swore that reading detective stories was more fun than writing them. He had a theory that people who didn't like mysteries were anarchists.

1381 Any spoke will lead an ant to the hub.
—Nero Wolfe's favorite saying, in his first book, *Fer-de-Lance*, 1934

1382 Never lay an ambush for truth.
—Ibid.

1383 War isn't politics. . . . It is indeed the only human activity that is rottener than politics.
—Mrs. Brown, *The President Vanishes*, 1934

1384 I am not a policeman. I am a private detective. I entrap criminals, and find evidence to imprison them or kill them, for hire.
—Nero Wolfe, *Too Many Cooks*, 1938

1385 Few of us have enough wisdom for justice, or enough leisure for humanity.
—Nero Wolfe, ibid.

1386 Nothing is simpler than to kill a man; the difficulties arise in attempting to avoid the consequences.
—Nero Wolfe, ibid.

1387 Courtesy is one's own affair, but decency is a debt to life.
—Nero Wolfe, ibid.

1388 A hole in the ice is dangerous only to those who go skating.
—Ibid.

1389 No man was ever taken to hell by a woman unless he already had a ticket in his pocket, or at least had been fooling around with timetables.
—Archie Goodwin, *Some Buried Caesar*, 1938

1390 We don't usually hang our linen on the line till it has been washed.
—Nero Wolfe, ibid.

1391 Innocence is a negative and can never be established; you can only establish guilt.
—Nero Wolfe, ibid.

1392 I rarely offer pledges, because I would redeem one, tritely, with my life.
—Nero Wolfe, ibid.

1393 My only serious fault is lethargy; and I tolerate Mr. Goodwin, and even pay him, to help me circumvent it.
—Nero Wolfe, ibid.

1394 A detective who minds his own business would be a contradiction in terms.
—Archie Goodwin, ibid.

1395 Don't you know that the air we breathe is composed of nitrogen, oxygen, and odium?
—A cynical career woman to Inspector Cramer, *Red Threads*, 1939

1396 Merely a drop of acid from rumor's unclean tongue.
—*The Broken Vase*, 1941

1397 He [Nero Wolfe] can't fire me because then he would never do any work at all and would eventually starve to death.
—Archie Goodwin, "Instead of the Evidence," *Trouble in Triplicate*, 1949

1398 The trouble with mornings is that they come when you're not awake.
> —Archie Goodwin, "A Window for Death,"
> *Three for the Chair*, 1957

1399 It's amazing what lengths a man will go to for envy.
> —Archie Goodwin, "Easter Parade," *And
> Four to Go*, 1958

1400 Tenuous almost to nullity.
> —Nero Wolfe, *A Right to Die*, 1964

1401 Tradition should be respected but not sanctified.
> —Nero Wolfe, *A Family Affair*, 1975

JOHN STEPHEN STRANGE 1896–

Pseudonym of American Dorothy Stockbridge Tillett. As Strange, author of more than twenty classic murder mystery puzzles; creator of Barney Gantt, George Honegger, and Van Dusen Ormsberry, each featured in his own series.

1402 The lack of consideration among the criminal classes is—well, it's criminal!
> —Van Dusen Ormsberry, *The Man Who
> Killed Fortescue*, 1928

T. S. STRIBLING 1881–1965

Pultizer Prize–winning American novelist and detective story writer; creator of Professor Henry Poggioli, philosophic psychologist.

1403 It's a shame we can't go in and look at the body. I paid my three bucks a day here, and they told me it included everything.
> —American tourist, "The Refugees," *Clues of
> the Caribees*, 1929

1404 Now when we analyze "hunches" we find they are composed of an instinctive correlation of facts which have not yet reached the surface of consciousness.
> —Henry Poggioli, ibid.

1405 The detection of crime is a damnable occupation. A man who follows it will become a monster.
> —Henry Poggioli, "Cricket," ibid.

1406 The force of adjectives, like gravitation, the speed of light, and the beauty of women, is relative.
> —Henry Poggioli, ibid.

JEAN STUBBS 1926–

English historical novelist whose detective novels are set in the Victorian era; creator of Ex-Inspector John Lintott.

1407 Life is a lottery. Pay up and take your chance if you desire a prize. You may not get it even then. You will never have it unless you pay with yourself first.
> —Advice to an artist, *The Painted Face*, 1974

1408 Each man carries his own justice with him.
> —Ex-Inspector John Lintott, *The Golden Crucible*, 1976

JEREMY STURROCK 1908–

Pseudonym of English writer Benjamin James Healy; in the United States his Jeremy Sturrock novels, presented as the memoirs of a Bow Street Runner, are published under the name J. G. Jeffreys.

1409 It is the company which makes the occasion, not the surroundings.
> —*Suicide Most Foul*, 1981

JULIAN SYMONS 1912–

Noted English man of letters and crime novelist. *Bloody Murder*, his history of the detective novel, won an Edgar, and he was awarded the Grand Master title by Mystery Writers of America in 1982. He claims he is "an addict, with a passion for crime literature that survives any rational explanation of it."

1410 Symons has said:
"The thing that absorbs me most in our age is the violence behind respectable faces, the civil servant planning how to kill Jews most efficiently, the judge speaking with passion about the need for capital punishment, the quiet obedient boy who kills for fun. These are extreme cases, but if you want to show the violence that lives behind the bland faces

most of us present to the world, what better vehicle can you have than the crime novel?"

—*Twentieth-Century Crime and Mystery Writers*, 1980

1411 When lies are no longer possible, then truth is the only resort.

—*A Three-Pipe Problem*, 1975

WILLIAM G. TAPPLEY 1940–

American detective novelist; creator of Brady Coyne, laywer for the rich.

1412 When you can win, you go for the throat. When you're going to lose, you go for the compromise.

—Ben Woodhouse, *The Marine Corpse*, 1986

ANDREW TAYLOR 1951–

English crime novelist whose *Caroline Minuscule* won the John Creasy Memorial Award for best first crime novel by an English writer; creator of William Dougal.

1413 Old habits die hard, even when you want nothing better than to see them dead.

—*Our Fathers' Lies*, 1985

1414 How bloody humiliating it is to bear the burden of someone else's self-sacrifice.

—Celia Prentisse, ibid.

1415 An old school tie wasn't just an article of dress; it shackled you to your past.

—William Dougal, *An Old School Tie*, 1986

PHOEBE ATWOOD TAYLOR 1909–1976

American detective novelist who also wrote as Alice Tilton. As Taylor, creator of Asey Mayo, the "Codfish Sherlock."

1416 Common sense . . . that's my maxim.

—Asey Mayo, *The Cape Cod Mystery*, 1931

1417 There ain't many whys without becauses.

—Asey Mayo, ibid.

WALTER TEVIS 1928–1984

American science fiction and suspense novelist; creator of Fast Eddie Felson, poolroom hustler and gambler.

1418 If you want the glory and the money, you got to be hard.
—Bert to Fast Eddie Felson, *The Hustler*, 1959

JOSEPHINE TEY 1897–1952

Pseudonym of Scottish writer Elizabeth Mackintosh, who also wrote historical plays as Gordon Daviot. As Tey, writer of mystery and detective novels; creator of Inspector Alan Grant, well-tailored Scotland Yard detective.

1419 Lack of education is an extraordinary handicap when one is being offensive.
—Mrs. Sharpe, *The Franchise Affair*, 1948

1420 You can't have a tin can tied to your tail and go through life pretending it isn't there.
—Robert Blair, ibid.

1421 Horse sense is the instinct that keeps horses from betting on men.
—Mrs. Sharpe, ibid.

1422 It's not possible to love and be wise.
—*To Love and Be Wise*, 1950

This title reverses a quotation from Shakespeare's *Troilus and Cressida*, Act III, scene ii.

LEE THAYER 1874–1973

American artist and prolific detective novelist, whose last book, *Dusty Death*, was published when she was ninety-two; creator of red-haired private investigator Peter Clancy and Wiggar, his snobbish English valet.

1423 Facts are stubborn things.
—*Murder Is Out*, 1942

1424 One must tighten one's belt over one's bowels of compassion.
—*A Plain Case of Murder*, 1944

LESLIE THOMAS 1931–

English novelist, author of the best-seller, *The Virgin Soldiers*, whose ventures into detective and espionage fields, *Dangerous Davies: The Last Detective* and *Ormerod's Landing*, make one hope he will make further contributions to the genre.

1425 Murder is a wound that time won't heal.
> —Dangerous Davies, *Dangerous Davies: The Last Detective*, 1976

1426 The terrier does not give the rat time to dig a hole.
> —Jacques-the-Odd to Detective-Sergeant George Ormerod, *Ormerod's Landing*, 1978

ROSS THOMAS 1926–

American writer of political thrillers, who also writes as Oliver Bleeck. As Thomas, winner of an Edgar for his first novel, *The Cold War Swap*, and another for *Briarpatch*.

1427 If you're in trouble, you're alone.
> —Stan Burmser to Michale Padillo, *Cast a Yellow Shadow*, 1967

1428 There has been a lot of nonsense written about childlike gazes, but Shartelle seemed to look out on the world with the lesson-learning grave eyes of a nine-year-old who has been told that he must save the ten-dollar bill he found under the bench in the park. Although he knows he will never find another one, he also knows that he will never again tell anybody if he does.
> —Peter Upshaw's observation, *The Seersucker Whipsaw*, 1967

1429 One of the keenest pleasures in life is to succumb to one's vices.
> —Ling Pang Sam to Eddie Cauthorne, *The Singapore Wink*, 1969

1430 To get better, it must get much worse.
> —Orcutt's First Law, *The Fools in Town Are on Our Side*, 1970

1431 Real grief often seems to parody itself.
> —*The Porkchoppers*, 1972

1432   Authentic detail can always be used to beef up unsubstantiated theory.

> —Decatur Lucas, *If You Can't Be Good*,
> 1973

1433   For some people the thought of suicide is a comfort. . . . It offers an ultimate solution to all their problems.

> —Harvey Longmore, *Yellow-Dog Contract*,
> 1976

1434   He Never Stiffed Nobody Unless He Deserved It.

> —Artie Wu's chosen epitaph, *Chinaman's*
> *Chance*, 1978

1435   You can't get old until you've got it made. Until then you can't afford old age.

> —Drew Meade's creed, *Missionary Stew*,
> 1983

Writing as **OLIVER BLEECK**, creator of Philip St. Ives, the go-between who gets things back for people.

1436   The world's nothing but a graveyard filled with old bones.

> —Julian Christenberry, medieval weaponry
> expert, to Philip St. Ives, *The Highbinders*,
> 1974

HENRY DAVID THOREAU 1817–1862

American man of letters, with a firm grasp of the rules of evidence.

1437   Some circumstantial evidence is very strong, as when you find a trout in the milk.

> —Entry of November 11, 1854, *Journal*,
> 1903

Sherlock Holmes quotes this line in "The Adventures of the Noble Bachelor," *The Adventures of Sherlock Holmes*. At least three mystery novelists—Hugh Holman, Michael Underwood, and Roy Lewis—have used *A Trout in the Milk* as a book title.

GUY M. TOWNSEND 1943–

American mystery novelist and publisher of *The Mystery Fancier*.

1438   Nowadays it seems that the mere fact of being married constitutes sufficient motive for murder.
—Reflection of John Miles Forest, *To Prove a Villain*, 1985

ARTHUR TRAIN 1875–1945

American lawyer, criminologist, and writer; creator of the believable lawyer-detective Ephraim Tutt, who never lost a case as he righted legal wrongs, and his unrelated partner, Samuel Tutt.

1439   Train said of himself:
"I enjoy the dubious distinction of being known among lawyers as a writer, and among writers as a lawyer."
—*My Day in Court*, 1939

1440   I cannot let an innocent man falsely admit under any conditions that he is guilty.
—Ephraim Tutt, "The Bloodhound," *Tut, Tut! Mr. Tutt*, 1923

1441   There are some people who simply can't learn anything by experience.
—"Tut, Tut! Mr. Tutt," ibid.

1442   The law offers greater opportunities to be at one and the same time a Christian and a horse-trader than any other profession.
—Author's Preface, *The Adventures of Ephraim Tutt*, 1930

1443   Never turn down a case.
—Ephraim Tutt's motto, "The Human Element," *Mr. Tutt's Casebook*, 1936

1444   Our duties as sworn officers of the judicial branch of the government renders it incumbent upon us to perform whatever services our clients' exigencies demand.
—Samuel Tutt's way of saying the same thing, ibid.

1445   Every dog is entitled to one bite.
—"The Dog Andrew," a story built around the old proverb, ibid.

1446   So far as we have any real justice in this world we get it less through the courts than by virtue of the inherent decency of our fellowmen.
—Ephraim Tutt, *Yankee Lawyer: The Autobiography of Ephraim Tutt*, 1943

LAWRENCE TREAT 1903–

American detective novelist, one of the earliest police procedural-ists; creator of Jub Freeman, Mitch Taylor, and Bill Decker.

1447   "What are you after, anyhow?"
"Facts. Just facts."
—Detective Jub Freeman and Walter Ivy,
Homicide, *H as in Hunted*, 1946

A few years later, on television, Jack Webb (as Sgt. Joe Friday of *Dragnet*) would be crying: "The facts, all we want is the facts. . . ." And long before, Sherlock Holmes was exclaiming: "Data! Data! Data!"

1448   Before society has the chance to progress, the criminal has to be neutralized. Police science is young and yelling. It needs new and better techniques. Once in a while my work gives me the chance to develop them.
—Jub Freeman, ibid.

1449   Dying can't be so bad . . . it can only happen once.
—Leda Vanderman, ibid.

1450   When a cop has his hands on cash, he usually keeps it. Not always, of course. It takes nice judgment to decide when you can, and when you can't.
—Opinion of Mitch Taylor, not a crooked cop, just one who takes a little cushion, *Big Shot*, 1951

WILLIAM TREVOR 1928–

Anglo-Irish novelist, whose *Fools of Fortune* tells the story of a family viciously murdered during the Irish "troubles" of 1918, an act of revenge, and the price paid for it.

1451   There's not much left in anyone's life after murder has been committed. God insists upon that.
—Father Kilgarriff, *Fools of Fortune*, 1983

SUSAN TROTT 1937–

American novelist whose books explore life in the rich counties north of San Francisco. *The Housewife and the Assassin* was her first suspense novel.

1452 Can you die and learn?
> —*The Housewife and the Assassin*, 1979

SIMON TROY

One of the pseudonyms used by English detective novelist Thurman Warriner. As Troy, creator of Inspector Smith.

1453 Compromise usually takes one half-way to nowhere in a long time, but it can be useful.
> —Inspector Smith, *Swift to Close*, 1969

1454 It's comparatively simple to renounce earthly delights when they're not available. It can be exhausting to deny yourself when they are.
> —Inspector Smith, ibid.

WILSON TUCKER 1914–

American detective novelist; creator of Charles Horne, a skinny, dumb-looking private eye, sometimes hampered by a supply of sentiment.

1455 Librarians are wonderful people. They should be in the detective business.
> —*The Chinese Doll*, 1946

MARK TWAIN 1835–1910

Pseudonym of American humorist and writer Samuel Langhorne Clemens; creator of Pudd'nhead Wilson, who was the first fictional lawyer to base his court case on the uniqueness of a person's fingerprints.

1456 A enemy can partly ruin a man, but it takes a good-natured injudicious friend to complete the thing and make it perfect.
> —*Pudd'nhead Wilson*, 1894

1457 No real gentleman will tell the naked truth in the presence of ladies.
> —"A Double-Barreled Detective Story," 1902

MICHAEL UNDERWOOD 1916–

Pseudonym of English barrister John Michael Evelyn. As Underwood, writer of crime and mystery novels, showing how the English legal system works; creator of Detective Sergeant Nick Atwell, Rosa Epton, and Superintendent Simon Manton.

1458   A failed alibi is worse than no alibi.
—*The Fatal Trip*, 1977

1459   "I've never heard of anyone being both frigid and a sexpot."
"In the same way you can burn your hand on a lump of frozen metal."
—Exchange between Rosa Epton and Sam Brazier, *Double Jeopardy*, 1981

1460   Provable lies are often better than the truth.
—Detective Chief Superintendent Everson, *Death in Camera*, 1984

ARTHUR W. UPFIELD 1888–1964

English-born Australian detective novelist; creator of Inspector Napoleon Bonaparte, more often called Bony, the half-caste detective of the Queensland Police.

1461   Never race Time. Make Time an ally, for Time is the greatest detective that ever was or will be.
—Inspector Napoleon Bonaparte's advice, *Mr. Jelly's Business*, 1937

1462   There are some blokes what was borned to be a husband of a nagging wife. There is other blokes what was borned to have sixteen kids. And there are some other blokes which are borned to be murdered. Kendall was borned to be murdered. The surprising thing is that he was murdered so late in life.
—Sam the Blackmailer, *Death of a Swagman*, 1945

1463   Life is what you get out of it, not what it likes to give you.
—Mike Conway, *Bony and the Kelly Gang*, 1960

1464   Never accept anything at face value.
—Inspector Napoleon Bonaparte, *The Lake Frome Monster*, completed by J. L. Price and Dorothy Strange, 1966

ROBERT UPTON 1934–

American playwright and private eye novelist; creator of Amos McGuffin, investigator and golf player, whose rule is: "Never drink while on a case."

1465   The only difference between Marian Boone and a vulture was nail polish.
>—Amos McGuffin's suspicion, *Dead on the Stick*, 1986

JANWILLEM VAN DE WETERING 1931–

Dutch detective novelist, now living in Maine, who mixes Zen Buddhism with his police procedurals; creator of the Commissaris (known only by his first name, Jan), Adjutant Henk Grijpstra, and Sergeant Rinus de Gier of the Amsterdam police department.

1466   Even an honest man gets tempted when faced by an idiot.
>—*The Maine Massacre*, 1979

1467   Suicide requires an act of will. It is easier to become careless.
>—Ibid.

1468   To live with guilt strengthens character.
>—Sergeant Jurriaans, *The Streetbird*, 1983

1469   Once everything becomes the way it should be, what do you do?
>—Sergeant Rinus de Gier's reflection, *The Rattle-Rat*, 1985

S. S. VAN DINE 1888–1939

Pseudonym of American writer and art critic Willard Huntington Wright. As Van Dine, detective novelist, creator of Philo Vance (who, according to Ogden Nash, needed "a kick in the pance").

1470   While his pseudonym was still a closely kept secret, Wright wrote:
"There is no more stimulating activity than that of the mind; and there is no more exciting adventure than that of the intellect."
>—Introduction, *The Great Detective Stories*, 1927

1471   He added:
"Crime has always exerted a profound fascination over humanity, and the more serious the crime, the greater has been that appeal. Murder, therefore, has always been an absorbing public topic."
>—Ibid.

1472 There is one infallible method of determining human guilt and responsibility. . . . The truth can be learned only by an analysis of the psychological factors of a crime, and an application of them to the individual. The only real clues are psychological—not material.
—*The Benson Murder Case*, 1926

1473 Crime isn't a mass instinct except during wartime, and then it's merely an obscene sport.
—Philo Vance, *The "Canary" Murder Case*, 1927

1474 As long as we're going insane we may as well go the whole way. A mere shred of sanity is of no value.
—Philo Vance, *The Bishop Murder Case*, 1929

1475 Vance was debonair, whimsical, and superficially cynical—an amateur of the arts, and with only an impersonal concern in serious social and moral problems.
—*The Scarab Murder Case*, 1930

ROBERT VAN GULIK 1910–1967

Dutch scholar, diplomat, translator of the old Chinese Judge Dee detective stories, and then writer of new ones.

1476 Trying to make a crime too perfect is a mistake of many murderers.
—*The Willow Pattern*, 1965

LOUIS JOSEPH VANCE 1879–1943

American author of hundreds of short stories and dozens of adventure and mystery novels; creator of Michael Lanyard, known as the Lone Wolf for his refusal to work with a pack of criminals.

1477 Love is unreasoning and unreasonable even when unrecognized.
—*The Brass Bowl*, 1907

1478 The three cardinal principles of successful cracksmanship: to know his ground thoroughly before venturing upon it; to strike and retreat with the swift precision of a hawk; to be friendless.
And the last of these was the greatest.
—Bourke's rules, *The Lone Wolf*, 1914

1479 What must be, must.
> —The Lone Wolf's philosophy, *Alias the Lone Wolf*, 1921

1480 Love is a fine art and marriage its last test.
> —*Encore the Lone Wolf*, 1933

MARIO VARGAS LLOSA 1936–

South American novelist who has used the structure of the detective novel to examine guilt and innocence and the corruption of law and justice in society.

1481 The truths that seem most truthful, if you look at them from all sides, if you look at them close up, turn out either to be half truths or lies.
> —Lieutenant Silva, *Who Killed Palimino Molero?*, 1987; English translation by Alfred Mac Adam

ROY C. VICKERS 1888?–1965

Prolific English writer; creator of the angelically beautiful Fidelity Dove and Detective-Inspector Rason of the Department of Dead Ends, an imaginary branch of Scotland Yard that scored forty-three convictions in ten years. Vickers wrote that "the impulse to murder is likely to seize almost anybody who has enough animal courage to see it through."

1482 Most criminals are fools. They keep me on at Dead Ends on the principle of setting a fool to catch a fool.
> —Detective-Inspector Rason, "The Man Who Was Murdered by a Bed," *The Department of Dead Ends*, 1947

1483 Self-contempt is one of the ingredients in the make-up of the murderer.
> —"Mean Man's Murder," ibid.

1484 Test an absurdity and you may stumble on a truth.
> —Detective-Inspector Rason's formula, "The Case of the Social Climber," *The Department of Dead Ends*, 1978

1485 Sexual charity is a virtue of which nature does not approve.
> —"A Fool and Her Money," ibid.

Two different selections of Vickers's stories were published under the same title, *The Department of Dead Ends*, in 1947 and 1978

VOLTAIRE 1697–1778

In *Zadig* Voltaire created the first systematic detective in modern literature, the progenitor of Dupin, Holmes, et al. The name Zadig came to stand for so much that in 1880 Thomas Huxley, in a series of lectures aimed at publicizing Darwin's theories, defined "Zadig's Method" as the making of retrospective predictions—common to history, archaeology, geology, physical astronomy, and paleontology. When causes cannot be repeated one must infer them from their effects.

> Zadig, the hero of the tale, had turned to the study of nature to console himself for his marital difficulties. One day, while walking near a little wood, fate involved him in a search for some most precious creatures.

1486 "Young man," said the chief eunuch to Zadig, "have you seen the queen's dog?"

Zadig modestly replied: "It is a bitch, not a dog."

"You are right," said the eunuch.

"It is a very small spaniel," added Zadig; "it is not long since she has had a litter of puppies; she is lame in the left forefoot, and her ears are very long."

"You have seen her, then?" said the chief eunuch, quite out of breath.

"No," answered Zadig, "I have never seen her, and never knew that the queen had a bitch."

—*Zadig; or, The Book of Fate*, 1748; English translation by Robert Bruce Boswell, 1910

> Just at this very time, by one of those curious coincidences which are not uncommon, the finest horse in the king's stables broke away from the hands of a groom in the plains of Babylon. The grand huntsman and all the other officers ran after him with as much anxiety as the chief of the eunuchs had displayed in his search after the queen's bitch. The grand huntsman accosted Zadig, and asked him if he had seen the king's horse pass that way.

1487   "It is the horse," said Zadig, "which gallops best; he is five feet high, and has small hoofs; his tail is three and a half feet long; the bosses on his bit are of gold twenty-three carats fine; his shoes are silver of eleven penny-weights."

"Which road did he take? Where is he?" asked the grand huntsman.

"I have not seen him," answered Zadig, "and I have never even heard anyone speak of him."

—Ibid.

The chief eunuch and the grand huntsman did not doubt that Zadig had stolen the animals. He was arrested as the thief, sentenced to a whipping and life in Siberia, and was saved only when the dog and the horse were found. The judges were now under the disagreeable necessity of amending their judgement, but they fined Zadig four hundred ounces of gold for having said "that he had not seen what he had seen."

Allowed to appeal, Zadig explained his deep and subtle inferences, and the court was amazed. Some, it is true, thought he should be burned as a wizard, but the king ordered his fine returned. This was done, with only three hundred and ninety-eight ounces of gold kept back for court expenses, and Zadig realized a fundamental truth:

1488   How very dangerous it sometimes is to show oneself too knowing.

—Ibid.

In a later chapter, as the king's prime minister, Zadig formulates one of the great tenets of justice:

1489   It is better that a guilty man should be acquitted than that an innocent one should be condemned.

—Ibid.

HENRY WADE 1887–1969

Pseudonym of English peer Henry Lancelot Aubrey-Fletcher. As Wade, one of the major figures of the Golden Age, though he continued to write well into the 1950s.

1490   It was never safe to turn one's back upon the most unpromising source of information.
> —As Detective-Inspector John Poole had learned, *The Duke of York's Steps*, 1929

1491   In cases of murder, it is the rarest thing in the world to have absolute knowledge of guilt—first-hand evidence; we have to rely upon the building up of a mass of circumstantial evidence. And yet, the majority of murderers are hanged and there is no known case of a man having been unjustly hanged.
> —Inspector Lott to Miss Nawten, *The Hanging Captain*, 1932

Perhaps this was true in England in 1932. But in 1950 an innocent man, Timothy Evans, was convicted of murdering his wife and daughter and then hanged. A prosecution witness, later found to have murdered six women, confessed to the Evans murders before his own execution. This miscarriage of justice was one of the reasons why England later suspended capital punishment.

CONSTANCE WAGNER 1903–

American writer, author of one international intrigue thriller.

1492   Avoid safety. The very word has a mean sound.
> —*The Major Has Seven Guests*, 1940

JOHN WAINWRIGHT 1921–

Prolific English police procedural novelist who often writes four books a year.

1493   We are the scavengers, the disposers of offal. We clean the streets of their filth. We are, I suppose, glorified garbage collectors.
> —Collins, a policeman who enjoys the chase but hates the kill, *Death in a Sleeping City*, 1965

1494   Murder. As a crime, it keeps the scribblers occupied, lines their pockets and, with luck, keeps one section of the reading public wide-eyed and wondering. Fictitious murder, that is, . . . bloodless, painless and, above all else, quite "acceptable" murder; murder which, within the next two hundred pages, or so, will be solved with a certain gay panache.

—*A Ripple of Murders*, 1978

1495 The real thing was as glamorous as an abattoir. . . . The real thing presupposed that some lunatic had nudged God from His pedestal; had taken over the business of life-and-death decision-making.

—Ibid.

1496 Something about "the fall of a sparrow." The balance of the world tilts a little; things are never *quite* the same; the equilibrium of nature shifts slightly and has to be compensated.
If this, for a mere sparrow, what for a man?

—Ibid.

1497 Straight up, straight down; two and two made four, and screw it around as much as you like, it didn't make three-and-a-half, and it didn't make four-and-a-half. It made *four*, period.

—Coop's view of life, *All on a Summer's Day*, 1981

EDGAR WALLACE 1875–1932

English writing "phenomenon," whose output was prodigious. While his public clamoured for the "Weekly Wallace," *Punch* started a joke about the "Midday Wallace." Over half of his countless books, plays, and short stories have to do with mystery and detection; creator of Mr. J. G. Reeder, absent-minded and old-maidish.

1498 This story about Wallace was one of his favorites:
"Edgar Wallace, world's most prolific writer, was called on the long-distance at the Marquery Hotel, Park Avenue. 'Sorry,' said his secretary. 'Mr. Wallace has just started a new novel.' 'Great!' said the voice from Cincinnati, O. 'I'll hold the wire till he's through.'"

—*The Wabash Monitor*, quoted by Douglas Thomson, *Masters of Mystery*, 1931

1499   We kill for justice. . . . When we see an unjust man
oppressing his fellows; when we see an evil thing done against
the good God and against man—and know that by the laws
of man this evildoer may escape punishment—we punish.
—George Manfred, *The Four Just Men*, 1905

1500   Fear is a tyrant and a despot, more terrible than the rack,
more potent than the snake.
—*The Clue of the Twisted Candle*, 1916

1501   That is my curious perversion—I have a criminal mind!
—Mr. J. G. Reeder, "The Poetical
Policeman," *The Mind of Mr. J. G.
Reeder*, 1925

1502   Love is a very beautiful experience—I have frequently read
about it.
—Mr. J. G. Reeder, ibid.

1503   The criminal mind is a peculiar thing. It harbours illusions
and fairy stories. Fortunately, I understand that mind.
—Mr. J. G. Reeder, "The Treasure Hunt,"
ibid.

1504   Coincidence . . . is permissible in stories but is so distressing in actual life. It shakes one's confidence in the logic of
things.
—Mr. J. G. Reeder, "The Strange Case,"
ibid.

1505   You're barking up the wrong tree.
—*The India-Rubber Men*, 1929

Burton E. Stevenson says, in *The Macmillan Book of
Proverbs, Maxims, and Famous Phrases*, that this is
the most common of all clichés in detective stories,
and cites many later examples.

R.A.J. WALLING 1869–1949

English newspaperman and Golden Age detective novelist Robert
Alfred John Walling; creator of Philip Tolefree, well-mannered
private enquiry agent.

1506   Seeing is believing says the most fallacious of all proverbs. It
should be reversed. Believing is seeing. The eye does not
control the mind. The mind controls the eye.
—*Behind the Yellow Blind*, 1932

1507 A politician's unlike other people—he's got to keep away from wet tar if he wants to stick to his seat.
> —Philip Tolefree, *More Than One Serpent*, 1938

1508 The less you understand the greater your faith.
> —*Why Did Trethewy Die?*, 1940

1509 The wiliest fox provides the best hunting.
> —Ibid.

JOSEPH WAMBAUGH 1937–

Los Angeles Police Department Detective Sergeant who wrote the best-seller, *The New Centurions*, followed by a series of novels portraying police officers as they deal with the horrors of life.

1510 See boys, there's just a million problems in this world that there ain't no solutions to and the cops get most a those kind.
> —Sergeant Dom Scuzzi of the Vice Squad, *The Choirboys*, 1975

1511 Most Big Events are decided by the falling of *less* than a sparrow.
> —Mario Villalobos, *The Delta Star*, 1983

"WATERS"

Little is known about "Waters" save that his name may have been William Russell. His yellow-back tales, immensely popular with the English reading public of his time, are important as the first supposedly true-life adventures of a London policeman. The first "Waters" story was published in 1849.

1512 Time and familiarity are such disenchanters.
> —"Murder Under the Microscope," *Experiences of a Real Detective*, 1862

COLIN WATSON 1920–1982

English writer of comic detective novels, coiner of the expression "Mayhem Parva" to describe the idealized closed little villages beloved of many detective and mystery writers; creator of Inspector Purbright and Miss Lucilla Teatime.

1513 A needle is much simpler to find in a haystack than in a bin of other needles.
> —Inspector Purbright, *Lonely Hearts 4122*, 1967

1514   Tact should not be confused with mendacity.
— Inspector Purbright, ibid.

1515   To tell the truth, it is regarding the physical side of marriage
that I have always been apprehensive. . . . There so
seldom seems to be enough of it.
— Miss Lucilla Teatime, *Charity Ends at
Home*, 1968

HILLARY WAUGH 1920–

American detective novelist, who also writes under other names. As
Waugh, one of the earliest and most distinguished of the police
proceduralists; creator of Chief Fred Fellows and others.

1516   I didn't go to college so I couldn't learn about people in
books. I had to learn about people from people. . . . I got
an education out of the Police Department.
— Detective Chief Frank Ford, *Last Seen
Wearing. . . .* , 1952

JACK WEBB 1920–

American detective novelist, not to be confused with Jack Webb the
actor; creator of Father Joseph Shanley and Detective-Sergeant
Sammy Golden.

1517   Watson, the needle!
— Shouts Holmes, the myna bird, *One For
My Dame*, 1961

JEAN FRANCIS WEBB 1910–

American historical, romance, adventure, and mystery novelist,
who also writes under other names.

1518   Love is like a mushroom. No roots and deadly poison.
— *No Match for Murder*, 1942

1519   The female of the species is more dead pan than the male.
— Ibid.

HENRY KITCHELL WEBSTER 1875–1932

American novelist, popular and prolific, whose output included
nearly a dozen "romances," as he called his detective and mystery
novels.

1520   The only certain knowledge is the inspired guess.
　　　　　　　—Arthur Jeffrey, *The Whispering Man*, 1908

1521   Consistency's a fourth rate sort of virtue.
　　　　　　　—*The Clock Strikes Two*, 1928

1522   When you've really learned to be serious about one thing you
　　　　 sort of naturally stop being a damned fool about others.
　　　　　　　—Camilla Lindstrom, *Who Is the Next?*, 1931

JOHN WEBSTER 1580?–1634?

Seventeenth-century English playwright; *The Duchess of Malfi*, his
greatest work, is a classic murder drama.

1523   Other sins only speak; murder shrieks out.
　　　　　　　—Bosola, *The Duchess of Malfi*, Act IV,
　　　　　　　scene ii, c. 1613

1524   Cover her face; mine eyes dazzle: she died young.
　　　　　　　—Ferdinand, ibid., Act IV, scene ii

　　　　 P. D. James (q.v.) and Hugh McCutcheon have both
　　　　 used *Cover Her Face* as a book title.

HUGH C. WEIR 1884–1934

American newspaperman and detective story writer; creator of Miss
Madelyn Mack, called a "petticoat detective" by rude policemen.

1525   A detective is always given certain known factors, and I keep
　　　　 building them up, or subtracting them, as the case may be,
　　　　 until I know that the answer *must* be correct.
　　　　　　　—Miss Madelyn Mack's method, "The Man
　　　　　　　With Nine Lives," *Miss Madelyn Mack,
　　　　　　　Detective*, 1914

1526   There are only two real rules for a successful detective, hard
　　　　 work and common sense.
　　　　　　　—Miss Madelyn Mack, ibid.

1527   How often must I tell you that nothing is trivial—in crime?
　　　　　　　—Miss Madelyn Mack, "The Missing
　　　　　　　Bridegroom," ibid.

ANNA MARY WELLS 1906–

American professor of English and detective novelist, creator of a
sleuthing team composed of a psychiatrist and his nurse, Dr. Hillis
Owen and Miss Pomeroy.

1528 Psychiatry's just a form of detecting—matter of putting two and two together and trying to figure out why the heck the answer isn't four.
—Dr. Hillis Owen, *Murderer's Choice*, 1943

1529 Of course I really like good literature, but naturally I don't get much time to read, and for when you just like to pick up something light, I always say you can't beat a good murder mystery.
—Miss Pomeroy's hairdresser, ibid.

CAROLYN WELLS 1869–1942

Prolific American writer of murder mysteries and other works, as well as the first how-to-write-a-murder-mystery manual, *The Technique of the Mystery Story*; creator of Fleming Stone, "a quiet, rather scholarly looking man, with a sympathetic face and good manners."

1530 Wells said of the detective novel:
"It must *seem* to be true as fairy stories *seem* true to children."
—*The Technique of the Mystery Story*, 1913

1531 If you knew anything about detective work, you'd know that the most seemingly impossible conditions are often the easiest to explain.
—Fleming Stone, *Vicky Van*, 1918

PATRICIA WENTWORTH 1878–1961

Pseudonym of English historical novelist and mystery writer Dora Amy Elles Dillon Turnbull. As Wentworth, creator of Miss Maud Silver, elderly female detective.

1532 A lie that is half a truth is ever the hardest to fight.
—*The Chinese Shawl*, 1943

1533 You cannot divide minds into sexes. Each human being presents an individual problem.
—Miss Maud Silver, rebuking Randal March for a platitude about the workings of the feminine mind, *The Brading Collection*, 1950

1534 The loving mother who spoils her child is preparing an unhappy future for both of them.
> —Miss Maud Silver, *The Benevent Treasure*, 1954

DONALD WESTLAKE 1933–

American mystery and suspense novelist, who also writes as Tucker Coe, Samuel Holt, and Richard Stark. As Westlake, best known for the wildly humorous quality of his books; winner of an Edgar for *God Save the Mark*.

1535 Westlake has said:
"A realist is somebody who thinks the world is simple enough to be understood. It isn't."
> —"Tracking the Genre," *Murder Ink*, 1977

1536 In any game, the worst players are always the ones most in a hurry to get at the next hand.
> —Charlie Poole, *The Fugitive Pigeon*, 1965

1537 One nude woman is beautiful but a nudist colony is only silly.
> —Fred Fitch, *God Save the Mark*, 1967

1538 Wealthy families begin with a sponge and end with a spigot.
> —*Nobody's Perfect*, 1977

Writing as **TUCKER COE**, creator of Mitch Tobin, ex-cop who must learn to live with the results of one major mistake.

1539 All situations are uncontrolled to one extent or another, except death.
> —Mitch Tobin, *Wax Apple*, 1970

1540 There was no choice. It turns out there never is a choice, and only the occasional illusion to keep us interested. Life is ten per cent carrot and ninety per cent stick.
> —Mitch Tobin, ibid.

Writing as **SAMUEL HOLT**, creator of Sam Holt, famous former TV star forced to turn sleuth.

1541 If coincidence didn't happen in this world, we wouldn't need a word for it.
> —Sam Holt, *One of Us Is Wrong*, 1986

1542   Indecision is the key to flexibility.
>   —Sign over a producer's desk, ibid.

1543   An insane person is simply a sane person who starts off with one firmly held wrong idea and then everything else has to flipflop to go along with step number one.
>   —Sam Holt, ibid.

Writing as **RICHARD STARK**, creator of Parker, a cold-blooded thief with a code of his own.

1544   "I'm only the messenger!"
        "Now you're the message."
>   —Exchange between Shevelly, bearing bloody tidings from the mob, and Parker, who shoots him dead, *Butcher's Moon*, 1974

1545   I've never seen you do anything but play the hand you were dealt.
>   —Handy McKay, to Parker, ibid.

DENNIS WHEATLY 1897–1977

English writer who started with crime and detective novels and moved on to the macabre and supernatural. With Joe Links, creator of the "Crime Dossiers" book games.

1546   Getting kisses out of a woman is like getting olives out of a bottle. The first may be devilish difficult, but the rest come easy.
>   —*The Scarlet Imposter*, 1940

ETHEL LINA WHITE 1887–1944

English detective and thriller novelist. Alfred Hitchcock took one of her novels, *The Wheel Spins*, and made it into his famous movie *The Lady Vanishes*.

1547   Everything that's worth having must be paid for.
>   —*Fear Stalks the Village*, 1932

VICTOR WHITECHURCH 1868–1933

English author of the first collection of railway detective stories, the first nine being "cases from the private notebook" of Thorpe Hazell, historically important because he was ahead of Francis Lynde's Scientific Sprague by a few months.

1548 Whitechurch said of one book:
"To begin with I had no plot. When I had written the first chapter I did not know why the crime had been committed, who had done it, or how it was done. Then, with an open mind, I picked up the clues which seemed to show themselves, and found, as I went on, their bearing on the problem."
>—Foreword, *The Crime at Diana's Pool*, 1927

1549 Digestion should be considered *before* a meal.
>—Thorpe Hazell, railway detective and fanatical vegetarian, "Sir Gilbert Murrell's Picture," *Thrilling Stories of the Railway*, 1912

1550 A little close observation and ordinary common sense, nothing more. Also an open mind.
>—Mr. Westerham's detective method, *The Crime at Diana's Pool*, 1927

RAOUL WHITFIELD 1898–1945

American detective novelist of the hard-boiled school, who also wrote under other names.

1551 Start theorizing—and you'll get lead in your lungs while you're thinking up nice words.
>—Phil Dobe, *Green Ice*, 1930

1552 You can't figure crooks—and you can't figure suckers.
>—Mike Donelly, ibid.

COLLIN WILCOX 1924–

American police procedural and suspense novelist, who also writes as Carter Wick. As Wilcox, creator of Lt. Frank Hastings of the San Francisco Homicide Squad.

1553 The introverts of the world—the practicing Christians— usually have more than their share of ulcers.
>—Clyde Briscoe to Lt. Frank Hastings, *Night Games*, 1986

OSCAR WILDE 1854–1900

Famous (and sometimes infamous) wit, poet, essayist, and play-wright who played with and around the mystery genre in several stories and essays. *The Picture of Dorian Gray* is a classic tale of murder and horror.

1554 The proper basis for marriage is a mutual misunderstanding.
> —Lady Windermere, in the title story of the collection, *Lord Arthur Saville's Crime and Other Stories*, 1887

1555 The world is a stage, but the play is badly cast.
> —Ibid.

1556 Women are meant to be loved, not to be understood.
> —"The Sphinx Without a Secret," ibid.

1557 A mask tells us more than a face.
> —"Pen, Pencil, and Poison," *The Fortnightly Review*, January 1889

1558 It was a dreadful thing to do, but she had very thick ankles.
> —Thomas Griffiths Wainewright, real-life forger and poisoner, explaining the murder of his beautiful sister-in-law, ibid.

There was also the matter of £18,000 in life insurance that Wainewright planned to collect.

1559 Perhaps, after all, America has never been discovered. I myself would say that it had merely been detected.
> —Mr. Erskine, *The Picture of Dorian Gray*, 1891

1560 Nobody ever commits a crime without doing something stupid.
> —Alan Campbell, ibid.

1561 Murder is always a mistake; one should never do anything that one cannot talk about after dinner.
> —Lord Henry Wotton to Dorian Gray, ibid.

CHARLES WILLIAMS 1909–1975

American mystery and suspense novelist, who used sea settings in several of his best novels.

1562 Barking back at a policeman is a sucker's game.
> —*The Sailcloth Shroud*, 1960

EMLYN WILLIAMS 1905–1987

Welsh murder mystery playwright and actor. *Night Must Fall*, a three-act play, was his great stage success. *Beyond Belief*, a nonfiction work, examines the Moors Murders that occurred in England in the 1960s.

1563 She'd cut 'er nose off to stop the dust-bin smelling sooner than empty it.

> —Mrs. Terrence, of Dora, *Night Must Fall*,
> Act II, 1935

1564 Murders a thing we read about in the papers; it isn't real life; it can't touch us.

> —Olivia Grayne, ibid.

But when it does, she says:

1565 That's murder. But it's so ordinary.

> —Olivia Grayne, ibid., Act III

1566 Who expects savor from a story of noisome evil? . . . There is in some people an instinct to avert the head and shovel the whole thing under the carpet ("I don't want to know"). But some of us *do* want to know, and it is salutary to inquire: The proper study of mankind is man. And man cannot be ignored because he has become vile. Woman neither.

> —Author's Foreword, *Beyond Belief: A
> Chronicle of Murder and Its Detection*,
> 1967

1567 The one mystery we shall never solve is the enigma of human identity.

> —Ibid.

EDMUND WILSON 1895–1972

American man of letters who didn't write detective stories. Instead, he wrote a famous trio of essays debunking the genre. He did like Arthur Conan Doyle.

1568 The reading of detective stories is simply a kind of vice that, for silliness and minor harmfulness, ranks somewhere between crossword puzzles and smoking.

> —"Who Cares Who Killed Roger Ackroyd?"
> *New Yorker*, January 20, 1945

DAVID WISE 1930–

American newspaperman, author of several excellent nonfiction books about intelligence, and more recently, spy thrillers.

1569 Secrecy is the end of intelligence. Not the means.
—Bill Danner, *The Children's Game*, 1983

CLIFFORD WITTING 1907–

English writer of detective novels. *Measure for Murder* is his best novel; creator of Detective-Inspector Harry Charlton and Detective-Inspector Peter Bradford.

1570 Squiring too many dames can be an expensive hobby.
—"Turtle" Tudor, *Measure for Murder*, 1941

1571 Real crime detection lies not in the microscope and test-tube, but in asking innumerable questions and weeding out the answers.
—Inspector Harry Charlton, ibid.

1572 Facts, not flummery.
—Superintendent Kingsley's maxim, *There Was a Crooked Man*, 1960

H. F. WOOD 1850–?

English newspaper man and novelist, frequently confused with other writers in bibliographic records. Three of his seven novels were detective stories.

1573 Where the prejudice is strong, the judgment will be weak.
—*The Passenger from Scotland Yard*, 1888

SALLY WOOD 1897–

American translator of French Resistance poetry and detective novelist; creator of Ann Thorne, one of the spinster sleuths.

1574 One is known by the type of woman who mourns for one.
—*Murder of a Novelist*, 1941

TED WOOD 1931–

English-born Canadian, former Toronto police officer; creator of Reid Bennett, one-man police force of Murphy's Harbor, Ontario, and Sam, his German shepherd.

1575   Pain hurts.
—Reid Bennett's axiom, *Murder on Ice*, 1984

1576   Never acknowledge the usefulness of information as long as it's pouring out freely.
—Reid Bennett, *Live Bait*, 1985

1577   When you hear hoofbeats, think horses, not zebras.
—Ibid.

SARA WOODS 1922–1985

Pseudonym of English-Canadian Sara Bowen-Judd, who began writing detective novels set in England after she moved to Canada; creator of barrister Antony Maitland.

1578   Facts in a court of law are what you can make the jury believe: no more, no less.
—Antony Maitland, *Malice Domestic*, 1962

1579   Hope can be so very cruel.
—Mrs. Henderson, *The Taste of Fears*, 1963

1580   "Well, that's very specious, Mr. Maitland."
"The truth so often is."
—Detective Inspector Sykes and Antony Maitland, ibid.

1581   Take care of the facts and the motive will take care of itself.
—*Error of the Moon*, 1963

CORNELL WOOLRICH 1903–1968

American crime and suspense novelist, who has been called "the poet of the dark night." Some of his most famous novels were published under the pseudonyms George Hopley and William Irish. Much of his work was adapted for movies and television.

1582   The title of an unwritten story could be taken as the theme of his work:
"First you dream, then you die."

1583   It's not taking on death that's tough, it's taking off life.
—Maxi Jones, "One Night in Barcelona,"
Mystery Book Magazine, Fall, 1947

1584 No place like it for living. And probably no place like it for dying.

> —Description of New York City, "New York Blues," *Ellery Queen's Mystery Magazine*, December 1970

Writing as GEORGE HOPLEY.

1585 Who hasn't at least one dream?

> —*Night Has a Thousand Eyes*, 1945

1586 God forgot to give us anything that would take away the pain that love can sometimes bring.

> —Jean Reid, ibid.

1587 He was *dressed in pajamas, in bed!* The height of time-wasting formality.

> —Shawn's opinion, ibid.

Writing as WILLIAM IRISH.

1588 Oh, Clock on the Paramount, that I can't see from here, the night is nearly over and the bus has nearly gone. Let me go home tonight.

> —Bricky Coleman's frantic prayer, *Deadline at Dawn*, 1944

1589 Time is a greater murderer than any man or woman. Time is the murderer that never gets punished.

> —*Phantom Lady*, 1942

1590 You cannot walk away from love.

> —*Waltz into Darkness*, 1947

1591 I don't know what the game was. I'm not sure how it should be played. No one ever tells you. I only know we must have played it wrong, somewhere along the way. . . . We've lost. That's all I know. We've lost. And now the game is through.

> —Heart-broken Helen, *I Married a Dead Man*, 1948

M. K. WREN 1938–

Pseudonym of American Martha Kay Renfroe; creator of Conan Flagg, rich bookstore owner and occasional private investigator.

1592 They take your money *before* you owe it—and that's just out-and-out confiscation—and never pay a damn cent of interest. . . . They don't pay any interest on *your* money, but they damn sure collect it when they think it's *their* money.
> —Brian Talley, blasting the IRS, *Nothing's Certain But Death*, 1978

ERIC WRIGHT 1929–

English-born Canadian professor of English and detective novelist; creator of Inspector Charlie Salter of the Toronto police force.

1593 Don't soak the rich, soak the poor. There's more of them.
> —*A Single Death*, 1986

1594 The trouble with letting it all hang out . . . was the difficulty of stuffing it all back in.
> —Inspector Charlie Salter, ibid.

E. M. WRONG 1889–1928

English historian, Fellow of Magdalen College, Oxford, and one of the first to apply literary criticism to the detective story. He also edited one of the earliest anthologies, *Crime and Detection*, in 1926.

1595 What we want in our detective fiction is not a semblance of real life . . . but deep mystery and conflicting clues.
> —Introduction, *Crime and Detection*, 1926

1596 Murder to be successful must be selfish.
> —Ibid.

ANTHONY WYNNE 1882–1963

Pseudonym of Englishman Robert McNair Wilson. As Wynne, one of the Golden Age detective novelists; creator of Harley Street specialist Dr. Eustace Hailey, who believes the only interesting crimes are those where the method as well as the motive is unusual.

1597 Circumstantial evidence which runs counter to experience is always to be doubted.
> —Dr. Eustace Hailey, *The Blue Vesuvius*, 1930

1598 Most murder mysteries are solved by study of the victim's life.
> —Dr. Eustace Hailey, *The Case of the Gold Coins*, 1933

WILLIAM BUTLER YEATS 1865–1939

Irish poet and dramatist.

1599   Referring to detective fiction, Yeats said:
"The technique is *supairb.*"
—Quoted by Barzun and Taylor, *A
Catalogue of Crime*, 1971

EDWARD YOUNG 1913–

English author of one first-rate thriller.

1600   Oh, I'm just a dreary old solicitor. I batten on the more
unpleasant sides of human nature. Our stock in trade is
anger, jealousy, spite, greed, insecurity, mistrust. . . .
We're stoppers-up of loopholes, purveyors of verbal quibbles,
debasers of the Queen's English. Our motto is: "I'm
covered—are you?"
—Peter Carrington, *The Fifth Passenger*,
1963

ISRAEL ZANGWILL 1864–1926

English Zionist who made one important contribution to the genre.
He thought it would be clever to "murder a man in a room to which
there was no possible access." He thought of a solution at once, and
wrote *The Big Bow Mystery*.

1601   Instinctively men are ashamed of being moral and domesti-
cated.
—*The Big Bow Mystery*, 1882

1602   To dash a half-truth in the world's eyes is the surest way of
blinding it altogether.
—Ibid.

THE INDEXES

Good old index. You can't beat it.
—Sherlock Holmes,
"The Adventure of the Sussex Vampire,"
The Case-Book of Sherlock Holmes, 1927

There are two indexes, a title index and a subject index. The former lists not only the titles used in citations but also alternate titles under which the works have been published. The latter includes the names of fictional characters as they occur in the collection, and keywords useful both for locating specific quotations and for finding thematic quotations on subjects such as "the possible" and "the impossible," "the probable" and "the improbable," "justice" and "mercy," "sparrows," or "two and two makes four."

The quotations in the collection are numbered sequentially; all references in the indexes are to quotations by number.

TITLE INDEX

SUBJECT INDEX

Careless, easier to become c., 1467
Carella, Detective Steve, 972
Carelli, Mary, 1168
Carner, Mary, 1168
Carpenter, Hanna, 1363
Carpet, shovel whole thing under c., 1566
Carrados, Max, 198–201
Carrington, Peter, 1600
Carruthers, 314–15
Cars, foreign c. big pain, 1349
Carter, Nick, 1369
Carter, Theodore, 56–57
Caruso, Enrico, 1171
Case, never turn down a c., 1443
Cases, c. decided in chambers, 788
    circumstances alter c., 482
Cash, cop has his hands on c., 1450
Cassella, Tony, 114
Cast, play is badly c., 1555
Castang, Henri, 612
Castleman, 1295
Castles, build c. in air, 646
Cat, c. chased by mouse, 128
    more ways to kill a c., 770
    mouse may feel superior to c., 134
    skinny c. pounces, 1351
    worst c. in village, 324
Catch, c. you where you catch, 30
Cats, c. for killing mice, 571
Cause, diverse effects from same c., 922
    law of c. and effect, 255
Cause célébre, junk their c., 1349
Cautious, criminal turned detective c., 1145
Cavendish, Miss, 160
Cavenett, Joan, 851
Caviar, more peanuts consumed than c., 1353
Cell, lock me in a c., 633
    worst c. of all, oneself, 713
Chambers, c. of six-shooter, 788
Chambers, Frank, 243–45
Chambers, Pat, 1359
Chambers, Peter, 877
Champagne, bad c. indicates bad morals, 852
Chan, Charlie, 141–47 passim
Chance, c. discoveries favour, 1042
    c. is a mystery, 1366
    c. most willing of goddesses, 1053
    c. never knocks, 393
    c. plays chief character, 594
    c. plays part in human affairs, 48
    didn't put in factor of c.!, 964
    don't usually rely on c., 1335
    first is c., 32
    games of c., 54
    we are servants of c., 1048
    we owe our success to c., 1054
    what c. did I stand, 451
Chances, world's full of people taking c., 150
Chandler, Raymond, bastard child of, 421
Chance, I cannot c. them, 536
    only c. can be for worse, 149
Character, guilt strengthens c., 1468
    man cannot escape own c., 727
    variety of c. in criminal, 1198
    who studies human c.?, 826
Characters, best clues to crime in c., 863
Chardonnay, trouble complex as good as C., 1068
Charity, love not indiscriminate c., 156
    sexual c. a virtue, 1485

Charles, Nick, 753
Charlton, Detective-Inspector Harry, 1571
Charm, c. of life in suspense, 1084
Chastity, c.'s a cold bedfellow, 176
Chauvinist, feminist needs a c., 432
Cheap, adultery is never c., 1229
    if I thought life c., 359
Cheated, c. if value on wrong things, 1073
Cheating, second is c., 32
Check, perforate like cancelled c., 115
Checkbooks, "self" most often used in c., 1196
Checkpoint Charlie, how long have we, 455
Cheerfulness, c. without humour, 303
Cheese, never eat holes in Swiss c., 248
Chequebooks, "self" most often used in c., 1196
Cherchez la femme, 541–42, 1020
Cherry, Edward, 589
Chess, riddle whose answer is c., 179
Chevy, take a 'fifty-seven C., 433
Chicken, deader than the c., 116
    where meat on c. is whitest, 1091
Child, mother who spoils her c., 1534
    murdering c. in various ways, 699
    people will like c. unless, 1227
Childlike, nonsense about c. gazes, 1428
Chinamen, C. have long arms!, 589
Chisler, penny-ante c. trigger-happy, 127
Chitterwick, Mr., 130
Chivalry, nine-tenths of law of c., 1307
Choice, c. between luck and brains, 449
    dealer's c. fair, 702
    some c. we made, 592
    there was no c., 1540
Choices, c. we make, 691
Choose, people c. guilts, 1023
Christ, C. serpent who deceiv'd Eve, 1
Christenberry, Julian, 1436
Christian, C. and horse-trader, 1442
Christians, practicing C. have ulcers, 1553
Christopher, Paul, 975
Chump, once a c., always a c., 747
Cigar, extravagance is two-dollar c., 239
Cinder, but to me a c., 730
Circumstances, c. alter cases, 482
    c. alter women, 136
    c. being favourable, 888
    c. connected with a crime, 707
    c. they could be tolerant of, 805
    distrust all c., 644
Circumstantial evidence, c. doubted, 1597
    c., that wonderful fabric, 194
    c. very strong, 1437
    c. very tricky, 508
    convict dog on c., 636
    mass of c., 1491
City, in c. thought of life as human, 984
Civilisation, how thin is protection of c., 223
    life lively in spite of c., 123
Civilization, c. is a conspiracy, 221
    good will of c., 330
    how thin is protection of c., 223
    life lively in spite of c., 123
    strikes at heart of c., 591
Clancarron, Lady, 852
Classes, all c. criminal today, 142
    among criminal c., 1402
    world made up of two c., 381
Clay, Colonel, 29, 30
Claydon, Mr., 831

Cleek, Hamilton, 758–59
Clement, Griselda, 324
Clement, Leonard, 325
Clever, c. enough to get that money, 304
 c. middle-aged man, 1047
 command handsome and c., 1147
 no one, however c., 802
 stupid man suspected himself c., 21
Cliché, c. truth repeating itself, 1113
Client, best I can for a c., 648
 c. incapable of crime, 650
 hand cut off than betray c., 657
 in business to serve my c., 723
 liable to risk neck for c., 1117
Clients, mortgage myself to c., 565
 our c.'s exigencies demand, 1444
 that's why they're c., 647
Clock, big c. running as usual, 575
 oh, C. on Paramount, 1588
Closet, remove skeleton from own c., 904
Clothes, with my c. on, 473
Clue, little accident c., 593
 looking for c. where it isn't, 261
 singularity invariably a c., 507
Clues, best c. to crime, 863
 c. lie where least expected, 1100
 deep mystery and conflicting c., 1595
 I picked up the c., 1548
 only real c. are psychological, 1472
 psychic c. studied like physical c., 978
 world is full of c., 222
Clunk, Joshua, 79
Cobb, Matt, 449
Code, private eye with a c., 564
 your own private c., 241
Coincidence, believing in c., 1165
 c. an elastic concept, 1337
 c. first thing people dismiss, 988
 c. must be held suspect, 428
 c. permissable in stories, 1504
 don't spurn c., 403
 if c. didn't happen, 1541
 no such thing as c., 268
 twice is c., 585
 you're c. prone, 1359
Coincidences, c. and magic in world, 875
 c. great stumbling-blocks, 1207
 c. of so marvellous a character, 1208
 c. worst enemies to truth, 947
 don't forget fortunate c., 10
 life made up of c., 619
Cold, out in c. all the time, 930
Cole, John, 676
Coleman, Bricky, 1588
Collector, c. has no conscience, 1098
 every c. a potential criminal, 161
College, I didn't go to c., 1516
Collins, 1493
Come, c. closer lads, 316
Comfort, innocence is great c., 901
 money root of all c., 349
 thought of suicide a c., 1433
 unhappy in maximum c., 1298
Commitment, most deadly c. to self, 1001
Committing, found himself c. vile action, 1210
 found out c. previous ten, 240
Common, in every highbrow a c. man, 163
 so long as it's not c., 39

Common sense, c. my maxim, 1416
 c. poor card in law court, 1125
 c. was right, 406
 hard work and c., 1526
 ordinary c., nothing more, 1550
 Watson's one quality, 527
Commonplace, most c. incident, 1282
 nothing so unnatural as c., 505
Company, c. makes occasion, 1409
Compassion, harsh in defence of c., 933
Complicate, point which appears to c., 528
Complicated, when a guy gets too c., 284
Complications, c. may trap you, 954
Compliment, c. better than truth, 181
Compromise, c. can be useful, 1453
 going to lose, go for c., 1412
 politicians know when to c., 8
Compromises, splitting ideals into c., 612
Conceal, something to c., 746
Concealment, c. principle of deception, 1258
Conceit, c. a mortal poison, 1018
Conception, it's beyond my c., 258
Concert, piano tuner's relationship to c., 868
Conclusion, c. without data, 617
Conclusions, then drew certain c., 1335
Condemned, than innocent one c., 1489
Condom, change emblem to c., 1297
Conduct, control one's own c., 69
 murder improper c., 464
Confidante, satisfactory for troubles, 627
Confidence, c. a good thing, 1018
Confidence man, rationalization of, 454
Confused, tact should not be c., 1514
Congress, only gentleman by act of C., 1035
Conned, never c. someone, 453
Conscience, accompanied by Official C., 1019
 collector has no c., 1098
 c. can make dyspeptics, 1333
 few of us have any c., 1281
 hardy c. quite easy, 621
 man can betray c., 385
 what shocks c., 354
Conscious, motive, c. or unconscious, 980
Consequences, avoid c., 1386
 c. determined everything, 212
 life has c., 427
 man may escape public c., 727
 undue exertion leads to c., 1036
Conservative, mystery last refuge of c. writer, 986
Consideration, lack of c. among criminal, 1402
Consistency, c. poor second to hedonism, 871
 c.'s fourth rate virtue, 1521
 false c. of events, 1221
 logic requires only c., 1151
Consistent, best men not consistent, 368
Conspiracy, civilization is a c., 221
Constitution, written down in the C., 1241
Consultant, c. borrows your watch, 1032
Contradiction, would be a c. in terms, 1394
Control, 929–30
Conventional, subscribe to c. morality, 228
Conversation, only c. remains, 821
Conversations, most c. are monologues, 1070
Conway, Mike, 1463
Cook, c. something and eat it, 1159
Coop, 1497
Cooperman, Benny, 562
Cop, c. has his hands on cash, 1450

instead of c., a crook, 1021
you're a c. of sorts, 241
Cope, things happen and we c., 1256
Cops, antagonizing c. stupid, 1245
    c. don't like me too well, 287
    c. get most a those kind, 1510
    lot of good c. around, 1334
    playing C. and Robbers, 970
Coquenil, Paul, 1083–84
Corleone, Don, 1247–48
Corner, The Old Man in the, 1136
Cornichon, Sebastian, 572–73
Corporations, no conscience regarding c., 1281
Corrupting, too much virtue c., 704
Corruption, savour of life from c.?, 630
Costs, money c. too much, 1012
Cotton, Clement, 850
Count, out-of-town doesn't c., 114
Country, c. worth living in, 353
    God made c., man town, 1025
    risk shameful death for c., 1063
Coup d'état, start their c., 1349
Courage, have c. of his sins, 1183
    stupidity rather than c., 525
Court, chambers of six-shooter instead of c., 788
    common sense poor card in c., 1125
    every man is own law c., 794
    facts in a c. of law, 1578
Courtesy, c. one's own affair, 1387
Courts, less through c. than by, 1446
Cover, c. her face, 1524
Covered, I'm c.—are you?, 1600
Cover-up, don't think I can't smell c., 844
Coward, one c. loves another, 391
Crackenthorpe, Cedric, 335
Cracksmanship, three principles of c., 1478
Crandell, Mrs., 1013
Crane, Bill, 915–16, 918
Crane, Lila, 166
Crane, Simon, 660
Crazy, all of us go a little c., 165
    anybody who kills is a c., 973
Credible, any motive c., 483
Creeds, sanctified as much as c., 842
Creighton, Colonel, 898
Cricket, play tennis instead of c., 909
Crime, can't do time, don't do c., 971
    commit a c., 561
    c. brings its own fatality, 370
    c. detection matter of, 869
    c. detection not secret art, 614
    c. does not pay, 700
    c. has exerted fascination, 1471
    c. has suffered more, 1131
    c., if of humourous description, 1029
    c. increases, 1195
    c. is a technical word, 1223
    c. is art of the unexpected, 296
    c. is common, 514
    c. isn't a mass instinct, 1473
    c. may pay, but, 269
    c. never pays. Not even, 1220
    c. not only pays well, 1105
    c. of beating a man, 764
    c. was coming back, 677
    detection of c. damnable, 1405
    difference between sin and c., 445

difficult c. to track, 524
from any c. a trail, 740
history of c. and detection, 594
I have lived a life of c., 758
justice will o'ertake the c., 537
let punishment fit the c., 687
make a c. too perfect, 1476
motives that instigate c., 1198
Napoleon of c., 526
need brains in life of c., 295
no c. successful without luck!, 327
no mystery in connection with c., 1136
nobody commits a c. without, 1560
nothing is trivial—in c.?, 1527
OUT—GONE TO C., 1343
over-precaution enemy of c., 577
person tired of c., 1102
prove c. did not pay, 677
psychological factors of c., 1472
science in detection of c., 1262
society accomplice of c., 366
solve c., or detective story, 1258
solve rather than commit c., 1015
solving of c. depends, 92
theft was a great c., 550
two parties to a c., 1050
we don't detect c., 62
with motive stoops to c., 765
Crime novel, better vehicle than c., 1410
Crime stories, c., appeal of, 343
Crimes, all murders are c. of passion, 768
    c. cause own detection, 365
    c. of which motive is want, 65
    c. tie themselves together, 1360
    half so many undetected c., 1137
    I planned c. carefully, 307
    little c. lead to big c., 701
    poverty mother of all c., 913
    real motive behind half c., 970
Criminal, all classes c. today, 1142
    between c. and detective, 638
    collector a potential c., 161
    c. and victim, 1050
    c. desires to establish alibi, 534
    c. has to be neutralized, 1448
    c. mind a peculiar thing, 1503
    c. mind rarely original, 200
    c. the creative artist, 302
    c. turned detective suspicious, 1145
    every c. leaves psychic fingerprints, 977
    evidences on mind of c., 89
    facts discovering c., 84
    first rule of c., 529
    got your c., motive or no, 1310
    I have a c. mind., 1501
    intelligent c. not different, 961
    Maigret's attitude towards c., 1327
    policeman has c. imagination, 1015
    variety of character in c., 1198
    well, it's c.!, 1402
Criminals, crime suffered more from c., 1131
    I entrap c., 1384
    imbeciles among imprisoned c., 1127
    magicians, c., and detective authors, 1258
    most c. are fools, 1482
    to run c. down, 750
Criminologist, c. obligation to question, 547

Machine, born-an'-bred fighting m., 291
Machine guns, ditto for m., 781
Mack, Miss Madelyn, 1525–27
Maclain, Captain Duncan, 881–83
Macrea, 679
MacWilliam, Mr., 763
Mad, all of us are m., 138
Mademoiselle, m., I have served, 1055
Maggiore, Charles, 567
Magic, coincidences and m., 875
Magicians, m., criminals, and detective authors,
    1258
Mahbub Ali, 899
Maid, felt like Macbeth's m., 566
Maigret, Inspector Jules, 1327–31
Maigrets, my very first M., 1327
Maitland, Antony, 1578–80
Mal de mere, when m., 326
Male, more deadpan than the m., 1519
Mallett, Inspector John, 762
Malone, John J., 1277–78
Maltravers, Augustus, 1280
Man, any m. might do a girl in., 555
    as a m.?, 1329
    created a beaten m., 764
    don't forget m. and bear, 830
    down these mean streets a m., 277
    each m. carries own justice, 1408
    enemy can partly ruin a m., 1456
    every m. has a sane spot, 1378
    every m. is own law court, 794
    every woman can gauge a m., 1092
    for the m. that's wronged, 81
    give me the hunting of a m.!, 638
    God made country, m. town, 1025
    heaviest sentence imposed on m., 1112
    honest m. gets tempted, 1466
    if dreams of normal m. exposed, 271
    I'm a m. and you're a woman, 741
    in the presence of a m., 708
    lengths m. will go to, 1399
    make m. sorry he's alive, 1003
    m. about to cross stream, 142
    m. accepts what lady tells, 27
    m. believes he is born detective, 220
    m. can shine in second rank, 640
    m. cannot be ignored, 1566
    m. can't measure up, 180
    m. finds it hard to realize, 519
    m. grows used to everything, 487
    m. indulges in murder, 1340
    m. is not truly alive, 1181
    m. knows he'll die, 792
    m. reads nothing but detective stories, 204
    m. should have courage, 1183
    m. strong enough to reject hope?, 73
    m. takes first drink, 787
    m. who cannot stand mysteries, 276
    m. who listens at doors, 539
    m. with grudge against world, 1130
    m.'s most open actions, 386
    m.'s wealth can be estimated, 625
    more likely m. done bad thing, 481
    never worry what you say to m., 322
    no m. dead til he's dead, 112
    no m. ever taken to hell, 1389
    no m. qualified, 904
    no stupid m., 21

    nothing makes m. as evil, 546
    obstinate as m. who half thinks, 1228
    one m.'s mate, 772
    prompt m. a lonely m., 942
    rare m. who isn't corrupted, 1235
    relieve m. of responsibility, 579
    sense of m.'s irresponsibility, 1327
    sex every m.'s loco spot, 1303
    stupidest m. may point to school, 144
    times when m. will lie still, 1294
    watch bad m. from all sides, 667
    way of life natural to m., 661
    what an ass a m. can make, 124
    what for m.?, 1496
    when a m. cares for nothing, 709
    when a m.'s partner is killed, 749
    when m. feels protective, 159
    when m. wants evil, 835
    young m. must be a shield, 24
Manchu, Dr. Fu, 1288–90
Manciple, Professor Gideon, 822
Manderley, dreamt I went to M., 543
Mandrake, Professor, 174
Manfred, George, 1499
Manhunter, I'm a m., 741
Mankind, attack on all m., 591
    beauty from m.'s undoing, 757
    misdeeds of m., 696
Manners, detective story a novel of m., 1308
    not excuse for bad m., 1074
    study m. of our age, 902
Marlowe, blondes went to Spade and M., 967
Marlowe, Philip, 278–87 *passim*
Marmeladov, 488
Marple, Jane, 324–38 *passim*
Marriage, basis for m. is misunderstanding, 1554
    m. a funny old carry-on, 1273
    m. balanced stalemate, 1189
    m. grounds for divorce, 1058
    m. its last test, 1480
    m. like pleading guilty, 1106
    physical side of m., 1515
    tragedy of m., 456
Married, both m. to same chap, 96
    in m. life three better, 846
    m. motive for murder, 1438
    only get under skin if m., 332
    silence relief in m. life, 1103
    worst of m. women, 31
Marrying, going ahead and m. them, 1279
Marshall, Detective Terry, 187
Martineau, Detective Chief Inspector Harry, 1243
Marukakis, 50
Mary Helen, Sister, 1128–29
Mask, m. tells more than a face, 1557
Masochist, m. make sadist of saint, 559
Mason, Perry, 647–57 *passim*
Mason, Randolph, 1223
Masterpiece, as if it were a m., 676
Masters, Detective Chief Inspector George, 340
Mate, one man's m., 772
Materials, work with m. at hand, 170
Mathematician, as poet and m., 1212
Mathis, 584
Maxim, an excellent m. unless, 919
    that's my m., 1416
Mayo, Asey, 1416–17
McBride, Rex, 4

McCorquodale, 1142
McCutcheon, Hugh, 1524
McFarland, Mac, 893
McGarr, Inspector Peter, 689–91
McGee, Fat Jack, 962
McGee, Travis, 994–1002 *passim*
McGing, Sergeant, 1015
McGuffin, Amos, 1465
McKay, Handy, 1545
McKenna, Patience Campbell, 1151–52
McPherson, Mark, 272
Meade, Danny, 1263
Meade, Drew, 1435
Meal, considered before m., 1549
Mean, Down these m. streets, 277
   word has a m. sound, 1492
Meanness, more interested in m., 93
Mediocre, someday she'll be m., 962
Mediocrity, m. knows nothing higher, 532
Meehan, Jack, 227
Meek, leaving m. to inherit, 1358
Melodrama, all murders have tang of m., 735
   unlikely m. likliest, 957
Memories, terrible face for m., 1014
Memory, good m. and play hunches, 1094
   he who is capable of m., 459
   nothing escapes my m., 153
Men, betting on m., 1421
   dirty jobs soil m., 674
   happening to unadventurous m., 218
   idiots and m. in love, 779
   instinctively m. are ashamed, 1601
   m. capable of every wickedness, 389
   m. do curious things for money, 1069
   m. have to *murder* wives, 663
   m. more law-abiding than women, 866
   m. more lovable for bad qualities, 1133
   m. not consistent in good, 368
   m. will not be nice, 320
   motives of m. moved to act, 926
   perfect young m. don't get murdered, 1075
Mendacity, not confused with m., 1514
Mercy, little justice and no m., 1250
   secret passion for m., 1011
Merlini, Great, 1258–59
Message, now you're the m., 1544
   warning m. arrived Monday, 59
Messenger, I'm only the m.!, 1544
Messenger, Adrian, 1005
Method, man has a m., 29
   m. and logic accomplish, 319
   reason m. to discover truth, 1226
   you know my m., 510
Meyer, 998
Meyers, Jane, 1284–85
Mice, cats for killing m., 571
Micro-ambition, man with m., 68
Middle-man, you might call m., 436
Mifflin, Roger, 1095–96
Milhone, Kinsey, 704
Milk, find trout in m., 1437
   once m. becomes sour, 653
Miller, Superintendent, 791
Millionaire, try being a m., 28
Milodragovitch, Milo, 423–24, 427
Minardi, Inspector, 818
Mind, also an open m., 1550
   chance favours prepared m., 1042

concentrate his m. on moving, 792
criminal m. peculiar thing, 1503
human m. thrown off track, 1287
I don't m. what I do, 39
I have a criminal m., 1501
logical in m. of killer, 227
mark of superior m., 1167
m. master of all things, 632
my m. a perfect b., 1199
no limits to which human m., 1254
official m., 1019
old-fashioned m., 82
open eye of open m., 9
stimulating activity of m., 1470
theory apt to dominate m., 1275
to great m., nothing little, 493
trained m. never bores, 774
what m. doesn't know, 135
Minds, cannot divide m. into sexes, 1533
   normal recreation of noble m.?, 1315
   recreation of noble m., 733
Miracle, m. a fact, 299
Miracles, in science m. repugnant, 548
   incredible thing about m., 301
   m. but divine experiments, 2
Misdirection, m. nothing more, 1259
   m. principle of deception, 1258
Misfortune, m. can happen to anyone, 878
Mistake, m. of doing something, 392
   m. of many murderers, 1476
   m. which has been rectified, 1138
   murder is always m., 1561
Mistakes, bad enough to make m., 1279
   owed to chance and m., 1054
   your m. will be mortal, 1166
Mr. Tibbs, they call me M., 88
Misunderstanding, basis for marriage m., 1554
Mitchell, Donald, 1016
Mitchell, Paul, 1236
Möbius, Johann Wilhelm, 548–49
Moderation, m. in all things, 99
Modern, mystery m. morality play, 854
Modesty, rank m. among virtues, 522
Money, Americans, no matter how much m.,
   1341
   clever enough to get that m., 304
   consulting doctors waste of m., 850
   curious things got m., 1069
   financiers make m., 263
   God pays debts without m., 253
   hang around m., 732
   he needed the m., 47
   I despise m., 335
   I've got enough m., 425
   jealousy—m.—revenge, 905
   m. costs too much, 1012
   m. doesn't bring happiness, 1298
   m. is only worth, 1363
   m. it interest me not, 197
   m.—lubrication for love, 810
   m. root of all comfort, 349
   m. talks, 13
   nothing like m., hot naked m., 694
   nothing like m., to keep, 111
   only kind of m. to have, 587
   people with m. find pitfalls, 438
   sex and m. all-dominant, 187
   sex and m.: root of evil, 1007

pill to change p.?, 1171
  shackled you to your p., 1415
  the p. arranges itself, 769
Patience, detective must have p., 1085
Patter, gaudier the p., 745
Pay, crime does not p., 700
  crime may p., but, 269
  don't p. by being dead, 1339
  you p. in money or time, 394
Pays, crime not only p. well, 1105
  God p. debts without money, 253
Peabody, Miss Amelia, 1187
Peace, we Saints are souls of p., 290
Peanuts, buy p. for monkeys, 446
  more p. consumed than caviar, 1353
Peculiar, except for p. persons, 11
Penalty, p. for pleasing one's self, 1364
People, can't run p.'s lives, 783
  evil in p., not money, 1006
  few p. so obstinate, 1228
  first thing most p. dismiss, 988
  hide things from p., 711
  intelligent p. succumb, 609
  justice keeps happening to p., 1011
  learn about p. from p., 1516
  less p. speculate, 777
  no formula for p., 927
  only happy p., 692
  p. aren't like arithmetic, 956
  p. can't learn by experience, 1441
  p. can't live without lies, 975
  p. choose guilts, 1023
  p. in dusk of history, 659
  p. miss all their todays, 995
  p. ought to retire, 1129
  p. who had hardly anything, 215
  p. will like child, 1227
  p. without brains, 1049
  p. you should like more, 557
  seldom loves p. for virtues, 782
  take p. as they are, 484
  way to rid of p., 155
  what you do to other p., 1010
Perfect, make a crime too p., 1476
  there are few p. crimes, 1131
Perfectionism, practice p. in murder, 256
Perkins, Mr., 664
Persistence, detection requires p., 855
Person, difficult p. to find, 201
  p. tired of crime, 1102
  you're a complete p., 771
Perverseness, p. primitive impulse, 1209
Perversion, that is my curious p., 1501
Peters, Jeff, 785–87
Peters, Mr., 51
Peters, Toby, 872–75
Peterson, 471
Peterson, Carl, 1031
Petrie, Dr., 1291
Petrov, Anatoli, 26
Pettigrew, Francis, 761
Philanthropist, p. killed by can, 90
Phipps, Miss Marian, 126
Phone, a watched p., 833
Physician, one's p. is a tyrant!, 61
Pibble, Superintendent James, 483
Pickering, Leslie, 212
Piffle, facts are p., 265

Piggot, Matt, 1321
Pill, p. to change past?, 1171
Pimpernel, that demmed elusive P., 1135
Pimpernel, Scarlet, 1135
Pine, Paul, 214–17
Pinkerton, motto of P. men, 1197
Piper, Inspector Oscar, 1148, 1150
Piper, John, 256
Pitt, Dirk, 432–33
Plans, making other p., 1077
Plato, 1145
Plato, we err with P., 267
Play, p. hand you were dealt, 1545
  p. is badly cast, 1555
Play fair, du Boisgobey failed to p., 1061
  people liked to p., 1367
  See also fair play
Players, worst p. in any game, 1536
Pleasures, keenest p. in life, 1429
Pledges, I rarely offer p., 1392
Plot, I had no p., 1548
  p. indecent, 986
Plots, one's plot improbable, 404
Plumbers, hires lawyers as one hires p., 416
Pocketbook, which touches on p., 154
Pocket-picking, p. wanted 'prenticeship, 480
Poe, the "Dupin" of P., 1323
Poet, as p. and mathematician, 1212
Poggioli, Professor Henry, 1404–06
Poidevin, M., 69
Poindexter, John, 709
Point, so pointless has to be p., 1280
Poirot, Hercule, 317–33 passim
Poirot, Hercule, use your grey cells, 409
Poison, conceit a mortal p., 1018
Poison, no roots and deadly p., 1518
  p. his master's dish, 1234
Poisoner, is worse than a p., 539
Poker, bad luck at p., 54
Police, British p. force run, 1138
  drab as p. business, 63
  enough to keep p. out, 936
  lawyers enemies of p., 681
  no place in p. work, 1338
  p. adept at detecting, 1366
  p. looking for man, 202
  p. pick obvious person, 761
  p. science is young, 1448
  p. work built on realism, 1337
  selected for "detective p.," 1143
Police romance, difficulty of p., 1376
Police-magistrate, God is not p., 1126
Policeman, as a p., I am bound, 1329
  barking back at a p., 1562
  I am not a p., 1384
  imagination what p. needs, 1015
  no one incorruptable to p., 16
  p. can't mind own business, 851
  p.'s lot is not happy, 686
  p.'s lot is not so hot, 1261
  terrorist and p. come, 384
Policemen, he was the best of p., 42
  p. repairers of destinies, 1330
Polifax, Mrs. Emily, 692
Politically, p. reliable, 53
Politician, p.'s unlike other people, 1507
Politicians, nuisance p. would be, 80
  p. know when to compromise, 8